Faraway Blue

Faraway Blue

Max Evans

UNIVERSITY OF NEW MEXICO PRESS

ALBUQUERQUE

11 10 09 08 07 06 05   1 2 3 4 5 6 7

Library of Congress Cataloging-in-Publication Data

Evans, Max, 1925–
    Faraway blue / Max Evans.
        p. cm.
    ISBN 0-8263-3585-3 (pbk. : alk. paper)
    1. Williams, Moses, d. 1899—Fiction.
    2. United States. Army—African American troops—Fiction.
    3. Indians of North America—Wars—1866–1895—Fiction.
    4. United States. Army. Cavalry, 9TH—Fiction.
    5. Nana, Apache chief, ca. 1806–1896—Fiction.
    6. Warm Spring Apache Indians—Wars—Fiction.
    7. African American soldiers—Fiction.
    8. New Mexico—Fiction. I. Title.
PS3555.V23F37 2005
    813'.54—dc22

                                2005007580

A Tribute
to a few old and relatively new friends who have *delivered*.

To
Producer Tim Bevan, co-owner of Working Title Films (*My Beautiful Laundrette, Four Weddings and a Funeral, Dead Man Walking,* and *Fargo*), who believed in *The Hi Lo Country*—only from the novel and a first draft screenplay—as a film and went to the mat for it with dignified courage.

To
Taos actor/producer Josh Bryant, founder of the successful Taos Talking Pictures Festival, and believer in my short novel *Xavier's Folly* for a high-class movie.

To
Writer/editor/critic John Bowman, who is a lover, with great taste and sincerity, of the written word and films of New Mexico, the Southwest, and the world.

To
Producer/director Bernard (Bernie) L. Kowalski, (*Barretta, Columbo,* etc.) who has been a kind-hearted, generous friend since the early sixties on Sunset Boulevard, in the Valley, and many working visits to New Mexico. We've sure had fun.

To
All those half-outlaw friends of the long ago who are now playing the wild cantinas of the sky: Cotton Lee, Big Boy (Wiley) Hittson, Luz Martinez, Benny Padilla, Elliot Calhoun, Sgt. Milton Rudio, Long John Dunn of Taos, John Sinor, Sam Peckinpah, Brian Keith, Chuck Miller, Mack Nunn, Clair Huffaker, Slim Pickens, and . . . quite a few more. Hasta la vista, amigos.

Faraway Blue

One

SHEELA JONES WAS AWARE OF NELDA'S GLANCES THROUGH THE adobe archway between the kitchen and the dining room as she folded the lace-edged, linen napkins preparing to set her own birthday table. She was a little embarrassed by all the extra fuss Nelda was making over her today. Both women knew that this was not actually her real birth date, but that little detail didn't matter to Nelda. She had special feelings for birthdays and anniversaries, and if there was no official date to celebrate, Nelda would make one up at least once a month.

Sheela's appreciation and love for this woman overrode any other sensibilities on this day that seemed more special to her benefactor than to herself. After all, Sheela owed her life to Nelda Nelson, wife of Lt. Gen. Joshua Nelson, retired supply commander during many major battles of the Civil War. Nelda was a giver and Sheela had been a grateful receiver of her largesse.

Sheela had been the daughter of slaves, and no doubt would have become one herself except for unknown tragedies or, perhaps, good fortune. She had no conscious memory of her ancestors, and today she knew she must not dwell on them.

Nelda had given Sheela this birth date the day she bought her from the Negro transients escaping to the Union side from the South. All they had told Nelda was, "Her folks is done dead. Nobody want her." Later the General's wife would feel guilty at having purchased the lovely, nine-year-old mulatto girl—and for five dollars at that. She kept this fact to herself, always; not even the General knew about it, even though he had once teased her about raising her own private servants.

Her cold wrath that greeted this teasing had convinced him to keep quiet about it from then on. She had said, "General,"—she called him that when duly agitated—"this is a special child. A very special child. If you do not wish to claim and respect her, that is your ignorance and your loss. I love her just as much as I do Brent and Robert." The latter were their ten- and twelve-year-old sons, who were away in private school at that time. Her statement had stood firm with the General.

She could not help watching as Sheela smoothly, expertly, set the dining room table. She was proud of her contributions to Sheela's life. She had grown into a talented and dangerously beautiful woman, by this, her nineteenth birthday. How the time had passed!

Now she also knew that someday soon she must give her up to some man waiting somewhere out there on the frontier. It was difficult for Nelda to think ahead about this because a mulatto woman was not fully accepted in their native Pennsylvania. And even here in a wild, wide land of many cultures, some joining peacefully, others often clashing, she wondered how her exquisite *daughter* would fare. She felt confident all would be well. At the thought of the word "daughter" her heart warmed.

Nelda could not imagine how she could love Sheela more. They had been together constantly as she grew and developed. Nelda, with a fine American and European education, had happily tutored Sheela in reading and writing fundamentals, but also in the art of gracious living—music, sewing, and all the practical skills of keeping a well-arranged, smoothly running household. Sheela's eagerness and ability to learn had always delighted Nelda. Now she listened as Sheela sang to herself. Her melodious voice had a rich feeling to it that warmed Nelda's being. She silently vowed to find her a fine voice teacher as soon as they were moved and settled.

Among the many things the gifted young woman did daily for the Nelson family was preparing the carefully planned, delicious meals, but today Nelda wanted to be the sole hands of invention and was pleased that Sheela had so readily allowed her to take over the cooking.

Tonight she was preparing wild duck, shot by the General, from some marshes along the Rio Grande just a short distance southeast of their town, Socorro, New Mexico Territory. She had fresh green beans, lettuce, and tomatoes from their garden, and rice from Lee Yan, the proprietor of the only Chinese restaurant in the Socorro mining district. There were already five bowls of caramel pudding in the canvas cooler that would later be topped with fresh whipped cream from their own milk cow. A serving for each—the General, their now-grown sons, Brent and Robert, Sheela, and herself. The five go-getting Nelsons. Her family. Her pride. Well, actually there were only four "Nelsons." The transients so long ago had told Nelda in their last words to her, "She is Sheela, with two e's, Jones."

Although she had wanted to adopt her under the Nelson name, something told her to leave the lost child this bit of her family history. For it seemed she would know no other. Now she was glad. She felt that she had been properly guided to do this.

* * *

There was a sign on the impressive brick building, NELSON MERCANTILE, and underneath the words GENERAL NELSON AND SONS, PROPRIETORS. The General had just finished briefing first one son and then the other about their upcoming move south to the Hillsboro-Kingston mining district. He looked with satisfaction around his large Socorro store as he talked. It was the best-stocked supply source in the area.

The mines and the sheep and cattle businesses were booming here in Socorro, and the railroad was on its way. The Billings smelter was going on-line nearby with plenty of flux ore secured from the mines near Magdalena—only a day's horseback ride to the west. However, the Apache wars still raged to the south and west of them all the way into Mexico. Any kind of travel out of the Socorro area could be extremely deadly. All this caused his sons to question their moving now, when everything was so filled with potential right here. The General explained that it was an expansion, not a move. One of the sons would stay here. The other would go with them to help set up the new Hillsboro Nelson Mercantile and would be left in charge there after it was established. The General, then, intended to move on westward and establish Nelson mercantiles all the way across Arizona and California—wherever mines flourished and gold and silver ore was found in abundance. The sons saw his vision clearly after a while, as the General knew they would.

There would be no disagreement about who would stay in Socorro. That would be Robert. He had been courting the handsome daughter of Manuel Martínez y Ortíz, a powerful political kingmaker and owner of a widespread sheep ranch. Both families knew they would join soon. The General was more anxious than most. He and Manuel loved to smoke cigars and drink brandy together, as both were ambitious and plotters extraordinaire.

The General was eager to expand into a literal chain of mercantiles, and Ortíz wanted to govern the territory when his political base was properly overwhelming. His connections were already powerful up north in Santa Fe and beyond. He knew the General's innate drive, along with the inherited wealth of his spouse, Nelda, could help him get there. They were by their desires compatible friends—*amigos* of convenience. And now their families would be joined by the recent engagement of the daughter, Luz Juanita, and the son, Robert. The future for both families would shine stronger and brighter across the west with the union of their young.

Already Manuel had helped the General get a troop of the Ninth Cavalry's "Buffalo Soldiers" assigned to escort Nelson's freight wagons south for his first expansion. It would take about a month to get everything ready for the trek. Brent had thought at first that they should just wait until the railroad was completed to Socorro and on south. The General carefully explained that in order to be first, they would have to risk the Apaches and the weather. After the railroad was in, all the world could easily move about. No, the Nelsons would be out front. Besides, his freighters were tough men and they were to be escorted by battle-seasoned Buffalo Soldiers. Brent got the idea.

The General was going home early for Nelda's and Sheela's special day. He asked his sons to close a little early and come on home for the dinner. "We don't want to make your mother wait, now do we, boys?"

He strolled around the Socorro plaza, taking a quick rub at his iron gray mustache and a brief pulling swipe at his carefully groomed goatee. The gray of his hair and the slightly pink skin gave him a look of both aged wisdom and youth. He was pleasurably conscious of this effect on people. Every permanent resident on the street recognized him, speaking either out of respect for a superior or from some unknown fear. Lt. Gen. Joshua Nelson liked this kind of attention. He knew he deserved it.

Now he headed up the two-block walk from the plaza where he had his fine home, his finely groomed and quietly elegant wife, and a hundred yards behind the house horse stables, private milk cows, and chicken pens to assure the family of fresh eggs, milk, cream, and butter. There was also a quarter-acre garden. He had two hired hands, recommended correctly by his good friend Manny Ortíz, to care for all of this. He rode his powerful, sleek, black horse at least twice a week for exercise—for both himself and the animal. Sometimes Nelda and Sheela accompanied him on other mounts from his stable. Both were fine horsewomen.

He was a proud, vain man. Then he could not help himself; his thoughts turned to the tar black eyes of Sheela, her golden smooth skin that seemed to caress the muscles underneath in an ancient and natural movement of enticement. He had wanted her for years now and fought the thoughts, first because it was wrong, and later because he was afraid Nelda might somehow become aware of the carnal craving that even his strong, regimented mind could not control. He was at war again, this time with himself, dammit. He could not risk losing the backing of Nelda's wealth on his soon-to-spread dream business. At the same time his breath seemed to hang in his throat at the thought of lying naked next to Sheela's golden body. He could not seem to reconcile the two consuming emotions. Often he would fool himself into thinking he could have both the great mercantiles and this Cleopatra of an ex-slave girl as well. Then he would fight the notion away. A standoff.

Well, he would work it out somehow after they had gotten established at Hillsboro and across the Black Range at Pinos Altos. By then he would have so much power he wouldn't have to worry about Nelda discovering his other passion. How could he, a respected general and businessman, even entertain these perilous thoughts of a mulatto girl-woman? How indeed?

The dinner was enjoyed by everyone. Even Sheela, feeling the General's eyes on her, hiding a volcano of feelings underneath his cleverly, pretentiously paternal eyes, enjoyed herself. She buried the dread of the inevitable clash of rejection with him, far more for Nelda's sake than hers.

For several years he had cleverly managed to rub against her in doorways. He had so smoothly brushed his hand across her bottom that, even if Nelda had been suspicious, she would not have known for sure if the touching was accidental or deliberate. Sheela had wanted to scream out the truth to Nelda, but could not bring herself to hurt the only sure love she had on this earth. So she had learned to avoid doorways and other close body encounters with the General. They both silently suffered her skillful evasions.

With her natural potent will, she buried the concern for today, and laughed and was truly thankful for all the gifts. Everyone was filled with delicious food and good wine from local vineyards and a controlled excitement about the upcoming migration south and new worlds to come. It was decided that Brent, Nelda, and Sheela would accompany the General on this new venture.

Nelda's classic face beamed her great pleasure at Sheela's dignified appreciation. She said a little silent prayer of thanks for her family, their good fortune, and the love they shared.

The hand-crocheted shawl from Nelda, almost the color of Sheela's skin, was admired by all, and they insisted she wear it the entire evening. She smilingly obliged, as well she might. The lovely adornment would remain with her as long as she breathed.

Two

THE MORNING OF SEPTEMBER 16, 1879, WAS A SOUTHERN NEW Mexico beauty. None of the black-skinned soldiers noticed the few frightening white clouds in the turquoise sky. Apache and Navajo scouts had found the trail of Victorio's raiding party. They were elated to know the sign was fresh. The great warrior had given the Buffalo Soldiers of the Ninth Cavalry Regiment death and misery over much of that part of the territory. They had raided farms, settlements, ranches, travelers, and troops with a planned randomness that had left the Ninth bloody, frustrated, and angry.

Over and over, the exhausted troops had thought they had Victorio trapped only to have the flesh of horses, mules, and some of themselves blasted apart by Victorio's rifles, lances, and arrows, with far more rifles than the latter. No matter how valiantly they fought, and they did, he gave them painful destruction with almost supernatural elusiveness. Even when the troopers had actually seen a warrior fall under their fire, they seldom ever found the bodies. This not only mystified them, but raised grave doubts in the Buffalo Soldiers. There would only be a patch of dried blood or a splattering, but no body as evidence of a kill. Somehow the Warm Springs

Apaches had a skill far beyond any reasoning in claiming their dead and wounded.

As one trooper said, "They disappear like they was turned into shadows."

Today, the Ninth had two companies following the scouts, who were hot on Victorio's horse, mule, and human tracks, and the support of two more companies coming. At last they would hunt him down and end the terror for the miners, farmers, trades people, and the Ninth itself. From evidence of the tracks, they had the Indians outnumbered approximately two to one.

As he moved his band into Las Animas Canyon, Victorio rode high up with the old man, Nana, his uncle, whom he respected so much that he called him "father," and his own younger sister, Lozen, who was called both Warrior Woman and Holy Woman. She had so much power in medicine, in spirit, in battle skills that she was the only Apache woman ever allowed to ride into battle without a husband.

Victorio had instructed a small number of the younger warriors to ride up the canyon, staying in sight of the pursuing Ninth. He spoke to Nana and glanced at the old warrior's oldest and favorite wife.

"Father, you and Nah-dos-te ride the game trail and take the other side of the canyon. Lozen, you split to the place where the canyon pinches its rocks together. I will take some men along here." And Victorio motioned the direction. It had been Nana's idea to send the young warriors along the bottom of the canyon as bait.

The troopers, under the command of Lt. Col. N. A. M. Dudley, led by Lt. Bryan Dawsons' Company B, and Capt. Ambrose Hooker's Company E, had spotted movement in the bottom of the canyon. The blood scent wafted through their bodies and dimmed their judgment. The trail- and battle-toughened soldiers rode hard to the final closure.

Nana's warriors kept just far enough ahead to give them the explosive adrenaline charge that comes to all men the moment before actual engagement to the death. It was the ultimate feeling of floating power. The troopers did not even notice the white-lathered horses and mules, nor the wide, air-gasping nostrils, nor the rippling, powerful muscles that were carrying them around trees and over piles of rocks and through brush. Nor did they pay any attention to the first shot that thudded into a tree next to the head of Private Freeland.

The young Apache warriors had secured their horses behind a series of indentations and boulders, where the canyon narrowed, and had taken position to do temporary battle. As instructed, they fired a wild shot now and then to give the troopers even more incentive.

When the soldiers were finally in easy range of the young warriors' guns, Victorio gave the signal to Nana and Lozen in their designated places and they, in turn, silently signaled those in their own groups. Then . . . then the fusillade of lead came cracking down into horses first—they were the larger targets—and then the men. The wounded horses screamed, falling, rising, dying, in a terrible cacophony, spurting and smearing their blood on the hard earth.

Colonel Dudley knew instantly his mistake—they were trapped—but he ordered his men to take cover and return fire. They did—or rather they tried—for the shots seemed to come from everywhere, and they only caught vague flashes of those above holding the weapons. Even Nana's young ones, who had baited the trap, were now on higher ground.

The troopers scrambled desperately for cover in rocks and behind trees, but there seemed to be nothing to protect them completely. Some part of their flesh was exposed to the Apaches' killing eyes.

They fired back until their guns burned their hands. The

cries of the horses were accompanied by those of wounded and dying men. In spite of the fatal trap, there were heroes that day. Men risked their lives to pull the wounded to cover. Some too late.

It was a hellish sound of battle symphony now, with the horses' cries, the shrieking wounded and dying, the snapping of limbs as bullets shattered them, along with the zinging crescendo of lead ricocheting from rocks and hard dirt, the men and their officers shouting helpless orders.

Company C and G arrived, and for a short time, it seemed they might have added enough weight to hold their ground, but Colonel Dudley saw that they would only add to the number of slaughtered and ordered a bugler to blow a withdrawal. The battle *out* of Las Animas Canyon was almost as deadly as staying in the trap, with the troopers trying to assist the wounded, save what horses were left, and with every man hoping to protect his own life.

Sgt. John Denny heard the cries of a wounded Private Freeland under his command. He turned, firing upward at ghosts, dodging from tree to tree, rock to rock, with lead singing and splattering all around him. Somehow he reached the thrice wounded Freeland. He hoisted the man's bloody body upon his back, pulling the private's arms together in front, carried and miraculously dragged him back for over four hundred yards through all the same obstacles and found safety in a rare crevice that afforded shelter from all sides. Then he checked the private's wounds—one in a lower leg, one in the side, and another that had shattered a hand—but nothing fatal for now.

Somehow Victorio sent a silent message to his warriors and the firing stopped.

An hour before this cease-fire, Lt. Gustavo Valois and Sgt. Moses Williams had led a scouting party of I Company of the Ninth about two miles to the north. They heard the distant shots and, knowing a battle was taking place, rode hard toward it. The unit only had seventeen troopers and scouts, but they could have observed the layout and ridden to attack on the rim of the canyon. However, the rough terrain slowed them and they arrived just as the guns went silent.

There was only the smell now of busted guts, drying blood, wafting gunpowder, and death. All they could do was volunteer to dig the graves and help with the wounded.

Colonel Dudley counted at least five dead troopers, sixteen or more wounded, three dead Indian scouts—their own—one of them Navajo, and thirty-two fallen horses.

Sergeant Moses and a few selected soldiers dug the shallow graves and buried the dead next to each other, covering the graves with rocks.

Lieutenant Valois said a short prayer: "God, bless these valiant men and take them home to rest." He paused a moment and then continued. "And please give me the strength and the privilege to choke the life out of Victorio with my bare hands."

Sergeant Moses flashed a tiny grin at his commander right in the middle of chaos. He understood. He had been there before. Sgt. John Denny, 2d Lt. Mathias Day, and 2d Lt. Robert Emmet eventually received the Congressional Medal of Honor for gallantry "above and beyond the call of duty."

If Victorio's band had suffered a single casualty, no one would ever know about it.

Col. Edward Hatch was a white officer who stood up for his men in every way possible. The men of the Ninth had fought under Hatch with much valor for a long time now, and they would as many times as he ordered them to in the future.

Dudley was a white officer the men disrespected. His actions of insulting the men of lesser rank by preening his colonelrey, and his thievery and chicanery in the Lincoln

County War, had imprinted disgust throughout. Colonel Hatch had long wanted to get Dudley out of the field but had been overridden by higher command. Now, because of the stupidity of the attack into the bottom of the canyon and the resultant disaster, Hatch finally had reason to demote Dudley to a desk job. He replaced him with Major Morrow. The men admired and felt comfortable with this fine field commander. All they asked for was proper respect and decent consideration for their sacrifices. No more, no less. Morrow gave them this respect and was a great tactician as well as a valiant fighter.

Earlier, while stationed at Fort Stanton near Lincoln, New Mexico, Dudley had illegally used his cannon and Gatling guns to scare into submission the participants in the infamous Lincoln County War—the political power conflict that had made Billy the Kid famous. He took Dolan's side against the opposing McSween forces because he had a half interest in one of his lucrative private businesses. Dudley also was known to trade horses and other goods with the proven crooked and powerful Santa Fe Ring—a powerful group of politicians, ranchers, and con men who controlled and profited from the trade of most of the territory. Hatch knew Dudley for a drunken, no-good son-of-a-bitch, and Dudley hated Hatch for knowing; but his all-powerful connections in Santa Fe and Washington protected him.

The fighting men of the Ninth were as happy with Morrow as it was possible to be in a land God, or the devil, had made for special kinds of killing.

Three

SGT. MOSES WILLIAMS CAME FROM A LARGE FAMILY, THE SON OF slaves, and he was a survivor. Because of his wide shoulders and powerful muscles, he seemed shorter than his five-foot-ten-inch height. There was a demeanor of assurance that made command come natural to him.

He had fought in the Civil War and in the Texas, Oklahoma, and Kansas Plains War against the Comanches, Kiowas, and others.

He had been wounded by a Comanche lance across his right side, by a Kiowa bullet in the left leg. An arrow had been extracted from his right arm after it completely penetrated the biceps, lodging in the pectoral muscle against his rib cage just above his heart. He considered himself a lucky soldier. Along with this presumed luck, he was also a very good, tough soldier.

Sgt. Moses Williams was given the extremely rare honor in the army of being called by his first name. He was known as Sergeant Moses or just plain Moses, to all, and he was the only one in the Ninth to be so honored.

Due to the high-quality fighting the black soldiers had

done in the Civil War, in 1866 the army had decided to form two black cavalry units for duty in the West. Col. George Armstrong Custer was offered the command of the Ninth. He turned it down and plotted instead to get the white Seventh Cavalry command to fight the Sioux and other tribes in Montana.

Moses was pleased when Colonel Hatch agreed to take command of the Ninth Regiment and thrilled that he'd been personally asked for by Lieutenant Valois, who was to command I Company. This tough disciplinarian had mellowed toward the men who had survived with him through the heat of many battles, many summers, in the Southwest, as well as the cold of the wind and death-chilled winters of the late war for the Union. Right now, the burying of the fallen at Las Animas Canyon was simply one of hundreds of distasteful duties the sergeant had performed.

The following week that onerous duty became the most exciting in Fort Selden. Lieutenant Valois, as always, had chosen Moses to head up a hunting party into the foothills of the Black Range to the northwest. They were to hunt deer to feed the soldiers. This fresh meat was extremely important to the health and strength of the fort's soldiers, and its delicious oak-brush flavor helped their morale immensely. Although Valois fought constantly to upgrade their provisions, they were always undersupplied, as the best supplies went to the white infantry and cavalry even when they didn't ask for it.

Moses's ebony, finely symmetrical face showed no expression, but his large black eyes had a gleam that the lieutenant and his best friend, Pvt. Augustus Walley, recognized: anticipation of the hunt.

The skinny Pvt. Augustus Walley was a hell of a soldier and friend, but a bad enemy. When he had a chance to drink, he became a dancing, laughing, joking pleasure until the moment that someone bothered—or he imagined they had bothered—one of his friends. Then he became a windmill of protective destruction, using whatever came to mind—striking, biting, kicking—as a weapon, until the offender was subdued. Even the mighty Sergeant Moses could seldom control him alone without using a rifle butt or a stick of wood to the jaw.

Walley had made corporal three times, but would no more. It was believed by all that that he would never be anything but a private. Just the same, both Lieutenant Valois, Moses, and all the men in I Company wanted him by their side in any battle. Walley put up with his place in the army because it was better treatment than he and all the others called Buffalo Soldiers—named that by the Apaches because of their thick curly hair and their bravery—could find in the postwar civilian world, despite all the stated "good intentions."

Because he was frequently in trouble didn't mean Walley was dumb. He and Moses had often privately agreed that the Civil War was not only fought to free slaves, as proclaimed worldwide, but the massive slaughter was actually about the land and the great potential wealth to be gained by both the North and South. Being in agreement makes friends. The sergeant and the private would die for one another and had nearly done so a number of times.

Moses was allotted seven pack mules to carry their hunting camp equipment and extra ammunition. He had his pick of ten horse-mounted soldiers and four camp and mule tenders.

Walley had a Springfield single-shot, 45–70 trapdoor rifle with a ten-power scope on it—the kind used in the late war and by buffalo hunters. It was protected in a sheepskin case of his own making to preserve the priceless sniping and hunting rifle and scope. He also carried into scouting, pursuit, and battle, a Marlin repeating rifle. It was extra weight, but he didn't mind. The private was the only soldier in I Company who could shoot as accurately as his sergeant.

Moses scattered the single-shot Springfield weapons and the repeating rifles among his party, according to each man's skills—the repeaters among good timber and brush hunters and the Springfields among the expert long-distance shooters.

As they rode out toward the lower semidesert foothills, a tiny smile finally came to Moses's lips as Walley said, "Hey, Sergeant, we've got enough guns and ammo to hunt all the way to the Pacific Ocean."

Moses answered, "Yeah, that'd be fun, except they'd put us to work picking cotton . . . besides . . . there're a million Apaches between here and there."

"Ain't nothing new about that," chimed in Corporal Smith. "They'd have our ball bags split and our legs run through the cut before we got to the Gila River."

Walley said, "You know, Sergeant, I s'pose between ole Geronimo, Cochise, Victorio, and Nana, they could have whupped both sides in the Civil War."

C. C. Smith answered, "They're sure makin' me old before my time; course I don't figure I had much of that time stuff to start with."

Moses said, "Gettin' old ain't nothing for you all to worry about, but staying alive right now is."

The soldiers' talk went on until they hit the high foothills. Then Moses raised his hand for silence. They might jump a deer or be jumped by the Apaches before they could set up camp in prime game territory. He sent Weta, the Navajo scout, who never changed expression except in a high wind, ahead to pick out the camp location near the deer territory and where they would be hidden from the Apaches.

The camp Weta found was in a random circle of cedars and a few dwarf pines. It had several rock outcroppings for battle cover if needed. It was in the oak brush foothills just as they bulged up, finally turning into the mountains of the massive Black Range. There was a spring nearby with sufficient water for men, horses, and mules.

That night Moses set up guard duties and they dined on beef jerky, hardtack, and water. The one blanket each soldier had left them cold in the high altitude. Even as the owls and night birds made their singular sounds, and the coyotes howled occasionally near and far, some dreamed of the green, warm lowlands of the Deep South and listened for the Apache at the same time.

Moses had paired up all, except the Navajo scout and the four camp tenders, assigning each to work the canyons. One would walk the bottom, the other the rim, trying to stay in sight of each other the best they could so they didn't shoot their partner—as had happened before.

The men felt good to be out of the high desert and around some evergreens. The fall reds and yellows of bushes had just begun coloring the landscape, and the distant aspen groves would shortly turn to glowing gold rivers through the thick blue timber of the high country.

Their mounts moved out eagerly, sensing the ancient hunters' adrenaline charge surging through their riders.

Sergeant Moses and Private Walley were paired and knew from long experience what to do. Wordlessly they tied their horses and the pack mule and checked their arms and ammo. Walley headed for the rimrock with the scope-mounted 45–70. The sergeant held back until he spotted the lean, quick-climbing figure of Walley moving now along the rim. Moses headed along the bottom, skirting boulders and brush with his Marlin repeater held ready. It was rough going at first. Then a game trail dropped down, weaving along the contours of the earth. Deer sign was heavy. Fresh pellet droppings were everywhere. The pointed tracks of does and the wider-spread tracks of bucks moved along the trail in and out of the brush. He saw several spots where the grass and brush was flattened for a night's bedding down. Prime deer country.

The second stage of the hunter's surge caused his heart to thump like a scared rabbit's. He thrilled at it. For a few moments he could forget that he had stalked, and been stalked, by the enemy for years now. There was no difference in the immensely heightened awareness, however. Whether Confederate soldiers, Plains Comanches, the Warm Springs Apaches, or living venison, the blood sang the same symphony of the ancient urge.

Moses saw Walley moving forward on the rim and the tracks in the game trail. He located each opening ahead just as it came into view. He could smell the living blood of deer as well as he could smell the Apaches. He knew all this without having to think. That's why he was still alive, awake, uncommonly aware.

The brush thickened just ahead as the game trail curved to the left out of his sight. Instantly, he realized that Walley was not moving ahead. His muscles bunched and he automatically raised the rifle as Walley's 45–70 cracked, creating a roaring echo through the canyon. Seven deer bounded out of the brush about fifty yards in front of him and made their mistakes. They bounced into the opening—uphill to the right.

The Marlin's sights were on the front of a deer's shoulder. The bullet left the muzzle of the Marlin, and Moses could actually feel it pierce the air, right into the back of the deer's shoulder. He knew it had gone through the heart and chest of the creature as it reared up slightly then fell sideways and down dead.

He levered another shell into the chamber and took the

last animal in line, dropping it not five yards from the first. As the third shell was fulcrumed into firing position, he lowered the rifle. He knew the rest of the deer had escaped to be hunted by someone or something else another day, another hour.

Without hesitation he charged up the hill, jerked the four-pointer and the spike buck's heads downhill, slit their throats deep, and watched as the clean, red blood flowed down, turning dark instantly where it found soft earth to soak into. The kill stage of the adrenaline—the highest high it gave—started subsiding. He was Sgt. Moses Williams, Buffalo Soldier, again.

He saw Walley walking swiftly, almost running downhill toward his target. Walley glanced up as he moved, feeling Moses's eyes and sensing his silent command. He motioned up, then down, pointing at the spot where he had shot. Moses knew Walley had made a kill.

When he reached the private, a couple of hundred yards ahead, he was surprised to find Walley had already dragged the deer up the hill out of the very bottom of the canyon, cut its throat, and was sitting waiting, about to take a chew of tobacco. He was grinning as wide as his mouth and face would stretch.

"Head shot. Keeps the meat clean."

Moses said, "Heart shots on mine . . . but *I* got *two.*"

Half the grin left Walley's face and he pointed down at the game trail. "There's the track of a buck that's biggern . . . biggern . . . a train engine."

"Yeah, I been follerin' 'im. Living long enough to get that big means he's damn smart. I guarantee you, he's watchin' us right now."

Walley's grin vanished as his eyes furtively perused the terrain. It was the same now as if an Apache was observing them. Walley said softly, "Lordy, Lordee."

* * *

It had turned into a fine hunt. Fourteen dressed out deer carcasses had been hung from tree limbs. The November nights had chilled the meat well. The hunting unit had feasted on the fresh venison as their own special reward. Today would be the last day of the hunt.

They left before sunrise as they would be working canyons and foothills more distant. About a mile from camp Moses had a sudden impulse. "Hey, Walley, I dreamed about that big buck we tracked the first day. I just gotta go try him out."

Walley grinned easily. "You done said he was smarter'n a hoot owl."

"I suppose you're right. I'm probably wasting my time, but I just gotta try."

They split up. Moses rode into the canyon where they had first struck the three-deer bonanza. There were lots of fresh tracks crisscrossing the game trail.

He observed the prints of a pair of lobo wolves, the almost round print of a bobcat, and some rabbits. The arrowhead-shaped track of a coyote came in and out of the trail as it, too, hunted in the brush and rocks. A mountain lion had crossed the trail in one spot and disappeared into the vegetation. In a small opening he saw the scattered feathers of a wild turkey where one of the predators had stalked, killed, and feasted.

As yet, he found no fresh deer sign of any kind. However, nature's newspaper was printed there on the earth for anyone who could read her own special language. Moses thought he was good at it, but the sight of the lion's tracks made him queasy. Maybe the lion had brought down the big deer in another canyon. Or maybe the wise old buck had moved on to another range. Still, he couldn't quit riding up and up.

Before he realized it, his horse was beginning to sweat a bit on the shoulders and in the flanks. He was now riding the zigzagging game trail in thicker timber and bigger rocks. It was harder to read and had less sign.

Suddenly, the horse snorted, throwing its ears up, muscles all bunched, looking down into a swale. Moses instinctively jerked his rifle from the scabbard and into firing position as he stared down at a large, black bear. At his movement the bear "whoofed" and took off with deceiving speed into a cluster of spruce, vanishing in its friendly shadows.

Moses kicked his horse on up, his hunter's nerves vibrating now. The horse calmed. He kept the rifle in arm. Then he saw where the old buck had dropped its large pellets as it moved across the trail. It was so fresh and so surprising—for in truth he was almost ready to give up—that he felt embarrassed at the sound of the blood pulsating in his ears.

He could see through the trees that a narrow meadow of golden brown grass was not far ahead. There was a chance— a very small one—that he could probably get one quick shot there, if at all. He quickly dismounted, tied his bay horse, Badger, and moved swiftly, smoothly, quietly along the twisting dim trail as if he was nearing the great Chief Victorio himself. The wind was southwesterly in his favor.

In one tiny clear spot in the trail he saw a single track of the buck. Huge. Near. Now the unfathomable zoned magic of all the elements that make up the world, the universe, the man himself, were in total harmony surrounding him. He floated forward. He did not need breath nor muscles nor bones, but he felt all. The contest.

Just across the meadow on a rise, an old Apache on a dappled gray horse was looking through a telescope. The treasured instrument he looked through was a prize from a leader of a small unit of cavalry guarding an ammunition wagon, foolishly disguised with hay. There had been a quick ambush. All were killed, but one Buffalo Soldier had somehow escaped to tell the tale.

Now he was watching through the glass as some of his younger warriors were readying to attack the hunting camp far below. It would be a swift strike for all he wanted today was ammunition. Ammunition, that was what *he* could smell. Some said he could smell it all the way through three mountains. He recognized the glimpse of the bay horse as one he'd once owned. He vowed to get him back.

He dropped the glass down with satisfaction. His warriors had come at the camp upwind and were ready for a swift strike. They would gather the ammo and meet him at the rendezvous spot far up in the high cliffs. His old eyes spotted a blurred movement across the narrow meadow. His rifle came up.

The huge old buck sensed something behind him, but he couldn't smell it or hear it for certain. He stopped in the last cover at the edge of the meadow, surveyed the opening carefully, and picked the nearest trees on the other side of the meadow and decided to move out across the open terrain as swiftly as possible.

Moses also saw a blur of movement at the edge of the meadow. There was no time for caution now if he was to get a shot in. He raced and dodged forward with urgent, desperate speed.

Even the Indian's aged eyes recognized the mightiest buck of his long life as it bounced out into the meadow. With no need for thought—he would have been unable to resist the chance at the prize of a lifetime anyway—he kicked his horse down into the opening for a clear shot.

* * *

All three experienced veterans made a mistake as the unexpected danger closed on the buck from two sides. Suddenly the buck swerved to his left and after three long leaps realized he had trapped himself. There were sheer bluffs at least twenty feet high. He whirled back now with no choice but to run the two-man gauntlet.

The Indian raised his gun with his horse turned sideways so the sound would not hurt the animal's ears. He liked running shots anyway, as the movement of his arms was smoother than trying to hold still for a standing target.

Although Moses was good either way, a running shot was better sport. More fun. Just as the great buck was almost exactly between the two hunters, who were as experienced as the buck, a triple moment of fatefulness occurred. The buck had been fired at many times and flesh wounded twice. He expected the same or worse in this suspended instant.

Moses's sights were on the buck and then, for the first time since his opening battle in the late war, he froze.

The old Indian saw his nemesis above and beyond the buck as it escaped downhill, and he, too, froze.

Neither one would ever be able to explain it to themselves or anyone else. Both could have shot at the same time and died. One might have shot the other first by a fraction. Moses's eyesight seemed to leap away from his gun sights and telescope for a moment of immeasurable speed into those of the Apache. The same happened to the old man. The Buffalo Soldier's face was slightly blurred to the Apache, but big and clear enough to remember forever. They both fired without sighting and missed each other. Both heard the crack of the lead-shattered air just above their heads.

The Indian whirled his horse for cover and disappeared as

Moses raced, almost leaping into the cover of some rocks. And then Moses's heart slowly slowed. He knew he had experienced some kind of event beyond his conscious body, but he could not explain it.

The old Indian knew it was not the time. They would meet again. Even he didn't know how *many* times.

Four

MOSES WAS NUMBLY RIDING DOWN INTO THE LOWER FOOTHILLS, when he spotted Private Walley and Cpl. C. C. Smith, about a quarter of a mile distant, with a deer on the back of each of their two pack mules. That was very good, considering how heavily they had hunted the foothills. Behind them, perhaps a half mile, were four more Buffalo Soldiers. He couldn't tell if they had scored meat or not. Somehow he wasn't cheered. How was he going to explain what had happened on *his* hunt?

That question was jarred out of his mind by sudden gunfire from the camp. He knew. He yelled across the hills with a warrior's scream all his men recognized and charged downhill.

Walley and Smith turned the deer-toting mules loose and spurred forward as hard as their horses could run, all jerking rifles out ready to fire.

Moses saw the mounted Apaches breaking out of the campsite and heading southwest. He yelled in another tone of authority, motioning to Smith and Walley to follow him. They did. He knew the other soldiers would soon be in camp to help any wounded. His horse was tired from the steep climb but valiantly pounded on, even though his nostrils were flared as wide as possible pulling air into his straining lungs.

There were seven Apaches and they had four cavalry horses in tow. It wasn't the horses that angered Moses as much as it was the large ammo pouch he recognized across the leader's shoulders. He was used to firing on the run the same as the Apaches, but he knew the leader was already out of range of his repeater. He swung it back and fired at an Apache warrior leading away two of the army's horses.

It was a lucky shot. The bullet went through the rider's lower leg and the horse at the same time. They rolled in a churning boil of dust. The Apache somehow fell free and screamed the name of the rider just ahead of him. The Apache's law, which cannot be broken, demanded that if a wounded fighter shouted a fellow warrior's name, he must return to recover that body, living or dead. The named man slid his horse to a stop and whirled back, yelling something. The wounded man stumbled upright, standing mostly on his good leg. The rider slowed, circled, coming back grabbing him and somehow jerking him up behind him, heading again for the hills and the Black Range. Home.

Moses had to admire this action while he fired twice more and missed. Walley had jerked his horse to a stop and knelt with the long-range Springfield to get the leader, but he was a fraction late. His prey had escaped with two hundred rounds of ammunition. That was a hell of a weight to carry and make such a run. They had heard some return shots snap above them and a few had dug dust wads from the earth. All missed.

Smith fired his repeating rifle until it was empty, but it was futile. The Apaches had the angle and had vanished into the hills they knew so well.

Walley had remounted and started to spur on in pursuit,

but Moses gave the come-back yell. He knew they were out-numbered and he had been sucked into far too many ambushes when he was overmatched. He wore the scars.

The Apaches had turned the other two horses loose. And two more horses had escaped when Moses's shot struck the rider leading them.

Moses yelled, "Go get our horses!"

He rode over and dismounted by the wounded horse. The animal tried to struggle to its feet, almost made it, and then fell back down with its neck raised and its head twisted back in agony, looking at Moses for succor. He pulled, aimed, and fired the revolver bullet into its brain as fast as possible. It always made him a little sick to his stomach to shoot a crippled horse. In all the years of battle he had never gotten used to the final act. He could kill a half-dozen men much more easily. He swallowed the sourness back, mounted, and joined Walley and Smith, who led two horses each.

Walley was mad at himself for not having dismounted earlier, even though Moses said, "Hey, soldiers, we got one of their horses, rescued ours, and busted an Apache leg all to hell."

"Well . . . yeah, but they got our ammo."

Moses knew there was no use of further discussion, Walley would have followed until he fell, even if he'd had to carry his guts in his hands all the way.

They rode up to the camp. One soldier had been pierced by an arrow in his heart and lay on his back as if he had been shot from above and pinned to the earth. Another man had three arrows in him. One had struck his Adam's apple, shattering his neck bones on the way out. One was in his stomach at an angle, and the third pinned his hand to his chest. Two had been shot but were alive and talking. Weta, the

Navajo guide, had been struck in the right arm and then knife-gutted like one of the deer that hung from the trees.

The straggling soldiers were already building travois to pull the two wounded men. They would live if they got them back to the base hospital or if infection didn't get them first.

Moses consoled the injured and realized that the ambush had been planned for bows and arrows, the Apaches hoping to silently kill the soldiers and have time to make off with supplies of the entire camp. The Warm Springs Apaches had been forced by greater numbers of soldiers and guns to fight hit-and-run. They had turned into great opportunists. But it was the Navajo scout who had fired back. Even though he missed, he had made the Apaches go to their guns, and that sound had brought Moses and the others down upon them.

Moses helped dig the three graves. It took awhile to get the holes dug and refilled, and he had half his men gathering rocks to pile on them. For a moment he wondered how many uncounted souls were scattered across this vast Mimbres and Gila River land in one, two, three to a grave, and even more. How many had only the honor of feeding the buzzards, coyotes, and worms who lived because of the dead? No one but the Great Mystery would ever know.

Moses said, simply, at the new grave site, "Oh, Lord, take these brave men home with you and feed 'em and drink 'em good. They fought and they died well. Amen."

On the long ride home, with the wounded in pain and their ammo gone west, the survivors were partially consoled by the fourteen dressed-out deer that would relieve the taste of hardtack for a few days for the men of I Company. There was nothing new on this trip that hadn't happened many times before, except, of course, the unfathomable meeting with the old Indian warrior.

At this thought, it seemed Walley had continued it or

maybe even answered it to a degree. "It wuz ol' Nana that planned that ambush. I knows it deep in my insides. Everybody says he can smell ammo through three big mountains."

Moses heard his friend all too well, but kept silent. Nana? Could it have been him after all this time of chasing, fighting, and trying to read his unseen mind? Yes, it had to be. No one else that old could have whirled his horse and vanished into the timber like the old Indian had. His heart increased its opening and closing speed a bit.

"Nana," he said, under his breath.

He had to clear Nana from his mind. He could imagine the Indian's powerful black eyes telescoped to a foot in front of his face, seeing into his brain, his soul. He thought, instead, of Bitch Moose's Hog Ranch. That's what the soldiers called the wilderness whorehouses. It wasn't out of disrespect they did so, for women were scarce, precious, and prized. It was said over a large area that Bitch Moose had the best women and the worst whiskey in the whole territory. Selling her own cheap, homemade whiskey so she could hire the pick of the girls was simply a wise business decision. Miners, gamblers, outlaws, and soldiers were not particular about either after long denial, but she had the most pleasing and profitable formula just the same. However, it was mostly officers and only a few entrepreneurial enlisted men who could afford her place. If they had enough money, she had good whiskey to go with the best women. Nevertheless, all dreamed of going there even if only a few had the wherewithal.

Lieutenant Valois would also be pleased with their successful hunt more than he would decry their losses. "Those ambushes happen several times every day out here, but it's not often that we have a week to ten days of feasting on fresh fat venison," he said.

Always, Valois gave the successful hunting party a three-day pass. There was not a survivor among the unit who hadn't thought of Bitch Moose's before they reached the fort, including the wounded. Mighty heavenly dice were being thrown for Moses now. He would learn that on the trip to the Hog Ranch.

Five

JOSHUA NELSON PROUDLY RODE POINT IN THE IMPRESSIVE CAR-
avan winding its way south. With him rode a unit of six Buffalo Soldiers. Gold coins passed to the proper political hands
had ensured the cavalry escort through the disputed Apache
land. Besides the drivers of the three freight wagons and a
smaller family wagon, he also had two personally hired white
scouts and one Navajo scout. All carried side arms and rifles.

He had been a major general in the "War against the
South," as he always called it. He and Nelda had first come
from Pennsylvania to Santa Fe, then moved south to Socorro
where they had set up their successful mercantile business.
He daydreamed over and over of his fertile plans. He was
certain the mineral strikes were in their infancy, and he had
a simple, but dedicated, business theory: just follow the
mines.

In just a few days, they would have their second store set
up somewhere in the Hillsboro-Kingston area, and if it was
successful, they would expand over the Black Range to Pinos
Altos near Silver City.

He was fifty-five but rode his majestic black horse as if his physical condition was that of a twenty-year-old and his mental wisdom that of a millenium. He was a tad proud.

He had left Robert in charge of the business at Socorro. Brent would take over the store in southern New Mexico. He wished they had had more sons. It would have put his expansion plans on a faster schedule.

Nelson rode just slightly in front of the family's four-horse wagon. It had a space in front for his wife, Nelda, and Sheela Jones. Brent followed slightly behind his mother's wagon.

While Sheela was trained to clean, cook, and all manner of activities meant to serve, Nelda had also taught her the art of fine sewing and embroidery and how to read and write, even though Nelson insisted this teaching was not to go beyond a certain point. Sheela being an orphan—but a free woman—the General wanted her to be polished only roughly so she wouldn't be tempted to leave them. Sheela, however, knew far more than she let anyone know—anyone except Nelda, of course.

Nelda was very protective of her, but Sheela's natural beauty was getting harder to hide and protect. Nelda observed all manner of men, from the crudest miners to the most sophisticated gentlemen, give Sheela that ancient look.

The thing Nelda did not know—because he was too smart to give himself away openly—was that her husband had tried twice in the past week to touch the girl when Nelda was away from the house. When the virginal Sheela had resisted, the General had covered by saying, "My dear girl, you've taken me all wrong. I only wanted to show the affection of a father to you."

Sheela knew better, but she also understood it was simply a matter of a moment of chance until he would try again.

She knew she was very lucky to have a mistress who respected her abilities and genuinely cared for her. She also accepted the reality, although she was treated like a true member of the family, that she was not a Nelson. Her blood carried the genes of the long-ago time when half her ancestry had raced through a great plains and bush, free as the gazelle, fearless as the lion, and graceful as the pink flamingos from the vast seasonal lakes. There was an unworded craving to be out on her own, as her healthy blood sent signals to her soul all the way from the primeval. For now, here in the jolting wagon beside Nelda, she was safe, and so she subdued any resentments and looked forward to the end of the journey.

Out in the lead, eyes working the foothills for any enemy, the General rode toward an out camp at the waterhole called Sweetwater Springs. He could see the cottonwood and other brush turning yellow and red a little over a mile ahead where one of the guides said they should spend the night. They might even rest and graze the horses and mules for a day here. They had not stopped during the daytime since leaving Socorro over a week ago. The General wanted to get into the area and have his business set up before the risk of November snows that sometimes came early and stayed.

The heavily loaded, eight-mule freight wagons made a constant groaning sound as if each turn of the wheels gave them both pain and some delight. There were brand-new buckets, tin tubs, and carefully packed dishes, hats, gloves, pants, dresses, long underwear, trinkets, and articles of need of all kinds in the great wagons. One was loaded with coffee beans, flour, cornmeal, sugar, sorghum molasses, and food goods of many sorts to please the mostly dried-meat-hardtack diet of the miners. At the very back of this wagon a space had been reserved for the newest hunting rifles of the day, plus knives and ammunition to sell with the guns.

Thus, a creaking, jolting mass of comforting treasure

moved determinedly across the semidesert, intending to shortly supply many tastes, needs, and demands of those who had invaded the land of the Mimbres and Warm Springs Apaches.

Six

NANA LOOKED THROUGH CAPTURED FIELD GLASSES, WATCHING the small caravan down below the foothills move along slowly in the dust. They seemed like four oddly shaped bugs moving toward some eternal rendezvous. He had given his folding glass to his favorite eleven-year-old grandson, Kaywayhla, whom he had been training as his own personal scout.

Nana turned to his *segundo*, Kaytennae, and the only Apache war woman, Lozen, and said, "They are rich with mules, these wagons, and I smell ammunition. They have more than one band of Buffalo Soldiers and perhaps that many more white guns. What do you think?"

"We have more warriors," Kaytennae said. He motioned toward the waiting band below in a swag.

Lozen said, "Uncle, allow me to use the big eyes and we will talk further."

Since Victorio's sister was respected by all Apaches as a great tactician, Nana handed her the glasses as she dismounted and crouched forward on the promontory above the springs. She held the glasses on the wagons for several minutes, studying the surrounding terrain as well. Then she stood with her arms stretched out to her sides palms up.

Those warriors nearest her watched as her palms turned red and her arms swung together and pointed at the small wagon train. The amount of time it took for her clasped, pointing palms to blush told of the enemies' whereabouts and, also, approximately how many there were.

She said, "What we see with our eyes are all." Then she scooted back, mounting her horse when out of danger of being spotted by the train.

Lozen said, "Grandfather, we can take them without many losses. If you agree, I will take half our warriors and ride back to an arroyo. We can come up unseen behind the wagons. We will be only a long spear-throw distance."

Nana said, "Ah, I see; then we will attack with much noise downhill, drawing their attention and their fire?"

"Yes, Grandfather," Lozen said—most called him this out of respect, some in actuality—"you must watch for my signal. If we time it exactly, we should be able to create a great surprise."

Nana spoke solemnly. "There is much we can use there, Lozen, much our people need."

There were many mules to ride, pack, and eat whenever needed; horses, saddles, and foodstuff, besides the guns and ammunition. If successful, this could be an extremely valuable raid.

No one ever questioned Nana about ammunition; that was his strongest power. Everyone, even the Buffalo Soldiers, said he could smell it through three mountains. It was said over and over, both in amazement and resentment.

Lozen raised her rifle, adjusted her heavy gun belt where it crossed between her breasts, and rode down to lead her part of the band, carefully seeking the exact position.

Nana and his *segundo* waited patiently, almost motionless, until the time was right. Then they split their forces and Kaytennae, with nine warriors, moved west perhaps a quarter of a mile, keeping out of sight of the train. The other eight warriors had joined Nana.

Nana had taken a prone position, twisting his right leg slightly so his long-ago crippled right foot would be more comfortable. He watched as the train neared the waterhole and waited for them to stop. He knew Lozen would not attack until they were busy unhooking the mules and horses from the wagons. That would be their weakest moment, when the small wagon train's escorts were anticipating the evening's food, water, and rest.

When the train had crossed the arroyo and the mules had dug in their hooves, pulling the loaded wagons to the prairie trail again, everyone felt more relaxed and the mules' breathing returned to near normal. Everyone was dust caked, and even more than food, they craved and delighted in the thought of the warm water springs to ease the dryness of their insides and cleanse their dusty outsides. It would be a luxury indeed.

As they neared the springs, Sheela studied Nelda's profile, her perfectly narrow nose and great blue eyes. She saw the glance of warmth and closeness above a quick smile that Nelda gave her as the wagons were haltingly, groaningly, formed into a half circle around the springs. That look created a warmth, a comfort, knowing the only person in the world she trusted and loved cared deeply for her.

For the last few miles, Sheela had stoically ignored that she needed to make water. There was a special hole in the wagon bed floor for the women, but somehow she had hesitated to use it today.

The wagons were in full stop position when she told Nelda that she would hasten to some nearby brush before they started unloading the cookware for the evening meal. Over her shoulders she wore the shawl that Nelda had made for her birthday. It always gave her a feeling of Nelda's protection and warmth. Security.

"Of course, dear, but watch out for snakes."

The soldiers dismounted and set up a picket line for their horses and all the others, and joined in unhooking the mules from the wagons.

Sheela felt the General's eyes hot on her back. She knew he would watch her fluid movements across the space to the heavy brush. A momentary dread brushed across her young body. At last she was safe in a deer's bed, where the brush had been pushed apart. She raised her long, full skirt and started pulling down her pantaloons so she could squat and relieve herself.

Lozen and her warriors were only a quarter mile or less around a bend in the dry arroyo when the last wagon topped out silently in the sandy bottom. They moved carefully forward until they were at a near point to the forming camp. She signaled Nana. He signaled Kaytennae. Instantly they attacked from the rimrocks, riding back and forth, creating great dust on the soft downslope, yelling and firing in a growing crescendo.

The soldiers, the mule skinners, and the General all grabbed the most available weapons; but not only were they completely surprised, they were now confused. Corporal Scroggins fell, with a bullet entering his eye and opening up the back of his head.

Nana wanted the General. As he rode past, an Apache warrior was knocked from his horse. A soldier's bullet had ripped a hole in his heart.

Nana was proud of his Winchester. He was the only one in his band to have one. It had been issued in 1866, but it had taken awhile for a few to move to his part of the West. Nana had heard that one could start shooting on Sunday and shoot all week.

Nana raised the 44–70 Winchester twelve-shot and fired. He missed. The General was down on one knee trying to get a decent moving shot in the churned dust.

Nana whirled his horse, levered in another shell, and

charged, weaving closer to the General. Although he was in his late seventies and had a hard time walking with his lame foot, once he was horseback he was home, as skilled as any young warrior, and far more experienced.

Now he saw the General swinging his rifle toward him. He knew he would get his horse first. Nana went into the *floating space* now. The vacuum of time stopped where everything hesitated for a fulfillment. The Winchester centered on the General's mouth, and Nana saw the lead leave his gun and his old half-blind eyes could see the bullet as it moved toward its target. The hunting spirit left his body and guided the bullet through the General's upper lip, knocking the roots of two teeth to bits and tearing apart the vertebrae that connected his head to his spine. Before the General fell backward, spewing blood on the ground, the hunting spirit had returned to Nana's soul.

It was too late for the small supply train. Lozen and her band came up from the blind side, firing with ease into the backs of those standing. The two or three who realized the trap had turned to fight too late.

The mules and horses screamed; two mules and three horses were down. Brent was shot from his horse with an arrow in his heart. He died instantly. One wounded soldier tried to crawl into the front of Nelda's wagon and Lozen charged right up to him. Saving a bullet, she plunged her twelve-inch knife into the center of his back.

Nelda, feeling death upon her, helplessly raised a cooking pan and hurled it at Lozen so hard she fell out over the draped dead soldier. Without a break in her movement, Lozen swung the knife with such force that Nelda's head hit the dirt and rolled a couple of yards.

The battle was over. Sudden death was more than common in the Territory.

The Warm Springs Apaches methodically, swiftly from long practice, gathered the surviving mules, horses, and what food they could use while moving away from the Buffalo Soldiers who were sure to come.

Nana was left alone to smell out the ammo. He went straight to the back of the General's lead wagon and there it was with many new guns. A great coup. They packed everything they could on the mules and whatever they could tie on their own horses and moved out toward the sun, still just above the ragged silhouettes of the Black Range.

The next day, or the next, was bound to bring the soldiers and their guns along the broad, impossible-to-hide trail. If they reached the mountains far enough ahead they could join their women and children high in the hidden sanctuary and, for a short while, celebrate the victory, feed their emaciated bodies, and love their families for a brief spell before it all started over again.

They left the scene with three dead of their own across the backs of mules and two wounded tied to their horses. Nana led the trek as he had done uncountable times. Lozen rode proudly by his side, knowing her brother Victorio would have exulted in sharing the day's victory; these were becoming fewer and fewer.

The dust around the column was golden for a tiny moment, then all vanished into a coyote night.

Sheela had just relieved herself when she heard the first shot. She started to make a dash for the wagons, but the fusillade increased instantly and the discord of shattered horses and men stayed her. A blur of horse legs pounded by her, throwing dust into her nostrils and eyes. Wrapping the shawl as tightly as possible, she crawled, shaking, deeper into the clawing, scratching brush, not feeling her skin tear.

The battle lasted less time than a prayer, but it seemed to

Sheela that the hands of a clock would have made three circles. Then the sudden short quiet that follows all battles was broken by the growing sounds of the Apaches' voices as they gathered the bounty of the raid and tended to their own dead and wounded. She tried not to breathe.

At last, when they had moved away and the sounds had faded in the distant, absorbing earth, she struggled free of the grasping brush and crawled until she could see around the edge. She had heard of these catastrophes, but now she was part of one.

Numbly, she stepped toward their wagon—hers and Nelda's. She tried not to look at the General, but her side vision revealed his body anyway. Then she saw Brent stretched out on his back with an arrow in his chest. In her numbed thoughts, he looked peaceful to her.

The only sound was a gust of wind just strong enough to rock the wagon a tiny bit and create a slight, lonely creaking. The very last rays of the sun reached around a corner of a peak of the Black Range just as she jerked away from the bloody-backed trooper halfway inside their wagon. Then she found the head of her beloved Nelda. For a singular moment the sun gave Nelda's eyes a semblance of life as Sheela looked into them.

Then the sun was gone. The twilight was complete. With a sob for the lost choked back into the pain of her chest, her heart, Sheela stumbled into the darkness away from her only anchor to life, to nothing at all.

Seven

THE PART OF THE NINTH CAVALRY KNOWN AS I TROOP AND C Troop of the Tenth had pursued the victorious Nana's wide trail for days. But now the trail was cold. Nana had left a few warriors to fire into the tired soldiers each twilight as they attempted to pitch camp, then vanish into the deepening shadows before the troops could return any effective fire. Moreover, the old Indian had split his forces so that the greatest tactical warrior on earth could not have been able to conceive of their true direction.

The Warm Springs Apaches would know when to move to their hidden spot among mighty bluffs with springs and grass and game. It had been their home, their hunting and loving and ceremonial ground, for hundreds of years. At any rate, the delaying fire wounded several Buffalo Soldiers and many of their horses were killed. Then the blizzard came surprisingly, as early fall storms often do, and the soldiers were blind for a spell in the almost total whiteout.

Sergeant Moses had lost his assigned cavalry horse and so had Private Walley and others. They had walked for days upward through the gravel and hand-sized stones of both dry and wet creek beds until parts of their feet were touching the earth through their worn-out boot soles. As they tried to find their way down from the failed chase, their feet left little spots of red in the snow. The white wind shot bullets of ice into the eyes, the lungs, the limbs, and numbed all—some eternally. Three of the wounded died from exposure.

They slid downward through the white, freezing blindness. Sometimes they broke the crust of frozen snow and turned ankles and bruised flesh and bone on the rocks beneath.

Moses yelled now, above the merciless, killing wind, cursing, cajoling his crippled troops to follow him and Lieutenant Valois. The lieutenant was walking on a fractured leg, and Moses helped him to his feet again and again. Finally, he got him mounted on one of the mules that, unlike the horses, were somehow able to keep their footing. It saved him.

Walley had, in his usual odd actions, taken it on himself to save the horses and mules by tying them together tail to bridle, leading, following, and talking horse talk to save most of them. All the mules, horses, and men left increasing spots and smears of red as hooves and shanks were cut and soles were ripped from the soldiers' feet. There was so much hurting that it became a oneness, but they could handle it together, and prevail.

Finally, the survivors staggered, limped, and even crawled down into the foothills, eleven bloody miles from the fort. A blind goat could have tracked them. The damage by the cold and, finally, the scattered trail, along with the deadly gunfire of the delaying actions, had been enough to defeat the two thin companies, but it was the white blasts of the entire mountain range that caused the real wounding.

As they buried those few who died and the surgeon amputated frozen fingers and toes, the healing process was almost invisibly underway. A few more horses had to be put down, but all the mules survived that had not been shot earlier by the Apaches. Lieutenant Valois was on crutches, but he was a fast healer. All suffered, but Moses's group seemed to be in better shape than most.

There was no time to grieve. They had to heal and reorganize to pursue again. Again. Again. And then, too, none of the hunting party had been able to enjoy their promised leave. They healed faster thinking of that. Later they would have time to swear at and hate old Nana and his warriors, along with a reluctant admiration that they all kept secret within themselves. It was difficult to hate and admire at the same time, but they did.

Eight

APACHES FROM DIFFERENT BANDS, TRIBES, AND DIRECTIONS raided the lowlands on through the winter. They fought soldiers, miners, farmers, ranchers, freight and stagecoach travelers, and, occasionally, even attacked small towns. The weather at Fort Selden was almost summerlike for about three weeks. The semidesert nights were often cold, but it was a respite for the members of the Ninth stationed there and helped their healing. In turn the enemy was able to hunt, feed, and strengthen just as they did.

Sergeant Moses had arranged that he, Walley, and C. C. Smith would go on leave together. When they had been stationed at Fort Bayard near Pinos Altos and Silver City, Moses had added a tidy sum to his small fortune now secure in the company safe. He had several sidelines for picking up extra money. He had rented out four fine mules and two horses that he'd acquired through capture and trade. He charged fifty cents a day for their use. He had also, along with several others, worked in the mines between battles at $2.50 per day—the highest wages available. These activities were forbidden by army regulations, but he was too valuable to court-martial. His entrepreneurial spirit was left alone as long as there were no official complaints. Who would be foolish enough to complain when Moses's best friend was the unpredictable Walley? All this, along with the ten cents he charged to write letters and agreements for the illiterate, created an accumulation of funds far beyond the savings of anyone in the company—including Lieutenant Valois.

The lieutenant didn't have any concern, as his own wife was wealthy. Christine Valois was born to a cloth-manufacturing family from Boston. Moses liked her; she never lorded it over any of her husband's men, and on occasion she organized plays, musicals, and other events to relieve the tedium of loneliness and the daily risking of life's blood among the Buffalo Soldiers. Christine Valois was appreciated.

Once Private Walley had nearly choked a new replacement into oblivion for making an untoward remark about Missus Christine Valois. Fortunately, six soldiers were present to pry his hands from the malefactor's voice box. It didn't help for long. The offender was shot in the Adam's apple in a running skirmish with Victorio's warriors a week later.

Moses sensed that something, over the long years, had to be helping him help himself. He couldn't pin it down exactly, but he felt he had a guardian angel or something that seemed to guide him just an inch away sometimes from certain death. Then, too, he had acquired the *warrior's warning* that all long-time combat men have—the sudden ice on the neck and the instant strange hum in the ears. But there was something else—a lifetime invisible something—a personal guide, maybe.

Now as they cleaned up their worn uniforms for their leave, and were issued other, used, boots, Moses could not explain why that invisible but ever-present power made him draw from his company account ten times as much money as he usually would. It still left him as secure financially as one could be under frontier circumstances, but still it was far more than he would use to help finance the party with Walley and Smith.

They rode for Mesilla, where there would be several drinking and dancing joints and where Bitch Moose ran the most famous, the finest, the most expensive "Hog Ranch" in the entire territory.

As she often proclaimed, "My drinks have the least water, my girls are the cleanest and most beautiful in the territory, so, fine gentlemen, you pay the price or stay home."

Those who could paid gladly.

Nine

THE SPANISH PLAZA OF MESILLA IN FAR SOUTHERN NEW MEX-
ico was constantly in movement. Traders and adventurers
up from nearby Mexico, miners, mine owners, prospectors,
stockmen, farmers, merchants, gamblers, whores, and a very
small scattering of ladies and gentlemen from all over the
territory came by stagecoach, wagon, and team—both
freighter and personal—by buggy, horse, and mule back, even
walking beside burros or just walking alone. This crossroads
along the Rio Grande would soon see the rail line reach there
on its route to tie in El Paso a few miles south.

There was a smell both instantly recognizable and at the
same time unique to the dry desert air. Scents from the sweat
glands of all these creatures, wild and domestic and of every
nationality and attitude, clung to the fine dust and permeated
the air breathed by all. A water wagon constantly traversed
the plaza road to keep the air breathable.

Some had come to fight the Apache because it was a better choice than they had had in the Civil War–torn land full
of hate they had left. Some came for gold or to trade with
those who had found it. Some came to take it away, by cunning or violence, from anyone who had it. Some had come to

love and caress the land into blessing them with bounties of mutton, beef, fruit, and other necessities. There were as many reasons for their coming West as there were particles of fine dust around the plaza.

Moses, Walley, and C.C. were aware of all this in only their subconscious minds, if at all. What they wanted to do was escape—to forget—the horrors of the uncounted Apache trails they had so recently, and for so long, endured, and miraculously survived.

They passed a bakery owned and operated by a Chinese family named Ho. The smell of fresh bread and sweet rolls filled their nostrils. The three Buffalo Soldiers could not resist the delicacies. They stopped, turned back, entered, and bought three loaves of fresh, hot bread. They tore into the crust and devoured each crumb to the grinning delight of Mr. Wong To Ho and his entire family. The soldiers craved more, but controlled themselves, saving space for a full meal.

Next, they entered an eating establishment and gorged themselves on steaming roast lamb seasoned with chili sauces, potatoes, and bread with thick milk gravy and lots of black pepper. This was topped off with a huge helping of moist wild berry cobbler and finished with a cigar. They then relaxed, content enough to visit for a bit—but not about anything worthwhile—and not for too long.

They walked outside with a rare fullness of the stomach and lingering of good tastes still in their mouths. They untied and mounted their horses and rode to the side of the plaza to the Red Barrel Saloon.

Moses led them to a corner table where they could survey the entire bar with little but adobe wall to their backs. After buying an expensive bottle of cheap whiskey and double shot glasses, the second part of the town party began. They toasted I Company, they toasted Mesilla, they toasted God, then they toasted the toast itself.

Private Walley said, "Now, here's to blowin' ol' Nana so far apart the magpies cain't find even a tiny little piece of 'im."

Corporal Smith said, with a big grin, "That ain't no good. Here's to gut shootin' 'im and lettin' the coyotes fight over his bones while we watch laughin' ourselves silly."

Moses lost his grin momentarily, solemnly raised his glass, and said, "I swear to y'all on the Bible," and he faked his hand on the good book, "and on my ol' mama's and daddy's graves, and on my own heart, that I'll put my sights on Nana's wild ass before I go to my reward."

The toasting and conversation about Nana ended when Walley said, "Hey, we come down here and eat all this high-class feed, and drink all this good stuff, and we act like we're still out in the brush chasin' Indians. Sheeiiit, we jist gotta forget about Nana for a spell."

Moses and C.C. nodded in affirmation. They had made a dent in funds paying for the expansively delicious meal and they certainly wanted to forget all those years of bullets, blood, and pain.

"Hey, soldiers, I'm feelin' *muy rico,*" he said, in two of thirty words of get-by Spanish he knew. "Your ol' sergeant's gonna treat you to the best gals at Bitch Moose's hog ranch."

"Bitch Moose's?" they echoed, looking at one another incredulously. This was so special they could not grasp it. No matter how wild they had dreamed, neither Walley nor C.C. ever figured on being able to afford one of Bitch Moose's selections. They thought their leader was kidding them. When they saw he was serious, the dreaming became real before it happened and affected them straight in their longing loins.

They followed their leader out to the horses like baby ducks follow their mama. They mounted and rode out to the edge of town to Bitch Moose's fortified hacienda.

As they rode along, Walley suddenly reined up. The other two horses automatically stopped. "Sergeant, it's sure nice of you to treat us to all this good stuff, but there ain't no use in goin' on." At the questioning looks he got from his fellow soldiers, he continued, "Lordy, Lordee, I forgot to tell you . . . I done froze my balls off in that blizzard on the mountain. They dropped right out of my pants soon's we got back to the fort. They broke up in such tiny little pieces when they hit the floor I just swept 'em out in the parade ground where soldiers and horses been trompin' on 'em ever since."

Walley bent forward in the saddle, covered his face with both hands, trying, unsuccessfully, to stop the roar of laughter that was about to escape from him. They all joined in and laughed away the many aches and thoughts of Nana, one Apache menace.

They reached their destination with such anticipation they could barely stand up after dismounting. A heaven had come down to visit the earth and picked three Buffalo Soldiers for the experience.

They were met by two armed guards, who took their mounts and tied them at a hitching rail beside two fancy horse-drawn buggies and several other saddled animals.

Bitch Moose herself greeted them as they entered the sanctuary. She was an awesome sight, towering at least two inches above Private Walley, the tallest of the trio.

She grabbed Moses's hands and shook them both with arms as big around as a gallon coffeepot, saying, "Well, if it ain't Sergeant Moses. Where you been so long, Sonny?" Her great blue eyes swallowed his being, as she continued. "We missed you. You're looking good and still mostly in one piece, huh?"

"Yes, ma'am, I'm *mostly* still Moses."

"Well, you young'uns come on up to the bar. The first drink is on Bitch Moose, by God."

Private Walley stared, stunned, by the massive white

woman. Her breasts would have made proper counterweights to a box of cannonballs. Her thighs bulged through the huge, purple silky dress, the legs somehow shapely even though a kick propelled by such power could have splintered a pine tree into toothpicks. Walley's eyes were so vision-shocked he could not see anything else and there was plenty to see. Bitch Moose's moist lips were so red and full as she talked, he was so dazed by their odd sensuousness that none of the details of her greeting registered in his brain. To Walley it was just a sound emanating from the body of the biggest, greatest, most beautiful woman in the whole world. This veteran of countless bloody battles was scared silly of her.

Jorge Campos, the Mexican bartender, served all three a double shot with dexterity and a certain elegance to match his eagle-faced demeanor. He said, "I only take one drink during working hours, boys, but here's to the dandy dancers, the whiskey wranglers, and the wild whore lovers."

It would have been impossible under any circumstances to refuse such a gratuity, but this booming yet silken voice, and the brown liquid smooth as an angel's caress, could only be accepted with great honor and pleasure to match.

Bitch Moose had to leave to greet another guest. All three stared after her amazing buttocks, whose movements would have ground walnuts to powder.

Walley whispered to Moses, "Can we afford her? Lordy, Lordee. She's the one I want."

Moses whispered back, "Jorge is her husband. He's got a crowbar and two Colt repeaters under the bar. 'Sides she's as true to him as the color of her eyes."

Walley felt sadly diminished until he had his second silky whiskey and the girls began to slowly circulate among them. The trio retired to a table to peruse the surroundings. The curtains, the wallpaper, everything seemed to be properly deep red.

A Mexican fiddler in a sombrero and white shirt, black em-
broidered vest, and tight black pants started playing an old
Spanish love song from a distant alcove. It was a cue for the
girls to come out of their own hidden rooms to waft about
along with the music. Bitch Moose insisted they wear subtle
perfumes so it would enter the nostrils and slowly infiltrate
the brain with strong hints of passion. The girls, like Mesilla's
citizens and visitors, were of many nationalities, sizes, shapes,
and attitudes. The women circulated only as they were asked
by potential patrons. There was no faking of phony drinks.
They all had water, tea, or coffee, and everybody knew it. At
Bitch Moose's, the customer got what he paid for.

C.C. led his Latin lady over to a corner table so they could
be alone away from the gaze of others.

Walley still watched his own *true* love—the madam herself—but was soon distracted by a half-Indian, half-Irish lady
called Maude. After a couple of more drinks his love shifted
from the boss lady to her employee. He had held her soft,
olive-colored hand in his darker brown one and looked into
her light brown eyes. She wrapped her personality around
him like a fishnet. He looked no more, and they soon de-
parted for her room, talking about things that would never be
known to anyone else.

Three women with enticingly different physical and emotional approaches had joined Moses. He had smelled their
delicate perfume, and impulses of the flesh had stirred him
almost to the snapping point as he observed what he had so
seldom had in his life of big and little wars—woman. He was
polite. He was caring. He needed one of them. He wanted all
of them, but something beyond any experience he had ever
had held him back. He didn't understand why. His body told
him with certainty that he could not restrict himself much
longer.

He looked around and saw that C.C. and Walley had both

gone their separate ways. And then the answer to the "why" of his hesitation approached.

Bitch Moose stood majestically in the center of the room and clapped her hands together. The fiddler stopped playing. All stopped drinking. All looked at the madam.

"I feel a moment of special time is here. A revelation, a treat for the weary and longing. We have Lieutenant Sanders of C Company of the Tenth. We have my old friend, Sgt. Moses Williams from I Company of the Ninth. We have His Honor, District Court Judge Samuel Carr, down from Santa Fe, and one of our area's leading freighters and merchants, Mr. Carlos Ortíz." She named all she knew, and those she didn't, she included en masse. "Gentlemen, have you ever heard the saying by someone, maybe it was me, 'Scarce as a virgin in a whorehouse'? Well, men of conscience and taste, here is the real thing."

At her signal the fiddler started playing a slow, haunting piece of love music. A curtain opened and a young woman walked shyly forward.

Moses saw her large, slanted, obsidian eyes before he saw the rest of her. He knew the true look of fear better than any man here. In spite of that, her natural walk was so sensuous that there was a mutual gasp for air in the blue-smoked, red-walled room by every male present.

"Gentlemen, I present my newest protégé, Sheela Jones."

Bitch Moose took Sheela by the hands and, with both their arms outstretched, moved in a complete circle. Sheela Jones wore a subtle golden dress that emphasized her smooth golden skin, her dark, angled eyes, and the sublime curves of her body.

Then Bitch Moose led her respectfully back behind the curtain and returned with her great red lips smiling proudly as their voices rose.

"How much, Bitch Moose? I'm first."

"No, you're not. I can outbid you, my friend."

"Don't listen to these gentlemen. I will make a better bid than anyone of them."

Then they all talked excitedly, lustfully, at once. Bitch Moose enjoyed casting a loving I-told-you-so look at her husband, Jorge Campos. He returned a knowing wink, smiling, as pleased as she.

"Now, now, my anxious friends. Calm your pounding hearts. If I were a whore with a heart of gold, I'd cut it out and put it in a steel safe." The nervous laughter rippled through the room in stuttered waves. She continued, "What you buy tonight is priceless. A thing of great beauty and class. To be her first is not just a question of money, for she has a say in this beautiful beginning. It must not be spoiled by pure lust or ego. Ah, no, this event must be consummated by a combination of money, a giving of honorable word for tenderness and care, and her own agreement to the first submission." She moved in front of the bar and leaned lightly against it as she continued, "All of us here in this room have suffered the sudden shocks and personal losses of frontier violence. But this lovely being you have just observed has lived through a sudden shock beyond any of our capabilities of survival. So I insist that the lucky winner treat her with extreme tenderness and sensitivity." Then she smiled and added, "If not, you will answer to me . . . to us." She cast one majestic arm toward Jorge, whose own smile complemented his wife's while both his hands touched the pistols under the bar. Everything here was clearly understood.

The clients of the establishment glanced nervously at one another, trying to appear confident. All, that is, except Moses. He was ready for war.

One excited client spoke up. "That was *our* deal and all in the territory know that the word of Bitch Moose—the madam—also known as Mrs. Jorge Campos, is as good as that of the Lord of Lords himself."

There were "yeahs" and "bravos" and then a voice above the others, "Please tell us, Madam Moose, how we apply, or contest, if you will."

"Of course," she said. "I shall interview each of you in my office. I will write down your reasons for thinking you qualify and present them to Sheela for her final decision. Come with me, if you can afford it, Your Honor," and she motioned for Judge Samuel Carr to follow.

It was her moment. This woman from the Saint Louis slums had a sense of history. She had bedded so many men who had made history or were in the process of doing so, working her way to becoming a famous madam, that she knew this night would be talked about for years. The word-of-mouth advertising of Bitch Moose's hacienda of momentary contentment would continue.

Moses sat stunned. He was the only patron in the entire hacienda that had remained voiceless. When his two happy soldier friends returned with their girls, passions relieved for now and still talking about sundry nothings, he felt a moment of joy for their good feelings and even attempted to explain what a monumental thing was occurring. They didn't get it and didn't care. They had dived into that world of temporary escape that becomes more precious to caring warriors than buckets of gold.

As Moses watched the powerful and wealthy go and come from the madam's office, he felt more misery than could be caused by a Comanche lance, or a horse rolling over him, or a bullet tearing his flesh, or walking with soleless boots bloodying the hard, harsh desert rocks with each step. Sheela's frightened eyes had possessed, yes, even obsessed, him. A strange combination of fear and courage emanated from them, filling the room, filling his heart. His body was numb all over. The air he breathed seemed heavy as mud.

At last he moved toward Bitch Moose's office door and pushed it open. Her mighty arms raised above the desk, her hands beckoning him with that vast landmark smile dividing her face.

"Come, come, Sergeant. What caused your hesitation? Forgive me. I should have known you were a man who would never give in without a battle. That's what you are, a fighter."

The sonorous voice enveloped him and washed away the numbness. Still, he didn't feel she would believe that a cavalry soldier would have a chance against the powerful military, political, and financial men vying for the prize: Sheela.

The name itself, even in his thinking, caused him to tingle like a first true kiss. The hesitation was over. All scouting of the mind that was possible under the restricted conditions had been done. He knew the enemy. He attacked.

Moses pulled a rawhide money poke from his pocket, opened the drawstring, took four ten-dollar gold pieces out, placing them to the side, as he said, "This is to take care of Private Walley and Corporal Smith until their leave is up day after tomorrow." He looked into the magnetic blue spaces of Bitch Moose's eyes and saw that she had agreed to his first move. Without hesitation he stacked three fifty-dollar coins, five twenties, and ten tens side by side. It was a fortune in those days and had been earned a gram at a bloody time, killing and nearly being killed, mucking gold and silver ore for twelve hours a day deep in the dusty near-darkness of deadly tunnels and shafts. He had captured and rented horses, and he had written hundreds of letters and agreements for his comrades at ten cents each. Sgt. Moses Williams now laid it on the line atop the walnut table. He looked at the madam. She had, from long practice, counted the money with just a glance.

The madam looked at him. In that instant they both some-how understood that their struggles in life had been equal.

Bitch Moose spoke as head-on as the soldier. "Sergeant, that will be sufficient for the first part of the bargain." He took a deep, sweet breath before she went on. "However, I must ask you, knowing the deprivation of female comfort soldiers of the Apache wars suffer, if you have the control to treat her with care? Since it is her first time, it should be done with patience and tenderness. You must, for this one night, give her real love. Sheela is unique, you see. You can-not imagine *how* unique."

Unbeknownst to the suitors, Sheela had been observing each one from a tiny crack in the door that led into Mr. and Mrs. Jorge Campos's own large bedroom. Her agreement with the madam had let her have the final say. The first choice would be made by Bitch Moose and the final by Sheela. Once the winner was chosen, there could be no backing out and both would have to live with it. Of course, it was a slightly one-sided deal, as Bitch Moose would have the front money and the continuing services—extremely profitable services if handled properly—of the girl as well.

Moses said, "I fully understand, ma'am."

"Just call me Bitch." She looked at him hard for an in-stant, rose up to her extensive height, adding, "Excuse me a moment, if you will, Sergeant."

"Yes, ma'am . . . Bitch."

She eased through the door and Moses stared at the back wall above the desk where a crude, but somehow lovely, *retablo*—a wooden religious tablet—hung. Painted on it was Our Lady of Guadalupe, the virgin saint. He stared at it as hypnotized as a ground rat is by a rattlesnake. It was both out of place and apropos. He had fought, hated, and admired the Apache so long that he had adopted some of their traits. One of them was patience. He put himself on hold. Clock time vanished. Earth cycle times vanished. Times of the turn-ing galaxies and the expanding universe ceased to exist. Sto-icism was perfected.

Then Bitch Moose returned with that face-ripping smile—her lips as red as fresh blood. "I hope you take no offense, Sergeant, but I stand before you amazed, considering the competition. You, sir, are the winner."

His brain only registered the last five words, but they were enough to scare him half blind as well as deaf. He followed her out through the curtains and down a short hallway, where it turned into a long corridor with several doors to the rooms of lust—each girl to her own. With a mighty arm, Bitch Moose gently tapped on a heavy, imported door with many designs of circles carved in it.

"Sheela, the sergeant is here."

The door slowly opened about two inches, and Moses stared at one dark eye, voiceless, motionless. He wasn't even aware that the madam was gone. The door slowly opened wider, with Sheela hiding her body behind it.

He entered, removing his service cap, and shyly looked around, surprised at how big and neat the room was. There was a heavy walnut bed with soft red covering, an armoire of cherry wood, a fine table, and two red velvet, cushioned chairs. There was a washbasin, drinking glasses, pitchers of water, and a half-body-size mirror hanging next to it, and next to that, a vanity table with a tilting mirror. A combination hat and clothing rack with a walking stick basket stood near the door; a folding dressing screen filled one whole corner of the room.

Subtle perfume cast its spell, but through it his Apache hunting nose detected again her own personal scent. This gave him the courage to turn and stare at her as she leaned on the now closed door. She stared at him, trying to push herself hard enough against the wood so he would not notice her shaking.

Sgt. Moses Williams had participated in the offerings of whorehouses in seven or eight states and Mexico. He had gotten drunk, relieved the pressure of his loins, laughed, fist-fought, and mostly had a hell of a lot of fun just as fast as it could be done before going back to his world of maiming and killing. None of this entered his conscious mind now. He started to speak, but she beat him to it.

"Madam Moose has spent a lot of money and time training me for this . . . this moment . . . so . . . you may do what you wish. I seem to have forgotten all she taught me."

"It's all right," he said, amazed at the sound of his own voice, as if he was listening to someone else speak. "It will be fine. Please, don't worry . . . please, don't be afraid." He noticed the oil lamp tea warmer on a corner table. "Maybe we can have some tea. I like tea. Do you like tea? I'll just sit down here, if you don't mind fixing the tea. I'm pretty nervous myself. I'd probably drop the pot."

He sat down awkwardly in one of the cushioned chairs, almost missing it because his eyes were now locked on hers, trying to see what she was feeling. As he righted himself safely in the chair, they both began laughing at the same time.

She took a deep breath and said, with growing confidence, "I'm glad it's not just me who's nervous. Maybe I can make the tea without burning the place down." She worked carefully at her task. "The water is already hot; it will take only a minute," she said, as she lit the wick with a match. The flame caressed the bottom of the tea pot as she brought one cup and saucer over, holding it with both hands to still the shaking.

He could not resist watching her move across the room. A

rhythm rippled up and down her body from her feet to the top of her head. She couldn't help it. A powerful sexuality exuded at each step. As she returned, he lowered his eyes out of respect.

She placed the second, slightly rattling cup, on the table next to her chair. She said with great relief, "There, that's done." Then taking a quick glance into each other's dark eyes, they had another laugh at how ridiculous each felt they appeared to the other. The laughter had eased their tension by half, and soon she poured them each a cup and set the pot in the middle of the table on a silver trivet.

Moses had, in his lifetime, drunk about everything in the liquid world, but this was the first time he had ever had tea in a whorehouse. There were many firsts facing the two of them this evening.

Slowly they relaxed, carefully at first, and then more freely talked of their pasts. He told of his childhood life as a slave in Georgia and the disappearance of his family, traded or sold, while he was made a houseboy to his owners. And she revealed her memories, so very vague, of her early childhood somewhere in the East. Her only true memory was of Nelda and the General.

He was not ready to talk yet of his war experiences in some of the great battles of the Civil War, nor about the escape and terrible travels to reach the Union side, nor how, with great irony, he missed the rich Georgia earth and woods even while being bought and owned by others. There was so much else to share with each other. Most young lovers-to-be find with weighty amazement that they have an unprecedented number of things in common. Moses and Sheela were no exception. They could find out later where they were different. They had no family that they knew of—strong reason by itself to pull them closer for company and comfort. They had both been fortunate to have been tutored by the well-educated in writing, reading, speech, numbers, and manners. They each savored the same foods . . . and . . . they both liked tea! They loved horses. How extraordinary that they shared a love for the last rays of the setting sun and then the quiet, peaceful twilight.

They were so alike that at last she told him of the massacre at Sweetwater Springs by Indians. She had a powerful urge to tell him of her escape and her terrible travails in somehow reaching Bitch Moose's; but no matter how hard she strained or how many times she tried, there were still only blurred, fleeting, and uncertain visions of what had happened. The shock had been too much for her mind to remember in much detail.

Then . . . then when he told her that his unit had been ordered into the pursuit of the terrible old man and of the consequent disaster and death, not only from gunfire, but the unfeeling blizzard.

They both realized they had found each other and were bound together by more than just coincidence.

Seeing the tears held back in her great slanted eyes, Moses could not resist touching her any longer.

He walked around beside her and pulled her head into his stomach, caressing the long, slightly wavy, dark brown hair with streaks of amber through it. He wanted to care for her forever. She reached around his hips, pulling herself tighter against him. If there was any sound in all the world beyond their own beating hearts they could not hear it. It was a moment alone together in all the savage and beautiful universe. A moment so special that only they could, or would, ever feel it. This they knew for certain like first real love everywhere.

Without breaking the enchantment, they stood naked together and each pulled the other to themselves. Then the nature of youth, the eternal, ancient drive that had kept humans on the earth for millions of years took over.

He picked her up and carried her to the bed. He kissed her softly as he caressed her smooth, golden body. She was afraid no more. All the tricks Bitch Moose had taught her were forgotten. She took his hands and put them on her breasts. He touched her dark V gently and probed its softness until it was damp, preparing for entry. She moaned so softly it was almost felt rather than heard. Her body now found a new, natural movement under both the soothing and exciting touch of his hands. Carefully, gradually, he slid inside her. Soon they were lost in the vacuum and vortex of undoubted, undeniable love.

Ten

THEY LAY ON THEIR BACKS STARING UP AT THE PATTERNS OF THE blue stitching in the red cloth glued smoothly to the ceiling. They were both exhausted and exhilarated.

Suddenly Sheela sat upright in the bed, pushed the sheets back, and moved swiftly across the room to the closet.

Moses propped himself up as she opened the cabinet doors wide. He saw the smear of blood on the sheet that signified the end of her virginity.

"Look, Moses," she said, pulling out and draping the dark golden threaded shawl around her neck and down over her breasts, where it also crossed over her stomach. "See, I do have something left from my past. Miss Nelda made it for me." She caressed it lovingly, looking at him for approval.

"It is beautiful. The most beautiful thing I ever saw."

"Thank you," she said softly, remembering how hard it had been to repair the damage done to her body and spirit during her mostly blank ordeal.

But he had not meant to praise the shawl alone but the entire effect of the dark golden cloth fitting the lighter gold of her skin. Her raven eyes gleaming with pleasure in the soft glow of the oil lamp sent invisible shivers through his war-hardened body. As she mashed the shawl against the curves of her body, his love for her turned to a sudden craving yet again. He could be a well-regimented man in control under the most stressful situations—that had been proven on many deadly occasions throughout the years—now he actually had to grit his teeth to the shattering point to keep from bedding her again. He must not. She would be sore enough tomorrow to temporarily forget the wonder of their embraces.

To prove his ability to control what was uncontrollable in most men, he got up and went to her and patted the material with both hands on her breasts.

"I will keep it always," she said with determination.

"Yes. Yes, you will." Feeling himself beginning to harden, he turned from her with great effort and started dressing.

Sheela forgot the shawl. "You're not going away, are you? I thought you had two more days of leave left. Please . . ." She cut the last plaintive query to one word.

As he pulled his boots on, he looked up at her where she stood nude, holding the shawl draped across her arm. "I'm not leaving right now. And I'm not leaving without you."

She swallowed. Her eyes and face showed enormous emotion and confusion. "What . . . what do you mean?"

"Just what you heard. I'm taking you with me."

Now her whole being was stricken. He did his best to ease her terror, saying softly, "It's simple, darling Sheela. I love you. I'm going to take you to the fort, and you will be my wife for the rest of my life."

"Your wife?"

"Yes."

"But Madam Moose, she saved me. She saved my life. She healed my body. She spent so much time and money . . . see . . ." She pointed at all the day clothes and the night clothes of promised whoring and hurried on as if her voice and reason might fail her. "Madam had all these made especially for me. She doctored me . . . she saved me . . . she . . ." Sheela reached in and pulled an eggshell-colored dressing gown of fine lace and sheer fabric and put it on. She pulled it around her fine body tightly as if she could explain and hide at the same time.

Moses's mouth was dry, but he said, "Sheela, no matter what, you are a free woman now. Hundreds of thousands of white people and black people died for that. All you owe her is your thanks."

"But, Moses, all the care and time and money she gave me for months."

"I will give her your thanks, and I'll pay her the money debt."

"We can't. Oh, God, we can't."

"Sheela please pack so we can leave when I come back."

"I don't have a bag, even if I could bring myself to . . ."

"Stuff them in the pillowcases," he interrupted. "Leave the whoring dresses, bring the others, and that gown you're wearing. I want to see you in it on our wedding day . . . or night. And don't forget your shawl."

He turned and walked out the door as she pitifully, pleadingly, cried after him, "Moses, oh, Moses, please don't . . . ," and her voice faded away.

He could hear the bed sounds and moans in a couple of the rooms as he made his way through the halls to the private office of Bitch Moose. She was not there. He sat down in the same chair as before and waited. Now he heard the muffled noise of drinking, talking, laughter, and he waited motionless. He waited and then he waited some more. It was interminable because he was afraid Sheela might go to the madam before he could return.

Then she entered with a box of money to put in the large safe against the wall in a far corner.

She smiled in her own singular fashion, saying without

hesitation, "Sergeant Williams, how could you leave your treasure so soon? I didn't expect to see you—except for food and drinks—until your leave was over."

He was just as straightforward. "Bitch, ma'am, I love Sheela. I really love that woman, and I want to take her with me and marry her."

She finished putting the money in the safe, undulated her great curves over, and sat across from him. He was surprised at her control. Placing her elbows on the tabletop and propping her head up with her hands, she said, "Of course you do. This happens at least once a week. I used to agree occasionally in my more innocent days and let the infatuated take a girl with him. Invariably, she was back in a few days, abandoned, her heart—and sometimes her skin—broken. No more, Sergeant . . . and especially *not* Sheela. As I'm sure you know by now, she is a jewel of great rarity."

"Yes, ma'am, she *is* that, but I'm taking her. You've got to understand, no matter what."

Her tone changed dramatically. "Don't talk to me about understanding a goddamned thing. That child came to my door out of her mind, scared to death, bruised and scratched all over." Her voice softened. "She had walked along the river for days, hiding in the thickets, starving, eating berries and even insects to stay alive. It was weeks before I could heal her body and mind enough so she could tell me what horrible things had happened to her. It was a miracle, Sergeant, her miracle, my miracle." She paused and spoke in a businesslike tone. "I damn sure intend to collect for my trouble. I didn't go into this business for my health. I went into it for money . . . for power. You know that."

"I'm sorry, Bitch . . . ma'am, but I ain't like the other men. You oughta know that. You sure oughta know I love her when I say I do. I have never felt this way about a woman in my whole life. Not once."

"You're a fine man, Moses. One of my better patrons over the years, but let me tell you something. I've known hundreds, maybe thousands of men—and there was only two of them worth lovin'. Real love always grows slowly, Sergeant. I *know* the difference between love and passion. You can trust me on that, son. It takes time, a long time. It takes living through tough events and many difficult times successfully together."

"I know you're right about the time thing, but I don't have the luxury. I've learned to make gardens grow fast. I sometimes have to make things happen so fast that you can't even see them. Wouldn't you die for Jorge if you were forced to it?"

"Well, yes, but that *don't* have anything to do with Sheela."

"Pardon me, ma'am, but it has everything to do with her." He stared his black eyes straight into the center of her walnut-sized blue ones, trying to project an absolute truth of his soul into her. "I'm willing to die for her in a second—so fast it would make your eyes whirl."

There was a silence as the staring continued in both directions with profound possibilities.

"There is no other choice for me, you see." He pulled out his money poke and emptied the two hundred and some odd dollars in gold coins in a small pile on the desktop without removing his eyes from hers.

"Death is *always* dancing on my shadow, ma'am. It gives you abilities most folks regretfully can't understand. We will need another horse. I'll send it back with my next man to get leave. Just tell Walley and C.C. the truth about this and tell them to enjoy the next two days of their leave."

They both stood up, ready to kill. Then Bitch Moose knew that the result would be bad business. The men of the Ninth and Tenth were highly respected, and they certainly covered the entire southern territory of New Mexico and Arizona. A battle such as this would become gossip and spread like the flu. It would involve her beloved Jorge.

"You, Walley, and C.C. have paid fair and square, Sergeant. I usually don't let my heart get involved with any of the girls—or the patrons—for that matter, but I have a certain feeling for Sheela." She stuck out her hand, saying with emphasis, "I don't expect to ever see either of you again."

"You won't, Bitch, ma'am. You surely won't." He left to get his woman, his love, almost in an Apache trail trot.

Eleven

MOSES AND SHEELA DID NOT RETURN TO THE FORT BY THE MAIN
trail, the one the Warm Springs Apaches knew so well, as did
numerous robbers and rapers of the area. Instead they trav-
eled along game trails and across the foothills that Moses
knew. Sheela's love for horses was apparent in the proud and
skilled way she rode, balancing her entire body with the
rhythms of the horse's stride. He wished he had bargained for
the buckskin gelding as an engagement gift for her; but a
horse like that, with a good rein, a fine distance-devouring,
running walk, and all-day muscles, would have cost a lot. He
consoled himself that he had ol' Badger for her from Nana's
band, which Nana, in turn, had captured from others.

Moses knew Nana must be downed. What his band had
done to Sheela's family and friends overcame his hidden admiration for the old trickster. When he looked at Sheela
under the late day sun, she was a precious apparition indeed.
All the dramatic and fearful changes in her life in less than
four months would have doomed most people to a future of
depression or madness. Here she rode expertly, confidently,
beside him across a wilderness so vast that away from the few
main trails a person could go for days without seeing another

human being or be attacked and mutilated swifter than the hawk's dive. How could she be so composed? The life of a Buffalo Soldier, even at the fort, was one of constant deprivation of good food and one of disease and great loneliness, with yearnings for things of comfort and safety that often seemed nothing but a far distant, dusty dream. Moses thought the truth of the soldiers' helpers—the wives who were washerwomen, cooks, housekeepers of the officers' quarters, and some who were used to service the soldiers as well—was far worse than she could imagine at this moment. It was her innate courage and the long, loving tutoring of Nelda Nelson that had given Sheela this outward appearance of felicity.

The dawning came to Moses suddenly. He had just doubled his responsibilities. He didn't want to get killed, but now he would have to worry about it for her sake and the sake of their future children. He also worried because he realized how hard this soldiering life would be for Sheela. They would just have to make the best of it.

Each time Sheela gave Moses a smiling glance from her dark, arched, silently speaking eyes, she felt as if she would melt into the earth with the insects. Of course, all this controlled appearance was just that. This man, who made her heart beat erratically and her body warmly prickle, had risked his all for her. She never wanted to cause him the least unnecessary concern. But underneath, she knew she was going into a harsh, unpredictable world.

She was suddenly filled with wonder—and some fear. She tried to visualize what Fort Selden looked like. What her responsibilities would be. Would she be capable of making a good wife for a combat soldier? What if he was killed? What would happen to her then? She would be all alone. Again.

Ever so slowly her horse was angling away from Moses as her outward vision turned opaque, like sugar frosting on a

cake. Her vision had turned inward, and she struggled might-
ily to see clearly what the shock had hidden from her on the
long trek from Nelda's severed head to Bitch Moose's healing arms. No matter how much she dredged her mind, only
scattered pieces evolved. There were flashes of her hiding,
afraid of all settlements, all travelers. She again felt the sting
of scorpions, red and black ants, and countless other insects
when she lay nearly dead from exhaustion. There were
cloudy remembrances of thorns and cactus spines penetrat-
ing her flesh. She remembered desperately trying to cut the
rancid meat from a freshly dead sheep with the edge of a
rock.

She remembered, in tiny bursts of light, drinking from the
Rio Grande and becoming sick so that she vomited until her
stomach bled. The river. Yes, that incident by the river was
the strongest blur of all. The three prospectors with three
burros had found her in a fevered sleep. What was it the one
with the rotten teeth and the smell of a year's sweat had said?
What was it?

"Well, look at this nugget I found here, boys."

Then the laughter. *That,* she could still hear like she had
just been dumped naked into hell in a cave full of murderers
and rapists.

"I get first assay, boys," he had said, reaching for her. She
had tried desperately to pull away, and in fact had. Then she
fell, crawling toward the river as the prospector walked beside her saying all sorts of things.

"Why, honey, I ain't gonna hurt you. Not none atall. Fact
is, you're gonna enjoy it like a heifer in heat. Ain't that right,
boys? Jist like a honeymoon, Abe. Only she's gonna have
three husbands 'stead of one. See how lucky you are, girl."

Those were the last words he would ever utter. Sheela had
reached the Rio Grande's banks and as the stinking man
jerked her up by one arm to embrace her, she came up with

a river rock in the other hand and drove it with all her will into his nose and forehead. If all else remained vague and confused, she would always feel the crunch of his nose and skull bones as she killed her first man. He had simply dropped straight down in a heap that unfolded limply into a motionless corpse.

The other two stared, stunned, at their friend's lifeless body, then looked at her with death in their eyes. She whirled and dived into the river, letting its current carry her across several bends far out of the dreadful sight of the men. She swam and floated on and on. Then, without being fully aware of all that happened, she awakened from a deep sleep on a small, grassy bank. The first thing she did was pull her tattered dress up and pantaloons down to stare at her crotch. There was no blood anywhere. She had escaped being ravished, but at that time she could not even piece this series of events together. The second shock was the fact that she couldn't find her shawl—her most treasured of all material possessions. She desperately felt and clawed around in the grass and rocks as if she could somehow conjure it up. A cold panic gripped her heart, and she placed a hand there to still the anxiety and felt the golden threads safely folded in the bosom of her dress where she had put it for protection days before. Although she was mostly dried out, she felt a sudden cool comfort from the still damp shawl and fell over in exhaustion.

The rest was a series of disconnected, unclear images. She had skirted like a lion-trailed doe around the very fort they were headed for now, but she could not make anything of the rest of the fragments.

Then there was nothing but Bitch Moose's mighty blue eyes swimming in a void above her and later, after all the sharp things had been removed by tweezers from her flesh by big Bitch's handmaiden, Beulah, she remembered the madam rubbing her body softly with a healing, aromatic oil and her voice caressing her battered mind as softly as the breeze from a butterfly's wings.

Moses had noticed her veering off right from the start, but recognized the glazed, great distance stare in her eyes. He had seen this look in the eyes of soldiers after a battle where some of their closest comrades had been blown apart. The protective, vacant stare of shock taking away the clear impressions that saved one from madness. He rode by her until the outer light suddenly returned to her eyes. She did not remember the inner voyage she had just taken.

He reined next to her and reached for her hand. The comfort that this strong, dark hand gave her caused a concealed fear to emerge.

"Moses, what happens if your commander refuses to accept me at the fort?"

He had already thoroughly thought this out. "I don't think that will happen, but if it does, I'll hide you in a spot near the fort that I know about. I'll withdraw our four hundred dollars in gold coin from the company safe and . . . I'll desert."

There was no doubt from his voice that he had spoken hard facts.

They rode on without speaking. There was no need for words now. They were totally committed to whatever came about. Whatever. Whenever. For this special moment, at least.

Twelve

ONE OF THE GREAT ACTS OF STUPIDITY DURING THE APACHE wars was so very simple to resolve. All the government had to do was allow Victorio, Nana, Lozen, and their Warm Springs Apaches to return to Camp Ojo Caliente, the reservation in the middle of their homeland where they knew how to survive off the land and properly worship the Great Mystery in the sky. Instead, they kept remaindering them to the San Carlos Reservation in Arizona and the Mescalero in New Mexico. A tragic mistake. The leaders and their loyal followers became disenchanted with these reserves, their hearts longing and hurting for their own place of ancient habitation. A belonging.

They fought with great bravery and extreme violence from the time the California gold rushers crossed their land and the miners, farmers, and ranchers; the opportunists and businesspeople who were followed in turn by government officials and the army to protect their claims. It had always been so, but seldom had so few fought so many so desperately as the Warm Springs Apaches did these invaders.

Mexican farms grew into little fortified towns with churches, businesses, and even plazas for leisure and celebrations. When gold and silver was found around and on the Mexican and Indian lands, booms started and the legitimate and the outlawed all moved in, armed themselves, and soon were supported by over a thousand armed, well-prepared veteran soldiers of other wars.

The Mimbres and Warm Springs Apaches were soon denigrated, called "bad neighbors," something to be argued over between the Indian agencies. The seasoned army and new settlers were angry at any attempt by the indigenous people to hold enough land to stave off starvation.

Victorio led Nana and Lozen and sometimes fought alongside Geronimo and Mangas Coloradas, outnumbered beyond counting, taking along the women and children. There were well over a thousand soldiers in pursuit of Victorio's band, which numbered at any given time between twenty and one hundred. The furor grew so great in the main towns and all the way to Santa Fe that railroads had started extending into the southern area of the state, as had telegraph lines, in an effort to outsupply and outmaneuver the Warm Springs defenders.

Newspapers blared headlines of terrible massacres by the Apaches. Entire villages were said to have been wiped out and slaughtered. If one-tenth of these claims had been true, the Apaches would have been alone in their lands again.

One rail line had reached Deming, near the mouth of the boot heel of New Mexico not far from the Mexican border. Entire boxcars of supplies could be shipped to the white and Buffalo Soldier troops. And so their advantage was becoming apparent, since Victorio and his bands had to scrounge, raid, hide, and do battle all over the Black Range and into the lower deserts just to stay alive.

Colonel Hatch, the commander of the Ninth Cavalry, passed orders down to Major Morrow to split up the men and make raids wherever he could find the enemy. Sometimes the soldiers of I Troop were forced to resupply and regroup at Fort Craig, Fort Bayard, Fort Cummings, and their favorite home base of Fort Selden just to try and keep up with the fast-moving, fast-attacking Apache warriors. Fort Selden was on the east side of the Rio Grande only a two-day ride north from El Paso and Mexico. Fort Bayard and Fort Cummings were west of the Rio Grande and the home fort by a two- and three-day ride over rough and varied terrain. Fort Craig was north, an easy three-day or so ride along the Rio Grande. This was not only hard on boot-sole leather and horses' hooves, but the few officers and enlisted men who had families or fiancées at Fort Selden were under immense extra worry and pressure.

Nana's band had escaped I Company's vengeance chase with few injuries because of the fortuitous gift of the sudden blizzard. They had also gotten away with most of the animals and goods from the highly successful raid at Sweetwater Springs.

Following the blizzard came a warm wind, and the secret camp among the bluffs and caves that had harbored and healed these struggling people for years now was for a while a true sanctuary. The women had gathered plenty of seeds and they had small, open, high grass meadows between the sheer cliffs to forage the stock. The mules made fine meat filled with life-giving strength. The precious warm winds melted the snow, and for a time the elk, deer, and other game returned for the band's hunting and feasting. It was a rare time—the time of recovery and blessings, the true time of thanks. For Nana and his tribe there would be only one more real respite.

Nana sat on some flat rocks with his treasured grandson, Kaywayhla. They looked out across a wondrous land. It was so big they couldn't see a single sign of the intruders. They knew they were out there in little far-scattered villages, mining camps, and military forts. But for just this moment they both pretended it was the time of the Warm Springs Apaches only. It felt good.

They were so high up that they looked down on the back of a flying golden eagle and lower caught the circling movement of hunting red-tailed hawks. The forested mountains of the Black Range rippled downward in snaking chains with uncountable, steep hidden canyons in between. Even with his worn eyes, Nana could see the mighty contours of the earth all the way below where the foothills were covered with scattered cedar and the brown grass of the earth showed through in ever greater patches right on into the fuzzy desert.

Kaywayhla put the glass to his eye and very slowly, as his grandfather had taught him, moved it until he found the green shrubbed trail of the Rio Grande and he followed it almost to Mexico before the earth turned to a blur.

A flock of mountain blue jays scattered from one tree to another just below, watching them. Nana had chosen this special day of rare warmth to be alone with his favorite grandson. He had things to tell him—things to clarify so someday he could voice these truths to *his* favorite grandchild to be carried on and on like the southwest wind.

"Grandson, I see you have learned to move the glass slowly so you see motion or different objects instead of the movement of the glass."

"I am getting better, Grandfather."

"That is good, for we will need you now more than before." Nana was happy to see that Kaywayhla was growing straight, tall, and swift of movement just as he, himself, had been in his youth, before the horse rolled over his ankle, crushing it into the rocks, and before the battles and wounds had bent and slowed everything but his will. That had grown stronger—much stronger.

Kaywayhla looked big-eyed and attentive at his grandfather's elderly, narrowed black eyes, which seemed to glint with power through the tiniest slit, and even though he sensed part of what he was about to hear he wanted to know every nuance.

"It was the gold that started it all. First, the Spanish craved it. Then when the others passed through on their way to the dropping sun, we let them move on as long as they didn't overstay or defile our water holes. But they just kept coming, and the Mexican farmers and sheepmen and cattlemen came too, followed by the businesspeople who began to build little towns to sell their supplies. Some stayed. Then more stayed. So, you see, Grandson, we decided to war on them in the meanest way we could so they would have great fear and go back to the place where the sun rose."

Nana paused a moment. Kaywayhla didn't move so as not to interrupt Nana's thoughts.

"We attacked on many small fronts, we screamed war cries, death cries, we slaughtered and butchered them, taking their scalps . . . and their guns and ammunition. We believed they would not like this treatment and go away and tell the others of all the bad things that would happen to them if they came here. We lost many warriors before we learned how to strike and gather their mounts, their guns, and their ammunition to fight in another place of our own choosing." He looked hard at the boy. "I tell you now, Grandson, that it did not work. They kept on coming and then they found gold on our land. Then the Buffalo cavalry and the white-eyes' infantry came to protect this metal, and more and more they came; and now I see that more and more will come. They are as endless as thought."

Nana looked now way beyond the desert at a single small cloud far, far to the east. The cloud grew bigger and others hatched out around it and enlarged. He knew it was a sign

from the Great Mystery of the truth of his telling. Out of respect Kaywayhla had sat as motionless and soundless as the
boulder under his bottom. He could not keep from speaking,
though he meant no disrespect.

"Grandfather, maybe all of them are here now. Maybe
there will be no more. Maybe we can kill them all a few at a
time. Maybe . . ."

Nana gave a swift rare smile at the enthusiasm of hope the
young must have to survive.

"I am sorry to tell you this, Grandson, but even our great
chief, Victorio, knows that we must make war with all the
force we have for a while yet. If the other powers do not hear
our plea for our homeland, we will terrorize them again with
the savagery they accuse us of and then we will go south to
a place in the Sierra Madres where we can be at peace.

"Now always remember this, for other tongues will tell it
differently. After the first scalpings and we saw that nothing
would slow them, we stopped the scalpings. Only a renegade
now and then would do such a thing. We were trying to send
them a small signal of consideration, hoping they would start
the same toward us. It didn't work.

"Our opponents fight for wealth, for power, for their pride.
We, my grandson, fight for the land that was ours. We fight
to be left alone on it. We fight now just to save enough of our
people to continue our blood. Already we are so few. But we
will survive somehow, so you and others can tell these truths."

Kaywayhla bent over, jerked a long-bladed knife from the
sheath on his knee-high moccasins, and held it in the stab-
bing position above his head with both hands.

"I promise you, Grandfather, that we will fight and we will
survive to tell your truth."

Nana was pleased. He arose with surprising agility for one
so aged and mountain and battle bruised, contented to now
make the final fight. He looked across the far eastern desert

mountains beyond the Rio Grande and saw the clouds were all one now and storming. But he was at peace because the final decision had been made in the sky. He would pass the word to Lozen, who would relay it to her brother, Victorio, who would see that Geronimo and all the other great Apache leaders of all the other tribes would know the message from the sky. There was no denial.

It was the time of a few fine days. Everyone ate a little too much for they had long trained themselves to survive on just enough food to fight well and seek flight well. They were just as proud of one as the other, considering both valiant fighting and skilled retreat all part of the same stick.

The women baked bread from stone-ground acorns and mesquite beans, and there was fresh elk and deer meat of most every kind of preparation. There were also caches of elk and venison jerky they tapped into as well as dried berries, some soaked in water to make a sweet bread dessert to be dipped in wild honey. They played games of all kinds and gambled heavily on them. They had cards made of rawhide and dice made of stones.

Once when Nana had been asked by a Mexican sheepherder friend why the Warm Springs Apaches gambled so readily, he had replied, "It is for fun. In the end what does it matter who wins. We share until all is gone."

He was proud of Kaywayhla entering the wheel games. The participants lined up in two runs each, ten steps apart, with a wooden lance. Wheels made from bending green twigs and small branches were rolled between the rows of lancers on the slightly downhill ground. Each participant had five or six lances—whatever was agreed upon—with his own personal mark carved on them. The old men rolled twenty wheels, or more, if decided, between the rows of lancers. The idea was to hurl a lance into the center of the rolling wheel and pin it, thereby claiming it as his own. After one rolling and lance throwing, the penetrated wheels were counted up. Then all participants reversed position and had the final equalizing contest.

The betting of blankets, guns, and the most precious of all commodities—war horses—went on raucously and with celebration.

When Kaywayhla was so young he could barely hurl a lance, Nana had spent much time rolling the wheel for him. It was not only a game to Nana, but he wanted to sharpen his grandson's eye to later kill moving targets. He showed him over and over exactly how to test the balance of the lance and where to hold it and how to bend his elbow at forty-five degrees to get the most accurate throw at the moving circles. All this had been preparation for the use of a gun—how to lead a target, how to "squeeze" the trigger, and much more, including the special and valuable use of the glass. The boy had learned well.

The wheel game ended with Kaywayhla the clear victor, and attention now turned to the footrace. All under forty could enter. In freer times before the Spaniards, Mexicans, whites, blacks, and other bloods and dilutions crowded them daily, hourly, they had room for running distances of a quarter of a mile, one mile, ten miles, and often even greater distances like the Zuni pueblo people. But here on the mountain, they would have to race a circle inside the bluffs for about a quarter mile. Sticks were driven in the ground to keep them on track.

Everyone knew that Lozen had won her first quarter-mile race when she was only fifteen, and every race since. This beautiful woman dominated this distance, so it was for second place that most of the bets had been made, although some were placed against her out of respect—even though she was a sure winner. No one wished to offend such a revered warrior woman, sister of Victorio. However, Lozen had been limping badly from a sprained ankle that was wrapped in herbal poultices. Everyone was surprised when she entered, gambling her repeating rifle and her prized sorrel horse.

The wagering was frenzied as almost everyone tried to bet on the runners who had come in second and third to Lozen before.

Nana knew she was courageous, but he knew she was no fool, so he took all bets he could handle with his meager belongings. Of course, he also owned many horses and mules as the leader of so many successful raids, and, too, he had control of captured guns and ammo, so he could call a great percentage of the wagers against Lozen.

At last, with the feverish betting still going on, the racers lined up in the positions chosen by drawing grass stems of different lengths from the hands of old subchiefs. Nana did not waste one bullet to start the race. That might be the bullet that would kill an officer of the army. Instead he cracked two sticks together, and they were off in a tight crowd.

Lozen limped along near the last racers until about midway and then she slowly started gaining, although obviously in pain. Nana's old heart was beating as if in the dead center of a great battle. It made his ribs rattle like dry snakeweeds in a sandstorm. His chest heaved like a blacksmith's bellows. He feared Lozen was never going to make it. She was seven runners back.

Then to the oh's and *yi yi*'s of the onlookers, almost without visibility, she increased her speed. Her limp had also vanished, and she passed one, two, three, four, five, six, and with mighty smooth-flowing strides left them all far behind. At the finish line she threw up her hands, ran to a small jumble of boulders, stopped, jerked the poultice wrappings from her ankle with a flourish to the crowd and like a young deer leapt upon the boulders, yelling, *"Yi yi yiaa,"* waving the poultice wrapping in the air like a captured adornment of the enemy.

There was a sudden silence. Lozen stood motionless now as well. Then there was a tiny giggle, another, more, and at last laughter rang and danced around the amphitheater of rocky bluffs into a crescendo of pure mirth. They had been had. Lozen had fooled them all, except, of course, her blood uncle, Nana.

She was honored now as if she had all alone defeated the entire Ninth Cavalry. Clay jars of chokecherry wine and mescal were opened. Such a ruse must be honored, must be given its great due.

There were ritual dances, such as the hunting dance and even the sacred victory dance, where each participant could crouch as if firing his bows or guns, pantomiming in this way manners of battle. Children ran about playing the games of children the world around. The celebration stirred the blood of the young, and even though the young women must remain chaste until married to one of their choosing, flirtations were many and unsaid engagements sealed.

The adults laughed, teased, made love, and the very old survivors, who were so few now, recounted other fast races, other times, and had dreams and visions of both the past, the now, and the future, which were also one in their most sacred thoughts. Lozen's ruse had given extra life, extra pleasure, extra love, and, for just a brief pleasurable pause, extra hope.

WHILE THE SHORT WARM SPELL WAS UPON THEM, THEY FIN-
ished building wickiups and a few tipis in front of the shallow indentations in the cliffs. There were many caves deep
enough for good shelter.

The women worked on clothing. They now wore two-piece
dresses made of calico with skirts long and full. Each wore as
many skirts as she owned, usually two or three. Each wore a
leather belt—many taken from raids—and each carried a
knife tucked into the belt or a sheath. Many wore cartridge
belts as well, ready to fight to the death to protect the few old
and the children left.

They repaired and made use of everything available to
them. They used the guts of dead horses to make circular
water canteens for the warriors to hang around their horses'
necks; they made an acorn-based hardtack and bundled this
up in cowhide pouches for the pack animals. Everyone
worked. Makers of bows, arrows, lances, and flint points were
kept busy. Young boys did most of the hunting, and these
weapons could noiselessly kill their game without giving away
their position. The horses and mules were fed mountain grass

tied with rawhide strings into bundles. There were also caches of sacked oats taken from raids of the past.

The young men and girls exercised the horses every day, playing at war and running short races. It was the time of fun for the very young, but a time of preparation as well.

Nana had a fine combination cave and wickiup. He was the leader here now. Victorio was still fighting his way out of the Mexican Sierra Madres, so this rock and stick house was not done out of deference to Nana. No, it was a place for councils, and too, he had many wives—the last being Nah-dos-te, Geronimo's sister. Once the Apaches had been mostly monogamous, but the wars of southern New Mexico and Arizona had put so many men in interment that the rest of them married the surviving widows.

The guards, mostly young men about to become full-time warriors, were always out, day and night, in places where any enemy would be spotted. Even though the soldiers, the miners, or enraged Mexican farmers and ranchers had never been able to find this sacred ground, caution was always taken.

Once in the morning, at full sun and at late sun, Lozen stood with her arms outstretched and waited for the coloration in her palms and the tingling that always pointed out the enemy. Her palms remained the same. They were safe that day and night. Many things were told of Lozen, who was considered a holy woman by all and the greatest of tacticians. Her brother Victorio, Nana, and Geronimo always insisted on the palm test before going into battle.

She strode now to Nana's place for council. She had overheard many times other women and a few men gossiping about her never marrying. They told of the Gray Ghost who rode mostly alone. He was of a great stature. When Lozen was a young girl, she had seen him fight in a huge canyon and outride and fool the pursuing soldiers. One of Geronimo's band signaled him the way to their camp. He rode a fine black horse and wore hand-beaded moccasins and shirt. He stayed the night and she fell in love, even though he was from a tribe far to the north. She wanted to run right through the council fire and fall upon him with kisses. The next morning he was gone, but not from her heart.

It was also said that once she had walked alone to the bluff overlooking another canyon to make the day's palm test and had seen the Gray Ghost run down and his body riddled with bullets. The shock of what this strong woman had seen happen to the love she had chosen for her entire life had caused her to vow to marry no man in this world. She would wait for the Gray Ghost in another. These things were told over and over.

Nana, Lozen, Kaytennae (his *segundo*), his grandson Kaywayhla, and two others sat and smoked a medicine pipe, one after the other. It made the boy sick, but no one knew. They made plans for spring attacks. There was no need for maps. They drew in the dust floor of the cave or mentioned this bend in a certain creek or a rock that looked like a cow, or a lightning-burned tree, or a place where game trails crossed. These signs were endless. They were etched in the elders' brains so deeply that no age affliction could dim this map made of the earth.

Kaywayhla sat respectfully back from the circle, but was allowed to hear. In the background, Nana's wives and many children gossiped and played.

Even the great Lozen gave Nana total respect because he had participated in an all-night victory dance long ago, and she and a few others had followed him up a sacred mountain where he had clearly seen Cochise, Victorio, and Geronimo rise up out of the earth, give him a greeting, and sink back into it. She and the others had seen it, although fuzzily; there was no doubt of Nana's power. And long before that he had gone to the sacred white mountain of the Mescaleros to visit the Dreamer, who was known by Chiricahuas, the Jicarillas, the Warm Springs Apaches, and the Mescalero Apaches. The Dreamer had broken bread with them and made a prayer to the white mountain. Then he told Nana to follow a game trail he would show him, and at a certain rock he would stay and fast for four days. If he was right, the Great Mystery would give him special powers. Kaytennae was not allowed to go with him.

Now Nana knew that many medicine men from all the Apache tribes had come to test the Dreamer, but few had been given powers beyond what they already possessed. Nana had no doubt his main purpose would be allotted him, and he eagerly ran up the mountain.

At the rock he waited and chanted his own private prayers. He never slept that he was aware of, but two or three hours before sunrise he saw the same great leaders as the night of the victory dance as well as Mangas Coloradas and Naiche, chief of the Chiricahuas, who had fought with them all at one time or another. They spoke in one voice, and he was told that he would have power over ammunition and rattlesnakes, besides the healing powers he already had. He would be responsible in making raids and guiding warriors to secure ammunition for caches from the Black Range and Southeast Arizona, all the way into Mexico. When he personally led a raid, no one had to look out for rattlesnakes, so they could fully concentrate on a strike of force.

It had been true. It was told around many campfires and in many tipis, wickiups, and caves that even as he neared eighty summers he could go with a handful of warriors and return with ammunition. When he led his own band, no one had ever been bitten by a snake. There were many battles that had been won because of a cache of ammunition made by Nana several years before. These mighty leaders said he would be respected for his feats and that he would eventually be called *Shit-su-ye* (grandfather) by all except Victorio. By blood Nana was Victorio's uncle, but the chief gave him his own special honor by calling Nana "Father."

Now, Lozen said, smiling, "I, Lozen, sister of Victorio, have heard your plans, Grandfather. I am anxious for the grass roots to suck up water from the earth again; then we will fight as never before."

"Yes, Warrior Woman," Nana said, "that we must do for the iron buffalo is bringing more and more men of war. We must make the Buffalo horsemen and the white-eyed walkers wish to ride the iron monster in the other direction."

Lozen, the master tactician, said, "Just before the grass greens, we should strike as far apart as our numbers will allow. We can tire their bodies and make the soldiers' minds weary as well."

"Agreed," Nana said, and he told his *segundo* to pick the best scout to ride and spread Lozen's word to all the Elders.

All made "agreement" grunts, even the grandson.

The meeting broke up. A furtive cheerfulness abounded even into the deep snows that soon came. The white flakes arrived with no wind. A gift. The Apaches warmed by their fires, with enough food for themselves and their animals, until the sun decided to rise higher in its circle to warm all. The soft, falling whiteness, which could kill under certain conditions, was a protection now, as they had sufficient food. It protected them from those on barren ground so far below. They would be ready and fit for the great bloodletting to come. Nana knew all these things and more. The word had been passed to the leaders across the land.

He could see the battles ahead clearly. The soft time would be short. The sky vision had been clear. Besides, the sky would never lie to Nana. Never. He snuggled up on the blankets in the cave, one arm outstretched over his youngest wife, Ya-do, and one over his oldest, Nah-dos-te, protecting both ends of his life.

Fourteen

IT HAD BEEN A DIFFICULT MOMENT FOR SGT. MOSES WILLIAMS when, while holding Sheela's hand, he had to face Lieutenant Valois—almost in defiance. However, his commander was as understanding as the army would allow him to be when it came to Negro enlisted men marrying. He explained patiently that the average time for acquiring permission was about a year. Moses knew that white soldiers got their papers in a fourth that time, but there was no use bringing it up.

The lieutenant was also strict when it came to Moses's fiancée. "Sergeant, you know the only way she can stay here at the post is to work as a laundress."

Moses took a risk, saying, "I understand that, sir, but it seems such a waste since she can read and write and, as you have heard, speak as well as anyone."

"I'm sorry, Moses. There are men and women who will become disgruntled and jealous if she were to start in a higher position. I have no choice."

Moses knew he and Sheela had none either, so he thanked Valois. Everyone on the post stared at them as they walked toward the laundry building where they would meet the head laundress.

Trying to console both Sheela and himself, he said, "I'll talk to the chaplain in a few weeks. He's trying to get a regular school started for illiterate enlisted men and the children of the fort."

Rev. Charles Pree was the only black captain in the Ninth. He was held in high regard by all the men. He had marched with them in combat, consoling the frightened and wounded, until the battles became so far scattered it was decided he could do more good at a single fort. Since he and many other Buffalo Soldiers had constructed a large part of Fort Selden and had built a special chapel with living quarters there, Pree chose it as his headquarters.

Moses explained to Sheela in the softest tones his voice could command, "I will look after you no matter what. We will just have to suffer through it until I can work it all out."

She was put to work immediately stirring the heavy dirty clothes in huge iron pots with a wooden stick. She had to carry the hot water from the ongoing fire in two gallon buckets.

After two days, her hands were blistered and bleeding. She wrapped them in cloth until they toughened. There were six other women working at the pots. Two kept the fires going. Over a dozen others were sewing, hanging, folding, and sorting. Often they had to clean battle-bloody uniforms as well as those that were muddy or just plain soiled. The lye soap was strong. Not only did it eat the dirt, blood, and other stains from the uniforms, the women had to rub their hands with melted tallow several times a day to prevent them from cracking like dead wood.

Mayo Lou, a huge Negress, almost as large as Bitch Moose, was the head laundress. She checked constantly on Sheela's work and often made her do it over—sometimes when Sheela knew it was unnecessary. Sheela had many urges to jam the stirring stick up Mayo Lou where it would do the most good, but thoughts of someday making a home with Moses kept her from getting out of line. Each day that passed made the verbal abuse easier for her to handle.

The washerwomen all slept in a long narrow room on little handmade single beds. The only cleaning permitted for their own bodies was a splash bath on Sunday. On that day they were allowed to carry their own hot water and bathe in a circular portable zinc and tin tub. Washing her hair, which was longer than that of the other women, was a problem because of the strong soap.

She found the food was almost inedible at first. Mayo pointed out that it was the same as that given to the soldiers. At Fort Selden they were served from the same pots after the soldiers were through eating. The women sat separately at two long tables in a corner, even though over half of them were married, and most of the balance were waiting for permission, just as Sheela was. Besides the Negro women, there was one Navajo, three whites, and two Orientals.

By the time they finished their evening meal, it was near eight-thirty. When taps was blown most of them were already asleep from pure exhaustion. No matter how much they craved to visit their men, they seldom had the strength or time. And if they had, it would not matter, for the men were usually training with their horses and weapons or out in the mountains and deserts using them for real.

The women who were able to stick it out would become tough as cedar wood. They were very appreciative of all small favors.

Sheela held on and eventually the jealousy over her natural beauty was replaced by admiration for her taking part in this form of slavery without complaint. The women quickly learned of her ability to read and write. She offered to write letters and poems for them to pass on to their men. Soon she became admired and treated with respect.

She still had to work almost as hard, except occasionally Mayo would whisper, "Yore pot's cleaner'n any of 'em." And she only gave a cursory glance on her inspection tours at Sheela's tubs.

Sheela lost some weight and her muscles toughened underneath, but the beauty of her body still remained, except for her constantly raw hands. She helped the Navajo woman, Wahee, braid her hair a few times. In return Wahee slipped her some precious yucca root soap that helped Sheela's hair maintain its shine and softened her hands as well.

She swore that she would hold on and better Moses as well as herself. She did. After what seemed like several years, but was only two months, she casually, in an offhand manner, mentioned to Mayo something about having sewn dresses and fine things for her patron and adopted mother, Nelda.

A week later she was assigned to a sewing table. The work was just as continuous and stressful, but it was still a gain. She was indoors and away from all the water toting and harsh soap—and the clothes she worked on were already clean. As stiff as her back and shoulders and hands became, she could add up the advantages of having half the sweat, and she could keep her hair shining and her tired hands softer in spite of the long hours—the same hours as the soldiers: reveille at 5:30 in the morning and taps at 8:30 at night.

Sheela silently exulted in her first step improvement while she prepared for another step up by occasionally and neatly repairing stitching in the laundresses' best dresses. The women got a three-day leave every three months, according to their work record, and they wanted to look their best to be with their men. It wasn't difficult to put in this little extra time and it made her feel good at the true appreciation from the women. When a person has nothing, the smallest gift of the heart or the hand is a bounty.

Fifteen

I Troop had been on a road of uncountable steps.

"Up and down, round and round," Private Walley complained, half-grinning, wishing to cry.

"Look at it this way," said Sergeant Moses. "You now have more experience than anyone in the army at both riding and walking. You are in such good condition you could run down a mountain lion, and you're so mean you could turn it into a parlor pet."

"You shore got a way 'uv puttin' words out perty, Sergeant Moses, but ain't nothin' you can say 'bout my shirt buttons bein' stuck to my backbone 'un my butt-hole ain't had nuthin' pass through in so long you couldn't shove a needle in it."

Corporal Smith added, as he reined his lean horse a little closer, "Jist think of the feast we're gonna have back at Fort Selden. Why my mouth's waterin' and my belly is laughin' out loud just thinkin' about it. Listen." Sure enough his stomach rumbled like thunderclouds on the other side of a canyon from neglect and anticipation.

Walley could not stop with that little useless information. "I dreamed that a scorpion that crawled in my blanket last night was Bitch Moose. Now there's an insult to a great woman."

C. C. Smith said, "Well, I didn't have no dreams about them red ants and that big ol' stinkbug and that ol' centipede what joined me for the night. No, siree, I knew *zackly* what they wuz."

Moses tried to put a stop to it. "You men are little tender-assed sissies. Ole Nana would have eaten those bugs for breakfast and belched in thanks."

They had fought and camped, pursued and lost pursuit, cut sign and been ambushed. Horses, mules, and two soldiers had died and many had been wounded. They had gone from Fort Selden to Fort Cummings, Fort Bayard, and Fort Craig in an egg-shaped circle of high desert, uncountable rocky canyons, and over mountains.

Sometimes they had had to lead their cavalry horses and pack mules on, literally scratching their way up and down, up and down. Days, nights, sunrises, sunsets had all become one until the trail of the Apache was hot. Then the surge of adrenaline always came and drove them into the lead and flint, firing, falling behind boulders, falling into whatever indentation the earth afforded them for even imagined protection from their enemy's fire.

At times they had been joined by white infantry units and Mexican settlers, as well as a few Apache and Navajo scouts. They had thought they were fighting Victorio at times, or any of a half-dozen other warriors, but most of the time they had no idea who the hostile leader was. It didn't matter anymore. The battles and chases seemed as if they would go on until the world had turned so many times it would fall apart from weariness.

At times as many as 2,000 soldiers and citizens were in pursuit of Victorio, who now had only a scattered band of

120 or so warriors, plus wives and children. As great as he was, he could never have covered so much ground. Nana, Lozen, Geronimo, Mangas Coloradas, and others fought along the borders of New Mexico, Arizona, and Mexico with such dedication that it seemed to their pursuers as if they had a band of warriors in every one of a thousand canyons.

The tattered I Troop was now headed home to Fort Selden to replenish supplies, heal bruises, broken bones, and wounds, and to rest a few days. They had to find replacements for their downed comrades and horses. Then it would all start again and again.

The Ninth and the Apaches had learned some hard lessons of warfare from one another. When they were fighting out of West Texas into the Guadalupe Mountains, they had learned that the supply, ambulance, and artillery wagons could not keep up in the rugged terrain. It was a waste of men and mules. Often it ended in lost lives and scarce necessities. The cannon was soon relegated mostly to fort ceremonies.

As they rode toward home now, Moses's mind went back to Texas. He hardly ever thought of those horrific days, but since he had met Sheela, he sometimes caught himself thinking into the future and back into the past. It seemed to give him direction for things to come.

Their principal duty in West Texas was supposed to be guarding the mail from El Paso to San Antonio and back, but it turned out that this was the smallest of their duties. Simply patrolling this vast region would have been difficult enough with its hundreds of miles of brush jungle paralleling the Rio Grande, great expanses of plains, soul-sapping deserts, and mountains. There the temperatures went from below freezing in winter to above one hundred degrees in summer. That mighty forbidding land was a favored haunt for Kiowas and Comanches raiding down from the north. From the south the Kickapoos, who had been driven into Mexico, crossed back over the border in seemingly endless bloody raids. The Mescaleros came down out of their nests in the Guadalupe Mountains in a ceaseless plundering of cattle, horses, sheep, stagecoaches, wagon trains, and any traveler moving or camped.

Out there were countless numbers of white ruffians ready to kill like hungry mountain lions, and urging them on were the vulturous Comancheros with trade goods, guns and ammunition, and whiskey to reward this riffraff of white outlaws, Mexican *bandidos,* and some Indians. There were vicious battles without letup from all these often demented and certainly merciless sources.

Moses and the Buffalo Soldiers had to fight all this and contend with horses discarded from white units and poor food inferior to other posts. The bread was sour, the beef of poor quality, the butter was suet, and the canned goods unfit to eat. Such sordid conditions have demoralized troops the world over, dooming them to destruction, but the Ninth survived and fought on with the lowest desertion rate on the frontier. Even their white commanders, especially Colonel Hatch, were pulled into court with eternal harassment suits because they stood up for the Buffalo Soldiers.

The Apaches learned that they could not stand toe to toe with the Negro troopers in head-on battles. They lost to superior firepower and training. So they reverted to their natural form of hit-and-run guerrilla warfare and made both living and dying far more miserable for their enemies.

With these widely varied sources of lead, lances, arrows, and knives constantly being hurled at them, it was a miracle the Buffalo Soldiers survived one year much less eight on the Texas frontier.

As Moses mused on the Texas wars, he dwelled only on the major battle skills learned and knew the Ninth was the equal of any regiment anywhere. They had learned to fight the Indian way and unlearned certain long-regimented army battle maneuvers.

He came out of the dust-fogged past, thinking of Miss Sheela. They were close enough to home now that he could allow himself this precious luxury.

Moses felt his third mount of the present campaign picking up the pace. No matter how starved, how exhausted the horses, when they were nearing their as-yet-unseen home, they managed to gather the speed of anticipation. Even horses that had never been there, mounts captured on the long campaigns, would throw their tired ears up straight and gather speed. That was one reason Moses had always known that horses talked in a silent language. To know even part of that horse vernacular, he had to become part horse.

The first thing Moses did after his debriefing with the officers and checking out all his men was to pay a visit to Supply Sergeant Weedly. He was a long-time friend and Moses had no trouble in arranging his absence from his room behind the supply quarters that night. Weedly had relatives still living in Mississippi, and Moses had written his letters home for free in order to get the best supplies possible for his unit of troops.

Then he bathed and went straight to the serving room where Sheela turned, staring as if Nelda herself had returned from the dead. She ran into his arms so hard that only the wall kept him from falling. He kissed her as if God had given him his own best dessert, savoring her taste, her smell, her golden skin, as he breathed her essence into his suddenly alert, and once again feeling body. It was so real it became a fantasy—a living marvel. The ending of such denial and longing became the beginning of a dream, a vision.

She had thought and yearned so long that the realness of his tree-hard body was not believable yet. How could she be so blessed? He was safe and here with her. Then she felt his warm soul join and comfort hers. She shed tears along with an ardent smile of sudden liberation. She, too, inhaled and absorbed him.

"Oh, Moses, you came home safely. You're all right," she said, touching his face gently with both hands.

"I love you. I missed you. I crave you," he whispered. He told her where and when they would meet.

"Oh, oh, yes," was all she could say.

Moses hurriedly tried to finish his food, such as it was, but it was not going down as well as with the other tired and hungry soldiers. Good or bad, hot or cold, it didn't really matter; he didn't taste it at all. His attention was elsewhere. His eyes flashed across the room to the laundresses' section, searching out Sheela.

As in every army before them and every one to follow, the soldiers griped their cavalry asses off about almost everything, but especially the food. The main cook was on sick leave along with two assistants who were also down with the flu. It seemed that dishwashers and the remaining assistant who had replaced them paid little attention to culinary details.

Pvt. Augustus Walley was choking slightly, trying to swallow his last bite. He leaned over, looking at Corporal Smith's plate, saying, "What do you think it is?"

C.C. replied, grimacing, "Looks like a combination of buzzard meat mixed with barn rats and baby skunks to me."

"Oh, I thought it was sumpthin' I couldn't eat," Walley said.

C.C. stared at a forkful of revolting food. "Somethin' this good, I like to take my time and eat it slow an' easy, so's to really enjoy it."

"Yeah, C.C., you're right. No use in rushin' a good thing."

Walley swallowed a bite with some struggle. "The secret is

to take little teeny-weeny bites, so's you can swaller it with-out chewin'.'" C.C. gave him a questioning glance as did sev-eral others within hearing distance. Walley continued, "It cuts down on the time you have to taste it."

All the new replacements were trying to survive under the Walley and C.C. tutelage, but they seemed more confused than enlightened. Walley and C.C. knew that the new men they would have to fight with, and maybe die with soon, needed encouragement, so they tried feebly again at pacifi-cation.

C.C. said hesitantly, looking around as if Colonel Hatch himself were listening in, "Walley, we cain't afford to hurt the replacement cook's feelings, bad grub's better'n none."

Walley valiantly tried to add something worthy to his friend's efforts. He twisted a very small spoon of the stuff off the plate, moving it slowly to his mouth, cleverly not breath-ing so as to taste it less. He rammed the tiny spoon of food in his mouth and gulped without chewing. "I could put up with it awhile longer . . . if I could just figger some way not to look at it." The new men listened and grinned. Walley con-tinued, "This coffee is colder'n a frozen foot and tastes just like one."

Even the old hands who were used to such goings on tried not to listen, and the new men struggled to lose their hear-ing and their taste all at once. It didn't do them any good. They were just getting started in this wonderful world of buf-falo soldiering.

Across the mess hall, the women had already exhausted their comments on the food and now concentrated on their personal gripes. It was a truth, but never voiced, that the few married women in the group could go sleep with their hus-bands if the men had been able to find them a private corner somewhere that wouldn't disturb the fleshly dreams of the single men. But they were not allowed to eat with them. The answer to this paradox had long been discussed with no results.

It was even more puzzling to the fiancées. They were neither officially allowed to dine or bed with their intended. Of course, they surreptitiously did the latter at every chance. The reasoning here, as in all armies, was resolved by the generals and the politicians who controlled them. It was simply kept close to their vests.

In the first place, having married enlisted men in the service most often created the birth of children. This in turn caused more expense and time taken from the pursuit of war. It was believed, in spite of a millennia of the opposite experience, that married men would have their minds on their families in the heat of battle and fail to properly execute their arms and their enemies.

Here, on the western frontier, nature itself was sidetracked by the belief that the more difficult they made it for an enlisted man to secure a marriage permit, the more likely the relationship would fall apart. That was true, but what was ignored was the fact that so would the love and lives of those who cared deeply about one another. A maze of red-taped tunnels were created to present often overwhelming obstacles against the inherent mating and irresistible reproductive drives of all young men and women. Of course, the generals and politicians and the white officers were immune to any such afflictions and restrictions themselves.

Shecla's eyes riveted those of her intended across the mess hall. She had to force them away by shaking her head to get out of the trance and rejoin her former sisters of laundry. She heard voices vaguely at first and then they became clearer as someone she recognized spoke.

Wahee, her Navajo friend, said, "I try to think hard . . .
maybe sometimes it is better to wash all day than not wash
at all."

There were glances around and some low, not very believing, mutterings of assent. Mayo Lou, the massive stir-pot
boss, nodded in slight agreement and then with dead seriousness added, "Most anything atall is better'n pickin' cotton
all day."

The volume of accord rose slightly at this for several present had suffered that back-bending, knee-peeling, raw-handed
ordeal. Sheela chimed in, with her resonant voice, "Anything
is better than cleaning latrines."

Now all felt better at this. Mayo Lou said, "I is in total,
wholeheartedly agreement."

They all relaxed and laughed for that was the one punish-
ment reserved for new men and others being chastised for
various misdeeds. That was one place at least that the laundresses had it over the soldiers—as far as undesirable labor
was concerned. Latrine duty in this primitive world was the
worst thing besides bloody battle one could pull. In some
soldiers' minds even the latter was preferred to the humbling
experience of trying to clean up the spillings from others.

The women gossiped about many things for a short spell,
now feeling temporarily good and momentarily forgetting the
bad food in their bellies. The soldiers were home. They survived on.

Sixteen

SHEELA FOUND MOSES WAITING AT THE DOOR TO THE SELECTED room. She carried two clean blankets. They entered without words and he turned the oil lamp down so that only a soft, flickering flame of light touched the two.

Sheela spread the blankets and they stood holding each other and kissing with released passion. His hands started rapidly removing her blouse. Then, shockingly to Moses, she stopped him. She put both of her hands on his chest as she pulled back from him, saying, "No, Moses." She sat on the bed and pulled the blanket tightly around herself. Her eyes stared at him in silent pain. "I can't. I can't love you."

Moses didn't know what to do. He stood helplessly, finally muttering, "What is it? What have I done? What do you mean you can't love me?"

"I do love you . . . I mean we can't make love . . . We're not married."

He thought a second. "Well, we would be if we could . . . and we will be soon."

"No, it's not the same thing."

"But we already did make love," he said, not understanding her reasoning.

"That was different. That was my job. I'm not a whore any-more . . . that's not my job anymore."

He was trying to understand. "I know it's been a long wait to get permission to marry, but I already feel like we're mar-ried. I have from the start."

"I love you for that." She held out her arms to him and he came to her.

"I'll try to figure a way to speed up our permit," he said. "There must be a way."

"Oh, Moses, I want that so much, but don't get yourself in trouble with your superiors. I can wait. Can you?"

"Sure. But it ain't gonna be easy."

She kissed him gently and then held his face in both of her hands, looking into his worried eyes. "Please, don't be angry with me, Moses. I wouldn't hurt you for anything in the world."

"How could I be angry with you. It's important to you. I do understand, my precious little Sheela." Moses felt a great protective love that he had never known existed.

They kissed and she snuggled into the curl of his body and they were silent and deep in thought.

Moses wondered how he could possibly be so lucky. He knew that God was too busy to bother with all the people of the earth individually. And he, a plain Buffalo sergeant, was not so outstanding as to be singled out and awarded this sub-limity.

At that moment he believed in his guardian angel, a guid-ing spirit of some kind. He had felt it before, in battle, warned somehow to fall just before a coming bullet caused him to do so; or to spring to the side from the saddle as a horse tripped or was shot into a full rollover. So many, many times he knew there was something unknown there, invisible, aware, but felt. His and Nana's faces had telescoped together so that their eyes were bigger than ponds and even clearer in their message of final intent that time back on the deer hunt.

Sheela did not think this way. She silently thanked whatever powers that were beyond her. She was deeply grateful that this man in her arms had come to her exactly when he had. She knew she had been both blessed and rescued. She did not question that part of it. The only part that puzzled her was that her own mind could never seem to allow her to escape from the horrible picture of Nelda's severed head. And with it—even in her love, her thankfulness—came the fear of losing all again. And *all* was Moses.

Then their beings and their bodies became so close that all else—even their natural, carnal cravings—were crowded out as they melded into a deep, calming abyss of pleasure that was themselves.

For the first time in his life, Sgt. Moses Williams's conscious mind failed to heed or hear the horn of reveille.

Seventeen

THE SNOWS DWINDLED AS THE SUN MOVED HIGHER EACH DAY, and although Nana liked to fight in the highest and most difficult mountain terrain possible, he moved his small band of about fifteen warriors into the scattered attack mode.

Lozen's vision of widely scattered and constant battles had long since been agreed to and planned on by the other Apache leaders.

The military reports started coming in to Colonel Hatch and his commanders: Four Mexican ranchers were killed in the foothills of the San Mateos Mountains just west of Fort Craig and the Rio Grande. Over thirty Indian-hunting ranchers were enjoying their dinner after a long day of trying to make sense of Nana's tracks, strikes, and movements when Nana's warriors caught them dining. They had swept in to the Red Canyon of the San Mateo Mountains and killed one man, wounded seven, drove off all their horses, and killed another Mexican as they raced out of the canyon.

Two days later nineteen Buffalo Soldiers, led by Captain Parker of the Ninth Cavalry, finally joined Nana's band in battle. The men of both sides fought from behind rocks, bushes, and anything that might give them cover. It was mostly gunfire, but as always, Nana had at least two skilled bowmen and sometimes the same number who carried lances. They could scoot along the ground like lizards and blend into the yucca plants or other bushes by camouflaging themselves. They would put small, leafy branches or bunches of grass in their headbands or in the openings of their clothing.

Nana knew that a soldier killed by an arrow or lance sent the message to the rest that his warriors were always capable of closely infiltrating the soldiers' territory. It was a strong part of his own psychological warfare, gathered from the longest fighting life of them all. It worked to a degree.

The lead shots chipped at rocks, zinging into space and often deflecting into flesh on both sides. The battle was brief. One soldier was missing, one soldier lay dead with a bullet in his heart, three were wounded, and many horses had been killed or disabled.

Captain Parker was so encumbered by the wounded, he could not pursue when it might have counted. When he did, he found only a few spots of Apache blood, but as always, no bodies. Nana's recovery of his dead and wounded was beyond the capacity of the soldiers or fighting civilians to ever explain. Trying to comprehend this seemingly supernatural ability haunted Nana's enemies.

It was true that the Apaches knew every crack, crevice, and cave in all this vast land. They interred most of their dead in the mountains and canyons all the way from the Sierra Madres in Mexico to the northern-most land of New Mexico, the latter fought for, and never lost, by the Jicarilla Apaches.

Now Nana had shown up on the rise just above Hillsboro, scaring everyone into near panic. There were mines recently discovered in what was known as the Hillsboro District of both placer and the underground lode types. There were riches being ripped from the abused hunting land of Nana and Victorio by armed miners. They were working over a huge area now, and at first they lived from game they killed. They cut trees by the hundreds of thousands to cook that game, construct their buildings, and to timber the mine tunnels. What had once seemed like a beautiful place of "the time of forever" was now being mutilated. The gold and silver were found and taken, and the madness in all the thousands of camps across the West—all the way to the Pacific Ocean—was no different here. The town of Hillsboro was where Nelda, the General, and Sheela had been headed when Nana, Lozen, and their band had stopped them.

About thirty miles south of Hillsboro, a cowboy, George Lufkin, had dismounted his horse to tighten the cinch and, purely by accident, found a strange-looking rock. The rock was so heavy, he had it assayed. To his amazement, the rock assayed several thousand ounces of silver to the ton. It changed the area and the Apache life forever.

Lufkin was so drunk when he made the deal to sell his find, he got only $10.50 for his share. The mine soon passed into other hands, and the Lake Valley District almost immediately became the site of the most remarkable discoveries of silver in the area. When the Bridal Chamber Mine was opened up in the now booming town of Lake Valley, it became not only the richest per ton in the territory but in the world.

These discoveries and the flurry of men and women moving and digging around like ants dancing in acid did not make Nana happy. He moved on from Hillsboro, burning and looting at every opportunity. Victorio and his main band had been seen heading into Gavilan Canyon south of Lake Valley. The area that was already mad over gold and silver now went into a frenzy over the Apache threat.

A posse arrived from Hillsboro under J. P. McPhearson. A

Captain Schmitt was there with a unit of the Tenth Regiment of both Negroes and whites. The superintendent of the Lake Valley Mining Company had gathered about twenty-five miners, armed and mounted. He was wildly accusing Captain Schmitt of not trying to find the Indians and was especially upset when it was reported by a scout that Nana had followed Victorio into Gavilan Canyon.

The fact that a lot of people had decided to liquor up and headquarter at Lake Valley was good for business, and the booze served enlarged some egos from plain miners into great warriors.

Gavilan Canyon is rough and narrow, with many rocks protruding. Nana had spotted the army scout and leisurely led his band after Victorio. He set up his warriors on both sides of the canyon and waited for the fools to come. They came.

Captain Schmitt and his men mounted their horses. In only a short time a hundred men, half of them drunk, followed with a disorderly, pitiful string of pack animals overloaded with bedrolls, pans, kettles, food, and ammunition. This circus set out for Gavilan Canyon. Many of the men were so drunk they were weaving in their saddles, hardly able to sit upright much less fight some of the most ferocious and cunning warriors ever known to man.

It can only be called extreme foolishness on Mine Manager Daly's part. Captain Schmitt knew better, but he had been insulted beyond reason, so both men rode into the perfect trap and fell dead from the first volley. With their leaders down, chaos followed.

As the rifles cracked from the rocks, soldiers and drunken miners literally fell from their mounts, seeking any cover they could find and firing blindly at the rocks above them. The wounded were moaning, and the confused were crying out for instructions where nothing existed but more confusion.

Wounded horses and mules screamed as they were

maimed and fell, scattering clanging pots and pans. Many of the white men were tenderfeet with no experience of battle aside from an occasional barroom brawl. A few stragglers had enough sense to rein back, thereby saving themselves. These were soon telling of the great horrors, along with their own heroic deeds, in Cotton's Saloon.

The pack animals, deserted by their owners, soon jammed the narrowest part of the canyon, creating a blockade. All of them were killed. Only four troopers had been killed but many more civilians were badly wounded.

The two sides were nearly even in numbers, but in skill and position the odds were heavily in favor of Victorio and Nana.

The surviving band of scared Lake Valley barroom warriors hid in the rocks and crevices wherever possible. The troopers who remained fired as best they could. They knew that only a miracle could save them for very long.

Colonel Hatch, having been made aware by heliograph signals while at Fort Selden, headed out for Gavilan Canyon with a contingent of fresh and battle-tested troops—including Lieutenant Valois, Sgt. Moses Williams, and a unit of I Troop.

One of Nana's scouts had seen them coming, and the Apaches split into small bands and somehow managed, as a last great insult, to leave with all the usable horses of a hundred-strong ragtags from the Lake Valley mines and saloons.

Hatch's men could only survey the battle site with professional dismay. Moses wanted to pursue, but could not get Lieutenant Valois to ask the colonel for permission.

Later Moses told Walley, "You know, I was wrong at Gavilan Canyon. My being pissed at Nana always escaping messes up my judgment."

"Yeah, Sarge, I know what you mean. That ol' bastard done away with all my judgments, too."

Just for the hell of it, completely out of range, a few Indians fired back as they victoriously rode away like desert ghosts in many directions.

Hatch ordered his men to help the wounded. He stared across the harsh landscape into a burning white sun and made a final silent vow to crush the Apache into the rocks they knew so well.

A few days later, camped near a spring and sitting next to Lozen, Nana surprised her by saying, "Once in a skirmish with some deer-hunting Buffalo Soldiers, I saw the big eyes of this sergeant. In those eyes I read that he would put his gun sights on me. This Buffalo man has a power, but he does not understand it. But I say to you, Lozen, that he will come when all the others are looking elsewhere."

"I hear you, Grandfather, and I will try to have a medicine vision to protect you."

"Ah, do not bother, Holy Woman, it was only the idle thought of an old man who sees odd things these days. Thoughts come that are as scattered about the mountains as the blood and spirits of our brave dead."

Nearly thirty new men had joined Nana's forces from the Mescalero Reservation. It had been a long time since he had had so many warriors at his disposal. As soon as they had been through a few raids under his command, Nana thought that maybe he could mount a creditable force of attack.

Eighteen

SHEELA JONES'S EMOTIONS WERE TWISTED FROM ECSTASY TO wrenching dread over and over by Nana and all the other Apache leaders. Moses and the men of the Ninth were in and out of forts and camps a week, a month, six weeks at a time, fighting occasionally, but mostly pursuing. The wounded returned to be treated or die in the infirmary. All day, all night she waited, watched, questioned her lover's safety, and ached terribly until his safe return. After the momentary bliss of holding him alive and well, he was taken from her again. Endless.

Others outside the Warm Springs tribe had taken Lozen's vision as an order from the Great Mystery. They attacked the ranches, the rancheros, the villages. At the great fortlike haciendas, the Spaniards and many Mexicans were being forced to bring their entire remuda of horses in from the pastures to the protected, walled-in compounds. Even with many armed guards, that was not always enough. Nana had long ago perfected a technique of the howling, barking coyote and lobo wolf sounds to draw the attention of the ranchers and even their dogs. Then one trained warrior—as Nana had done when younger—would silently drop over the wall among the horses with a leather riata. Then he and a warrior on the other side would saw back and forth down to the rock foundation until two such cuts were made in the adobe walls. Then pushing it over, they would chase the entire herd of horses outside for the waiting band to drive away into the darkness. Sometimes, the inside warrior would be caught and killed.

The very newest haciendas started mixing broken glass into the mud in their adobe walls and the Indians' riatas were cut and useless. So it was that the older, longest established patrons suffered the greatest losses.

Nana, always the gambler, pointed out the odds—the risk of one man against an entire remuda of fine horses. With that remuda they could move and save the lives of many women and children and have food as needed. He caused his followers to understand how many white-eyes and Buffalo Soldiers they could destroy riding their enemy's own animals into battle.

It would seem the greatest mistake that the Spanish conquerors made was introducing the horse to the Indians. Somewhere from the time before history, the Indian people had known these animals only too well, for these long-ago eras spoke to their souls of the life-and-death bond between the four-legs and the two-legs. This rapport was deeply understood and skillfully and fatefully executed by the Indians.

Among the ironies of these days was the one of the Apache relationship to the lonely sheepherder. They left them mostly unharmed. There was an understanding between them. First, sheep were too difficult to drive at any speed, and the Apache had never had time to develop a taste for the animals. The Apache would leave the sheep and their masters and dogs alone. The shepherd, on many occasions, with a slight nod of his head, the raising of a certain number of fingers or a glance, could tip off the warriors as to the location and movement of a unit of soldiers. On such little things hang the breath or death of many.

Sheela knew little of these things. She was tortured as she checked the infirmary, not only for Moses, but his two closest friends, Walley and C. C. Smith. Then she gradually came to recognize his entire unit—who had died and who had been replaced.

At every opportunity she asked the chaplain, Reverend Pree, if he had heard anything from the telegraph about the troops in the field. He was a comfort and a dismay at the same time, for the telegraph only occasionally seemed to get a message through that was straight. It was so new to the area and had been strung and set up swiftly without full knowledge of its installation and use. Mistaken tragedies occurred daily because of this. Colonel Hatch had rarely benefited from the telegraph as he had hoped. The major problem with the telegraph was a lack of trained personnel. Many messages were garbled. Sometimes there no messages at all, for Nana had learned how to sever the wire close to the pole and tie it back with a piece of rawhide. The Indians' method of sabotage was very hard to detect and time-consuming for the soldiers to repair.

Sheela often looked across the river above Leasburg—a bad whiskey, crooked cards, and cheap whorehouse village— where the barren brown rocks of Robleda Mountain was crested with a heliograph. But her hopes that this mirrored signal machine would keep her in touch with Moses were wasted.

The heliograph had been mostly a failure in the war against the unpredictable Apache, although it was used with some success to keep one fort in touch with another. At first it had put some doubt in the Apaches when Geronimo proclaimed, "When the white man can talk with light, we are doomed."

The wise old warrior had been wrong for once. The instrument did them minimal damage and was no help at all to Sheela Jones.

The reverend's soft words to have faith in God's will were both soothing and maddening to Sheela. She had a profound belief in the higher power or powers, but it was difficult for her to relegate this to a single prayer or event. Even though she had the fortune of born beauty, that too had almost become a curse. True, her dear mistress Nelda had loved, educated, and used her services, but only the slaughter of the wagon train people and the murder of the General had spared Sheela from the General's eventual attack on her. This seemed to have a significant meaning and proof of a higher being looking out for her.

She then thought of all the miracles that seemed to surround her. The river trip, that was mostly a bruised, bleeding blank, had brought her to the door of Bitch Moose—another savior who had treated her like precious jewelry while healing and training her for a new life of protected slavery. Then there was the godlike rescue, the impossible odds that occurred at the arrival of Moses; her near slavery here that she had overcome by courage and extra skills to get herself away from the dreaded wash pots into finally heading up the sewing room. Before that she'd had to take jealous insults for her beauty again, as well as jealousy of her skills, but finally she had earned the loyalty, and even love, of both the laundresses and sewers.

There were the longed-after moments with Moses. Moments surely stolen from eternity. The more precious the moments, the more burning painful the absence. Her struggle for balance was near-stupefying to Sheela. She studied the other women who had come here before her. How did they handle it? She could not tell, for some seemed impassive, some withdrawn from the truth of the tedium of their lives and lovers.

It got worse. She often thought she had gone mad. Finally it took the massive heart of Mayo Lou to help at all.

"Honey, I'se been seein' you runnin' 'round to the infirmary and the reverend and all. I'se been watchin' your heart meltin' with love and dryin' up from fear. I'se done had four soldier husbands. Two killed by the Comanches. Two by the Apaches. Now I got none. But I remembers 'em. You try'n remember that. Sgt. Moses Williams done outlived all my husbands, and they fought in the same battles. Ain't no Apache gonna get him less'n it's plain meant to be, an' cain't you or him neither do a diddly damn 'bout that."

With many questions, Sheela looked into Mayo Lou's white-rimmed eyes that had seen much suffering and kindness. She saw the huge breasts and arms that had lovingly held these unknown men unknown to herself.

Mayo Lou continued, "I loved each one of 'em in a different way, honey, but I miss 'em all the same. There ain't no gettin' used to it. Quit tryin'. Quit tryin', right this minute. There is only waitin', workin', and a little lovin' in between out here. Thass all. It's the work what saves us. So do it best you can and be proud of yourself and your man, livin' or dead. Don't matter what nobody tells you, no preacher, no officer, nobody. Life is skunk shit and peach cobbler. You gonna get some of both no matter how you plan it."

Mayo Lou had helped her realize that simple appearances most often hide the buried truths of wisdom. She was grateful beyond speech for the painful effort it must have cost the older woman. She hugged her and let tears silently wash across Mayo Lou's shoulder.

Mayo Lou held her close and hummed the sound of eternal consoling that mothers have always made to their babies. Mayo Lou had lost five of those to different diseases and a rattlesnake's bite. This she could not speak of, not even to Sheela, but just for this moment the beautiful young woman in her arms represented all her lost men and all the babies they had made together.

The ancient female hum entered Sheela and she was comforted beyond any womanly sense she could recall. She felt an aged warmth, part of which would stay with her always. Mayo Lou was her mother now, and Sheela was all of Mayo Lou's children in her one lovely, kind-souled body. A need. A blending.

Nineteen

THE NEWSPAPERS OF THE TERRITORY NEVER LET UP NOW. RE-
ports of the Warm Springs Apaches having been seen as far
north as Acoma, Socorro, and other towns almost screamed
off the pages. Headlines and stories told of the slaughter and
mutilation of twenty-seven out of twenty-nine workers on
one ranch . . . then nine more here . . . fourteen there . . .
then entire villages sacked and burned, and their people
killed.

The pressure from Santa Fe and Washington was coming
to bear heavily on Colonel Hatch. He had taken temporary
field command of the Ninth. Because there was some truth
in the headlines, he shared the field command with Major
Morrow.

Victorio and Nana were hitting every possible target over a
wide area consisting of at least twenty thousand square miles.

Nana was keeping up the ammunition caches by ordering
his warriors to attack wherever his vision told him. Sometimes he sent only a few men, sometimes all would go. He
was relentless in keeping his part of Lozen's visions as well.

There were so many continuing raids scattered over such
a wide area that the miners, settlers, and soldiers felt at times

as if every one of a thousand canyons was inhabited by angry Apaches.

Lieutenant Valois and Sergeant Moses had led a unit of I Company back and forth from the mining camp of Chloride in the middle foothills of the Black Range where Nana's raid had killed four miners and wounded several more. The Apaches had escaped all the way south to the Gila, with nine horses and four mules. No matter how hard Lieutenant Valois led his unit, they seldom got a full engagement.

The high command dispatched other units of both the Ninth and Tenth Cavalry to the rail headings as many workers were threatening to quit without some military protection. Valois's unit was too good a fighting group for this bodyguard duty.

The cavalry finally got a fresh trail in the Mogollon Mountains. One of their Apache scouts read the sign and said they would be easy to catch the next morning because there were only eight or nine warriors and they were driving a large herd of newly captured horses and mules.

There were many problems facing the unit. Half their horses had worn-out shoes, and their hooves were tender from endless miles of semidesert and the jagged rocks of the canyons. Some of the unit were walking, leading their mounts, and the leather of their boots was worn through to the bare foot. Due to the scattered and extremely skillful attacks and trail deceptions of old Nana, the supply wagons had long ago quit trying to keep up with the troops.

The scout picked out a spot at the head of a canyon, where there was a small spring, for their night camp. He said the signs showed that Nana was already out on top in a small side canyon. So Valois and Moses agreed to hold council when they reached camp and plan the attack. For now, they were still two hard miles from the site.

Moses limped along and spoke aloud while it was still safe

to do so. "Hey, men, maybe we'll get that old son of a bitch tomorrow."

Private Walley said, "Lordy, Lordee, I been hearin' you say that so long I done forget the first time."

"But tomorrow's different—it's my birthday."

Cpl. C. C. Smith, who was limping on both feet and leading a horse limping on three, perked up. "Shore 'nuff, Sarge? Well, maybe you're right. Maybe we'll get to celebrate by skinnin' ole Nana like a fox. Hell, I bet his hide'd sell at auction fer . . . fer . . ."

Walley finished his thoughts for him. "That wrinkled ole hide wouldn't bring more'n a dollar. Couldn't even patch a pair of gloves with it. Now his brains—if we just had some way to bust them outta his head an use 'em—I bet the commandin' general would give all his pay, his pension, his wife, and his kids fer a set a' brains like that."

Happy he had gotten the men's minds back on killing Nana instead of their sore feet, Moses said, "Yeah, Walley, I'd give a year's pay just to borrow them for ten minutes before we attack in the morning. Just ten minutes is all we'd need those brains, as fast as that old fart thinks."

Walley grinned in spite of the many places on his long, skinny, hungry body, that hurt and said, "Sarge, you been promisin' to put your sights on him now for . . ."

"Don't go into that again. I *will* do it, but I don't want to hear about it anymore from you rock dancers." And some of them did appear to be doing bizarre little dances as their sore feet touched sharp, hot rocks.

Walley changed the subject back to the beginning of the conversation, "How old you gonna be tomorrow?"

Moses answered with a purposely solemn face. "I'm gonna be one thousand and thirteen years old tomorrow, and I lived most of it on this trek right here." Before any reaction could interrupt, he went on, "You see, you fancy dancing soldiers, if we don't get the old ghost tomorrow, I might die of old age before I put my sights on his killing heart."

Walley said right back, "Lordy, Lordee, don't worry about his heart. Jis' blow his ole ass into so many pieces he can never set on a horse again."

"Hey, Private, you're smarter'n you act. If we could get the old bastard afoot, we could wind this war up in a week."

Walley was no longer distracted by Moses's instigations. As they neared the campsite, he limped heavier and hummed an almost inaudible little newly invented tune:

> Sergeant Moses shot ole Nana right in the ass
> All his parts flew about in the grass
> We rode and rode, round and round
> but none of Nana's ass could be found
> Where did it go, the mean ole shit?
> We know for sure he ain't gonna quit . . .

Private Walley continued his composition down to a whisper as they watered their horses at the spring.

There were a couple of rocked-in grassy swales where they could corral the horses and let them graze on the rich grass. The soldiers had a little bit of old beef jerky and one piece of hardtack for their dinner. They would have only stale jerky for breakfast. There was a little coffee left in the one solid, still half-healthy mule's pack, but they couldn't risk even the tiniest fire to heat the water to make it.

Lieutenant Valois had been tricked and trapped in canyons so many times he seriously asked Moses if he had any ideas.

"Well, sir, just in case our scout is wrong about our surprising them . . . maybe we'd better risk four or five men up the canyon. I'll do it, sir."

"I suppose you intend to split our forces to move to the top of each side of the canyon ahead of the bottom unit?"

"You read my mind, sir. We'll stumble and creep along at the same time. Maybe Nana will be certain we're the stupid soldiers he thinks we are anyway."

The lieutenant managed a weary smile. "Between just the two of us, Sergeant, he has made us seem a bit more than foolish at times, huh?"

"Many, many times, sir. So did the Comanches, but we finally beat 'em."

"That we did, Sergeant, but I could not bear thinking of trying to again."

"Nor I, sir. Nor I."

Moses dreamed of Nana's eyes in a fitful sleep and the old warrior's had just changed to the slanted ones of Sheela, his love. Just as he reached for her, he threw the blanket off his upper body and knew it was time to do battle. It was not yet light.

It was a struggle to get all the men up and in any mood to move at all, much less fight the greatest trickster they had ever faced.

But Moses did it by whispering to his men, "It's my birthday. We'll dance on Nana's grave before noon."

Whether they believed it could not really be known, but soon they were checking their arms and ammo while they tried to chew and swallow the last of the jerky. One way or the other those who lived would be heading home to the fort. Their food, their mounts, themselves, had finally run out of string on this long journey of disappointment. The two leaders, along with C.C., got all the men as ready as they would ever be at dawn.

As sore as their feet were, some even blistered and cracked to where each step left a little blood on the grass, the dirt, the rocks, they were relieved to leave the lame horses feeding. The proud cavalry had become limping infantry. They had just one crippling charge left in them. Had they known that this battle would long be known as "The time the sky turned to stone," they might not have tried. No one would ever know. They moved out in three tiny units, straining their last hungry, exhausted muscles near the tearing point by sheer will and a little bit of battle anticipation still pushing them up the steep slopes.

Lieutenant Valois hoped they were finally going to catch the old man of the boulders sleeping, after all these years, all these uncountable skirmishes and battles.

On the opposite ridge Corporal Shield, Private Walley, and their battered unit suddenly began to believe the possibility of "putting the sights on him," as Moses had said. They halted every little bit and listened. They could hear no sound of human movement.

In the wild canyon, scrambling over and around boulders, through brush that clawed and tore at them like cougar claws, Moses, C.C., and three privates advanced with great effort. So difficult in fact that Moses forgot for a moment about killing Nana himself and made silent prayers that Walley, or any soldier at all, would down him. His thoughts were as scrambled as the surface of the canyon. Now he was suddenly able to see Nana's giant eyes hovering over them all even as the sky turned from dawn to daylight.

He became jubilant when he heard the cracking of rifle fire to his upper left and a moment later again on the upper right. The two units had made contact in a pincers movement. Surely, surely, they had him at last. Moses was suddenly so elated that he felt he could stretch his arms all the way up to heaven and shout a victory yell that would shake the earth.

His elation quickly turned to caution as the firing moved farther out to each side, until the sounds of battle were dimming and the shots more scarce.

"The old bastard," Moses muttered to himself. It seemed impossible, but Nana had done it again. He had known they were there, split his forces to each flank, and now had no doubt vanished into the vastness yet again. Before Moses could worry about the casualties at the upper firefights, he saw C.C. and the three privates staggered apart below him.

Then that thing—that spirit, or whatever the hell it was, the *warrior's warning,* caused him to look up to see that the sky was falling. It had turned to stone.

He fell back against a boulder that sloped outward above him and stared through the deflected rocks as C.C. was smashed down suddenly and disappeared under the stones faster than a bullet could break skin. He watched helplessly as the torrent of rocks buried Privates Frazier and Altomont. Private Wiggins had been knocked sideways by a bouncing rock that broke his lower leg in several places but also saved his life.

When the rocks stopped crashing, Moses raced and clawed, falling and getting up over those stones that had been meant for him, to Wiggins's side.

In spite of his agony, Wiggins grimaced with much struggle, asking, "How many, Sarge?"

"Just you and me, Wiggins."

"Oh, God," Wiggins said and tried to struggle to his feet but fainted from the pain that now was overtaking the first numbness.

"Yeah, he did it to us again. He thought he'd get us all." The last statement to the unconscious man was certainly the only consolation of the day.

Moses crawled on his hands and knees to the edge of the pile of rocks that had instantly killed and permanently buried one of his two best friends. At first, a great rage overcame him and he shouted into the sky from a kneeling position with his rifle raised above his head. There were no words in his cry to the sky, only feelings. Feelings of loss and anguish that he had long ago controlled, but because of the vision of Nana hovering above, he could no longer contain the terrible frustration of helpless rage. The one thing a soldier cannot do is feel guilt at others dying when he had been just as vulnerable but was somehow spared. That is a foolish luxury with no answer, but it had happened and now his sky sounds slowly turned to a wail of personal loss and then to tears of silence. The sky stones had done what bullets, knives, arrows, and lances could never do.

Suddenly he felt a hand on his shoulder. Wiggins had come to and somehow dragged himself to Moses's side. The only comfort he knew to give was a touch on the shoulder that said all there was about caring.

Lieutenant Valois and Private Walley finally arrived to find Moses using a fist-sized stone to chisel three crosses of the church, one for each of the dead, into the overhanging sandstone bluff that had saved him. Wiggins was sweating with pain.

Moses turned a face now full of acceptance to Valois, who asked, "How many?"

"We have three wounded, one bad, and one dead."

"Nana?"

"I don't know. We found three smears of blood."

"That's all?"

"That's it."

Moses took off his hat. All followed his lead.

"Dear Lord, wherever you are, be good to these men buried here. They were fine soldiers and even better human beings. Amen."

All who were able said "Amen" after him.

Then the survivors wove, stumbled, and a few were carried, moving toward the spring where the tired horses still grazed, having a short rest and enjoying themselves for the first time in weeks.

Twenty

COLONEL HATCH AND MAJOR MORROW WERE SHUFFLING THE Buffalo Soldiers of the Ninth Regiment back and forth, from fort to fort, camp to camp, using all the intelligence they could gather from scouts, civilians, heliograph, and the telegraph, to pursue, intercept, and anticipate full and final engagement with the Apache warriors. The pressure was enormous from their superiors, the press, the civilians, but most of all from themselves.

From Civil War times each trooper carried, besides his ordinary kit, five days' rations in haversacks, thirty pounds of forage for the horses, seventy-five rounds of ammunition, and two extra horseshoes. But here in the desert and high canyons of the Black Range everything had been cut to a minimum—most even left their beloved sabers behind to save any weighted burden possible. The men, animals, and energy it took made the Gatling gun useless in the terrain of Nana's band. They made do with a boot knife or the issue shovel-bayonet. Most of the time now they were riding far from their wagons with only jerky and hardtack for food. Often they rode and fought until there was nothing to eat and they were forced to turn back before hunger weakened them to the point of no return.

Even so, they made do, resting, cooling, checking for wrinkles in the saddle blankets and sore feet and backs on the horses, taking better care of them than they did of themselves. Veterinarians often performed surgery, and medical doctors treated horses as well as men. The Buffalo Soldier "made do" and moved on.

So many men and mounts were lamed and worn out from the unceasing movement of the Apaches it was hard to get enough replacements to fully, properly fight.

Hatch and Morrow had one thing going for them, however, that transcended all else with the Buffalo Soldiers. They knew they truly cared for them and fought the various bureaucracies constantly to overcome their inferior supplies and equipment.

None of this was on Moses's mind for the moment. It would be at least two weeks before his unit of men and horses could be healed enough to move out again. If there were no replacements available, he knew he and Lieutenant Valois could depend on Major Morrow to transfer some men and horses to them somehow. They had survived and fought under him over the years. He would do his best to take care of his best.

Moses's losses bothered him badly—three dead and one permanently injured, without the honor of firing or being fired at in the last defeat by Nana, was a terrible loss and insult. The strange combination of reluctant admiration and an ever-growing hatred, inflamed by helplessly seeing one of his best friends being killed and buried by Nana's trap, did nothing to defuse the growing rage within his battered body. But being a career soldier, all that was set aside, for a short while.

* * *

Sheela had earned her every-ninety-day leave, and Moses had no problem getting a three-day pass from Valois. The two of them had ridden since daylight side by side for hours and had turned to a certain cedar-dotted hill that Moses knew.

She had said eagerly, her great dark eyes radiant with anticipation, "So, you have a surprise for me?"

"Maybe. We'll see. Be patient for a while."

"I can't, but I'll act as if I am."

"Good," he said, smiling, reining next to her and taking her hand in his for a reassuring squeeze. Just that little contact with her flesh sent goose bumps rippling through him. He must stay with his plan or his craving for her would overcome him.

Moses was extremely proud of his future wife. She had adapted to the rigors of army life with good cheer and expertise. Still, he was a little worried about their future—especially letting Sheela know his new plans. With difficulty he brought it up.

"You know, honey, I've been so busy fighting that I've neglected part of my business. I haven't had time to write letters for the men and collect my charge fee."

"And here I've been doing it for the girls for free," she said.

"Oh no, that's fine. I still have my horses working, and we've got a nice little starter nest egg, but not enough. I just want you to know that soon as the fighting's over, I'll get back to it. I want to be sure we've got enough money to get us a little place and set up some kind of business when I retire. That's not so far away, you know? And the best news of all is that Lieutenant Valois volunteered the information that he was personally working to speed up our marriage permit."

She turned her head and stared a moment at him, sighed a deep breath, and smiled almost invisibly.

"Reverend Pree says that as soon as the war is over and we

are assigned to a permanent post, I'll be able to draw a salary
for teaching."

"Well, that's good news. Between the two of us this world
hasn't got a chance."

"Precisely," she agreed, with a smile.

Now Moses raised his hand in the halt signal out of long
habit. There in the scattered cedar they looked across a rolling
valley of grass, chamisa, and scattered greasewood bushes.
Just a few miles north, the hills started rising up in seeming
countless contours into the Black Range. It didn't look so
huge, so high, so deep, so deadly from here. In fact, just the
opposite. It undulated across the far western skyline in all
shades of almost welcoming blues, hinting at its hidden spots
of paradise instead of deadly deep canyon traps of death and
devastation. Both views were true.

Today, Sheela looked hypnotically across the immense
spaces, absorbing the beauty rapturously, while knowing underneath the feeling of dread that the great dark blueness
might at anytime take her love away for eternity. But now she
breathed in the clean, cool air deeply, lifting her breasts as
well as her spirits, and she had suddenly, happily, made up
her mind on another important matter.

She stared into the far distance of the deceivingly faraway
blip of the Black Range. She said softly to Moses, "It is so . . .
it's immeasurable."

"Yes, if it was flattened out, I suppose it would be as big as
Texas."

They watched as three red-tailed hawks circled slowly,
widely apart, then the center nearer one suddenly dropped as
if dead from the sky, flinging its wings wide the instant before
hitting the earth and then rising at a low angle with a cot-
tontail rabbit safely in its claws. The others circled on as if
the sudden deadly survival event had not occurred at all. Forgotten as swiftly as it had happened.

Sheela thought to herself though that this act represented all that had happened in the high desert and supporting mountains and all that ever would or could happen anywhere.

Moses knew it without thinking. He had something else on his mind as he slowly moved his field glasses across the land spread before them from horizon to horizon. He watched for movement of any kind, especially birds. To his satisfaction he had seen none except the flash of a single magpie's wings. The sun was high enough now that most wild creatures were seeking shade, shelter, or hidden spots to dine on its night or early morning prey, just as the hawk. The rolling, golden, often blue-grey, hills were prominent in the shadows cast by the eleven o'clock sun. If one stared at it long enough, he would realize that the shadows and lights, ever-evolving, revealed the earth, the universe, in never-ending movement. If someone closed his eyes a spell or observed a person or object nearby it all seemed still, peacefully quiet and soothingly permanent, but of course one always had to look again and see the moving, circling truth. Sheela was in a reverie, a torpor that she was absorbing from the earth, its smells, its soft breeze, its calling. It was almost the same feeling she reveled in when she lay still in Moses's arms. It was the treasure of the young. They could absorb and deflect the hard blows that in turn made these moments so special. Sheela was making the most of it. It was her nature and her learning. She knew now that being close in flesh would only intensify their love and give them the one escape they might survive on.

Then Moses broke her musing with, "Sheela, see that second ridge . . . see the opening between the trees?" He was pointing and she leaned over, sighting down the side of his arm the best she could.

"The opening just to the right of the two rock outcroppings?"

"That's it. Now you wait here. I'm going to ride over there. Now listen carefully. After I disappear over the first ridge, you wait and watch for me in the opening between the trees. If I show up and wave, you ride across as straight as you can to me. All right?"

She was puzzled, but kept it to herself. "Yes. All right."

"If I don't show up by high sun, ride on back to the fort. You understand?"

"Well, no . . . but I promise."

He turned his horse's muzzle to her horse's tail, reached one hand behind her head and pulled her lips to his. He kissed her with the utmost tenderness, looked quickly into her eyes, reined his horse away, and disappeared down the side of their lookout hill, weaving through the brush and trees. Then he came into sight again riding across the valley in a snaking arroyo. She watched him with no boredom whatsoever. Just seeing him out there healthy, alive, hers, was the purest joy.

At last he disappeared over the first hill. For just a moment she felt a shudder of aloneness pass through her. Then it vanished and she knew he would show up at the appointed opening.

Moses reined to the right toward the highest point on the chosen hill. He had seen Apache, Pueblo, and Navajo scouts use this place to survey a vast area of the foothills. The powerful hindquarters of his chestnut sorrel, Reno, made the last surge onto the half-hidden place.

He stepped down, tying the reins to a dead branch of a cedar, took the field glasses, and easing up in tall grass and rocks, began his magnified survey. As before, he watched for a sudden fearful flight of birds. After fifteen or so minutes, he was sure the area was safe.

Moses knew that Lieutenant Valois had received a telegraph saying that Nana and Victorio were raiding south and west around the San Mateo Mountains; but knowing how they split their forces, he had to be certain this area was clear before signaling Sheela. He knew she had to be puzzled, even as she sensed what he was doing.

He arose confidently now. He had done all he could to assure her safety so there was no use worrying. It would serve no purpose but to lessen the pleasure of this special day.

He rode now through the terrain happily to the spot to signal his woman. At first, he didn't think she had seen him; then he spotted her winding through the trees out onto the rolling ridge that rose almost straight across the valley. He put the glasses on her and marveled again at her beauty, at his being blessed with her. He admired her natural rhythm of riding the bay horse, Badger, in perfect sync and balance. If ever a soldier had a proud few minutes, this was it.

A dust devil was twisting its precarious way across the valley. It looked for a moment as if she would meet it as it crossed, but she kicked the horse into a long lope and it passed behind her. The sun shining through her multicolored hair as it streamed out, flipping in the breeze behind, appeared to capture the sunrays and create a flickering aura around her head. He was proud of her. He loved her so much. Sometimes he thought the warm, unfulfilled ache would cause him to dissolve and blow away like the dust devil slowly whirling itself out of existence.

Now she was here, right before him, smiling widely with questions in her eyes.

"Follow me," he said.

They rode around until they found one of those little hidden paradises scattered throughout this otherwise harsh and unforgiving land. There were green bushes and three small cottonwoods encircling a pond of turquoise blue.

They dismounted. They walked down and stared at the jewel of a hot-water spring seeping up from the molten guts of the earth through a tiny seam in the rocks. It ran out over the smoothed stone for perhaps twenty yards and formed another pool of pure, cooler water. There was a patch of thick green grass curving around a sheer little palisade for another thirty or forty yards.

"Oh," she said, clasping her hands together as her eyes and mind tried to take in the totality, the specialness, of this high-desert oasis. "It's so beautiful."

By the time they had unsaddled the horses, and he had watered them at the lower pond, then hobbled and turned them loose to feast on lush grasses, the sun had reached its apex and entered the western half of the sky.

They placed their blankets in a soft spot next to little bluffs where the grass was thick. Sheela had unwrapped their food of several slabs of roast beef, and Mayo Lou had gotten her two loaves of fresh bread, a small jar of honey, and two tins of sardines. She placed their canteens and the food in a shady indentation in the cliff. As she finished checking all this out, she turned to see Moses's uniform in a pile and he was sitting half under the hot water, smiling a big welcome at her.

She dropped her clothing next to his and just for a minute posed in the bright sunlight; then, giggling, she slipped slowly into the hot water beside him, sighing luxuriously as its heat-mineralized water seemed to dissolve her bones and her body became one mass of fused contentment.

She closed her eyes for a spell, voluptuously rubbing cupped hands full of the water on her neck and her breasts where it coursed back to the pond in arcs, circling around her dark brown nipples as they firmed and pushed out from the rest of her roundness.

It took all his willpower to keep from joining the water around her breasts. However, control right now was full of pressure. He had something so singular to share with her that physical passion would have to wait.

With her eyes still closed, Sheela asked, "How in God's world did you ever find this magic place?"

"Luck, just plain ole Moses luck." He didn't want to change her mood by mentioning the Apache scouts who knew the observation point nearby and must certainly have known this sybaritic spot for countless centuries.

"Oh, yes. I'm so happy you were so lucky."

Before the sun moved too far west, Moses crawled out of the pond and reached down and took Sheela's arm. He slowly turned her around, then with his hands, starting at the neck, dried her body, moving across her shoulders then slowly down the entire length of her arms. He moved to her chest and around both breasts with both hands down, down, over her sides and belly, kneeling to smooth his palms down her legs to her feet. He rubbed slowly back and forth down the inside of her smooth thighs all the way to her ankles. Now he could not help but move his hands slowly up the inside of her thighs. He was pleased that she was not pushing him away or resisting his lovemaking.

She helped pull him to his feet, where they moved their bodies together. Although he had thought he would pick her up and carry her to the blankets, it was not to be. She slowly collapsed on the tall grass, pulling him down with her.

Their moans of pleasure melded into one and were absorbed by the cliffs before they woke the sleeping coyotes.

They lay there in the loving position for a long time, their clean-washed skins gleaming with new perspiration as the sun turned the thousands of tiny droplets into rainbowed diamonds. Later they held hands and looked up at the cerulean sky as it pulsated with almost unseeable violets and light greens as far as the eye could see up into the spaces so vast they were beyond anyone but the Great Mystery's description. Then one tiny white cloud formed above, just for them, and they watched, silently delighted, as it grew a bit and then broke into little pieces and vanished.

"Sheela, have you ever thought about how much of the world is colored blue?"

"Well, the blue sky is bigger than the entire earth."

"And there are the oceans, streams, lakes, and even most shadows."

"That's right," she agreed. "And the blue spruce forests."

"Azurite copper."

"And turquoise."

"There must be millions of people with blue eyes."

"Yes, but I like brown ones." She smiled at him.

He went on with the game. "Gun-barrel blue."

"Cavalry uniforms," she added. "And bluebirds."

"You know the Black Range is not black, it's blue."

Then in a suddenly solemn tone, Sheela said softly, almost in a reverent whisper, "Yes, the faraway blue."

They were side by side, quiet, still for a few moments with their own private thoughts.

Then, as one, they sat up and were suddenly full of a new hunger—for food. They dressed and Sheela served their little meal using Moses's trench knife to cut the bread and meat. He opened a can of the wonderfully oily sardines. Then they feasted. The roast beef, the little canned fish, the fresh bread later smeared with honey was beyond compare.

No matter at all. No matter anything. It was the most delicious meal either had ever experienced. They leaned back against the warm sun-absorbing bluffs and visited. They talked of dreams of their future when the Indian Wars were over and they could be together as it was meant. And they spoke of silly things that made them laugh and before one could stop the other would start.

For a moment Sheela was silent. Several times she started to speak but pulled back.

"What?" he asked.

"Nothing," she said, then opened her mouth, shook her head, and then reluctantly uttered, "Moses, you know the night you were bidding for me? I . . . I was watching you through a slit in the doorway, praying you would be the one. Otherwise I planned to escape . . . to run away somehow; but when you won, I couldn't think anymore. And then after we talked and everything . . . I was so afraid I'd never see you again that my mind just froze. I can't believe now that I hesitated to go with you when that was what I wanted most in all the world."

"Who can blame you for the confusion after what you'd been through?" he said, softly touching her lips with a forefinger. "My God, darlin', I have no idea what I said to Madam Moose. All I know was I'd finally found the answer to my life . . . you."

"Me, too. I knew you were the person I'd been waiting for all along. Oh, thank you, God, and thank you, Moses, and thank you, Bitch Moose."

They held hands as if it were the very first time.

Then the sun ran away for the day, hiding behind the hills, but still leaving its rays bluing the sky for a while.

Sheela leaned back against the bluff, looking out across the pond, seeing great things that not even the open sky above could possibly show her at this moment.

Moses caressed the bronze red streaks in her dark hair and

inhaled deeply the scent that was just hers in all the world, and now was his to share.

As the sky faded from the disappearing sun, a coolness descended upon their little utopia. Moses unhobbled and watered the horses again. Then he gathered wood and risked a small fire. They ate again. And stared wondering at each other across the flames, and their dark eyes caught the light of the moving flames and tossed them softly back and forth, each to the other, and then they bedded and loved. Afterward they stared side by side again into the uncountable stars.

She said in a whisper, "I suppose we aren't meant to see the stars during the day even though they are there."

He knew what she meant without saying more and she in turn understood that he did.

The fire burned down to one tiny glow, and the moon tipped up over the other side of the world and turned the tops of the rocky spires a rich faraway blue, the light slowly moving down in a line across the darkness just above their knees. Some crickets chirped. A night bird called from over the hill, the horses chewed and occasionally snorted in soft satisfaction as they went on eating from the great bowl of grassy dessert. A coyote howled so near it seemed it was on top of the rocky spires and then another and another, and they talked on out of hearing of the world around. And then, just as occurred in the so-called heat of a battle, there was a sudden total silence. Straining to see as far into the stars as he could, the moment Moses had waited for came with the sudden silence.

"This is it," he whispered. "This is what I wanted to experience with you, my darling." She turned her head to him, eagerly awaiting his next words. "I just wanted to see what it would be like if you and I were the only humans left in the whole world."

They turned together and held one another. Now they both

knew. Passion, euphoria, and the deep sleep of peace was theirs this night. The moon moved on in its perpetual circle, and just before the day broke, the coyotes sang in their dreams once more.

Twenty One

IT IS THE BIG EVENTS, THE TURNING POINTS, THAT ARE MOST often thought of as history; however, it is often the seemingly small things that start events cascading out of control—or lead to a solution.

Sheela presented her handwriting and reading skills to Rev. Charles Pree. The reverend had a tiny study off the pulpit area in the fort chapel. He looked and listened carefully.

"Good. Very good, Sheela."

"Thank you, Reverend."

"You cannot imagine how long I have tried to set up a real . . . a permanent school here at the fort for those who have never had a chance at an education. So far I've only succeeded in getting permission to teach one evening a week myself. The soldiers are too tired at night when they've finished training. And as you well know, war comes first. It takes time to get the men interested enough to put in that extra effort after a hard day. The children, of course, would get along fine."

"I understand, sir," she said. "When Missus Nelda was tutoring me, we worked at least two hours a day, five days a week—and that was just on reading and writing." Then she explained about Nelda.

"Yes," the chaplain said, with some regret edging into his mellow yet powerful voice, "regular attendance is the only way to capture those dormant imaginations. Of course, with the Apaches raiding so widely now, there would be almost daily interruptions."

Sheela could see the present problems, but Moses had said the wars could not last at this intensity for much longer. She did not interrupt with this bit of prophecy, but listened patiently as Pree talked in his sonorous preacher's voice of his dreams of education for the career soldiers and what it would do for their personal respect and advancement. Then he went on at length about the soldiers who would go back into civilian life with great disadvantages without a basic education—especially the Buffalo Soldiers who were such a short time out of the recent war.

Sheela was so stirred by his talk of truth and sincerity that she ventured an unsought-after opinion. "Well, you are a captain. It seems to me that should give you the clout to organize your school."

He laughed, rubbing his tightly curled black hair as if to show her why, but verbalized anyway. "I'm no longer a fighting man of the field, my dear. I'm a post preacher, a counselor of the wounded and dying and a frustrated educator. I'm afraid that clout you speak of only exists in others' imagination."

"I wish I could help."

"I know you do, and when we somehow get it started, I'm sure you will be a big part of it."

Sheela arose, saying, "I'd better get back to my sewing or my friend Mama Mayo Lou will beat me with a big stick."

"I doubt that. Mayo Lou is forced to show bluster to get the laundry done, but she has a heart of much compassion. I've heard her prayers for years and years. They are always made for others."

"I know. Thank you, Reverend Pree, sir. I have faith that you'll get your school."

"I have strong faith, too. It's my business, you know?"

They had propped each other up. Each giving the other fortitude to continue their dreams. Sheela went back to her labors with a slight bounce to her naturally sensuous walk. She was glad to have another friend, a compatriot of dreams and real plans.

It was the time of preparation. Almost all the men, horses, and mules who could be healed were. It was absolutely necessary to get the men and animals into battle with whatever small advantages they could gather against the cunning of the earth-worshipping enemy. It had always been so, and Moses was certain it always would be.

Moses trained his troops relentlessly, overhearing their gripes of "Why are we riding these horses to death here at the fort when we're going out into the hills to do battle anyway? It's the stupidest thing I done ever heard of." "We been trainin' by travelin' and fightin' for years. This here's plumb stupid." And on and on, the complaints mounted and with half-right reasons, they griped.

Sometimes, Moses himself, and even Lieutenant Valois, silently agreed with the complaints, but each knew that new horses had to be trained with the older, experienced ones. And the new men, the replacements, had to be wearied so they would automatically respond to commands and follow the seasoned veterans into the hazards of battle—all hoping they would survive long enough to become veterans themselves. The one exception was target practice for the replacements.

The veterans needed none of that, for it would waste ammunition that they could professionally send in the direction of the Apaches.

In a rare moment of observing the troops, Moses now ventured a statement to his long-time friend of many shared battles. "Lieutenant, do you think it possible that Sheela could help Reverend Pree establish a school for our uneducated men?" He knew he was out of place asking this in spite of a blood-letting kinship with Valois. One never knew how frontier authority would come down.

Valois did not turn his head from observing the horse drill of I Troop. "Sergeant, the Reverend Pree will get his school when these damned wars are over, and not before. Colonel Hatch is under the kind of pressure that would break lesser men, and we must give him our total support." Then he smiled warmly at Moses. "Of course, you know that?"

"Yes, sir."

"Well," he added, "if it will make you feel any better, the good reverend harasses me at least once a week on this very subject. Let us get our battles done first."

"Yes, sir. I understand, sir."

How words spread about small things remains a mystery in the army. They seemed to fly around in the air randomly seeking ears. A series of small events rapidly occurred now that made the handling of larger, more deadly duties appear easier for Moses.

Overnight, Lieutenant Valois's wife, Christine, lost the tutor for her six-year- and eight-year-old daughters. The tutor married an officer in the Tenth Regiment and left. Christine was distraught over the loss. She was a good-enough mother, but as a diversion from the worries of her life, and duties, as a military officer's wife, she enjoyed organizing, directing, and putting on musicals and small plays for the troops. Taking time to tutor her children, in addition to these many diverting activities, would upset her method of surviving her husband's absence. The thoughts of battles must be subdued. So many of his men never returned, or if they did, often were terribly wounded and most would perish from infection.

As she was carefully explaining what the loss of their tutor and her lack of needed time might mean to the morale of his troops, the lieutenant interrupted her. "You're familiar with Reverend Pree's obsession about opening up a school for the troopers?"

"Yes, of course," she said. "He even mentions it to me on occasion, hoping, I'm sure, that I could influence you in turn."

"Well, yes . . . I know . . . but he just yesterday was telling me what a wonderful reader Sergeant Moses's fiancée, Sheela Jones, is, and what beautiful handwriting she has."

That did it. The decision was made for Christine to interview Sheela immediately.

She was not only pleased with Sheela's bearing, but astounded at her reading and writing skills. As the conversation progressed, Christine was further delighted to learn of Sheela's sewing expertise. She considered this bonus to be a miracle, a true blessing for her entertainment pursuits. Sheela could help her with all the costumes. It added up to be her greatest time of joy and relief in all the long years of duty with her husband and his beloved I Troop.

"What a waste is being perpetrated," Christine told her husband, and Sheela was immediately transferred to the small, but serviceable tutor's quarters in the Valois household.

The two Valois daughters, Danielle and Stacy, were enamored of Sheela's beauty and her soft but strong authority. They looked forward to the four hours of study each day.

4 M S

Sheela was very appreciative of the gain in quality of living quarters, food, clothing, and respect, and her true enjoyment in tutoring the two children; but it was soon brought to Christine's attention that Sheela was also a fine cook. Sheela soon found herself overloaded.

After a quiet discussion it was decided that Sheela needed help. She secured the talents of Mayo Lou as the chef for the Valois family and, though a bit crowded, moved her into her own quarters.

Lieutenant Valois allowed this and, in fact, encouraged it because the Apache wars had reached such an intensity, that having fewer concerns about the welfare of his family was a valuable relief.

Moses was even more delighted and relieved by this progression than his superior officer. His beloved was doing what she enjoyed. She was now provided with, not only better creature comforts, but the companionship of Mama Mayo Lou— her adopted mother. He, too, felt suddenly blessed. He allowed himself to marvel at the chain of events: the rescue of Sheela from Bitch Moose's high-class "hog ranch," her advancement from the wearing position in the laundry of pot woman to sewing and sorting, right on up to being the tutor and seamstress for his respected commander's household. And today he had just received the long overdue payment for the use of his horses and mules in the Central City mines near Fort Bayard. The forty-three dollars added to the two hundred in the company safe helped his possibilities of further enhancing Sheela's life after they finally got their marriage papers.

"I do believe that I'm the happiest man at the fort," he said, with a little strut in his walk.

The only one in an authoritative position who was momentarily dismayed by all of this was Reverend Pree. He felt his prize teacher had been taken from him before he could get his long-craved and fought-after school going. He consoled himself, like everyone else, by assuming that the wars would soon be over and everything would work out. He was sure he could convince Lieutenant Valois that Sheela would somehow make the time to help him teach the troopers.

So all dreamed on pleasantly for a brief spell. Too brief.

Twenty Two

LIEUTENANT GUILFOYLE OF L COMPANY, WITH TWENTY TROOP-
ers and some Indian scouts, had been dispatched by Major
Morrow in desperate pursuit of Nana, who had ambushed his
supply wagons while scouting near the Texas border. The Indians' first strike killed two pack animals, ridden by two Buffalo Soldiers. The soldiers used the bodies of the dead
animals as fortifications and did a magnificent holding job.
One trooper was wounded, and after capturing three mules,
Nana's band moved on.

The attack had so angered Guilfoyle that he led his troops
on a long, vengeful pursuit of Nana through Dog Canyon
and along the edge of the great White Sands. It was a chase
across forty miles of roasting desert. All living things that
moved that July day breathed air that seemed as if it would in-
cinerate their lungs and reduce their feet to ashes.

The troopers caught up with the Indians as they were taking a short breather in the San Andres Mountains. L Company had a temporary victory. They captured two horses,
several mules, and wounded two of Nana's few warriors.

Nana then led Guilfoyle across the Rio Grande, killing
three civilians in his wake, before he turned north to the San

Mateo Mountains. Guilfoyle trailed Nana in what turned into harassment by the pursued.

Finally, Guilfoyle had to give up temporarily. His men were at a point beyond exhaustion. The horses' shoes were worn and torn by the hot desert rocks, and the same had happened to most of his men's boots. He stopped at Fort Craig to rest, to heal, and to resupply before moving out again.

Only eight miles from where Guilfoyle and his worn troop were recovering, Nana made three raids in only three days, burning a large, supposedly fortified ranch house and killing ten civilians.

The old cliché of adding insult to injury was repeated many times. The greatest goad was the destruction and death Nana left along his trail for the troops to observe. It both disheartened and angered them. Nana was causing the entire area to boil with confusion and rage.

Headquartering at Fort Bayard, a unit of B Company, including fourteen privates led by Sgt. David Bodie and a few scouts, engaged a roving group of Nana's band in Nogal Canyon east of the San Mateos and resulted in two wounded and three horses killed by Nana's warriors.

Three days later, Lt. George W. Smith, leading the remaining soldiers of Company B, fought Nana's band in Gabaldon Canyon. Three of his men were killed in the battle and a Private Hawkins was badly wounded.

A few days later, nineteen men of Company K, led by Lt. Charles Parker, fought Nana again at Carrizo Canyon, perhaps twenty-five miles west of Sabinal. They were outnumbered by Nana this time. A rare event.

In the hour and a half battle the troopers put up a valiant struggle before the old Apache disappeared to fight at the next better opportunity. Even so, his warriors had killed nine horses and two troopers. Three had been wounded and one captured.

Company K reported one Indian killed and three wounded, but, as always, the only real evidence were four bloody streaks as Nana retrieved his stricken warriors.

Colonel Hatch had the telegraph working somewhat better; and he kept a series of scouts moving messages and orders to Major Morrow, back and forth across the immense and rugged land the best he could, trying to move the most troops against Nana from as many different positions as possible.

The manner and skill Nana had in splitting his band for brief, glancing attacks and then gathering them back together to make stronger stands kept Colonel Hatch and his far-flung units in constant anguish and turmoil. It had become an enormous but scattered cauldron of unprecedented conflict. Never had so few fought so viciously across so many vast horizons.

The word of all these engagements—and many that were missed, and many more that were exaggerated—came to the ears and minds of Lieutenant Valois and his I Troop men, where they were encamped at Cañada Alamosa, near a Mexican farming community, awaiting their turn to head for battle.

Private Walley said to Moses, "Sarge, I know you want ole Nana for yourself, but . . ."

Moses interrupted. "The way he's made a fool out of the whole western army, everyone from the cooks to the generals are having dreams about different ways of killing him."

"Lordy, Lordee, I s'pose you're right, but I wuz jist gonna tell you my way." Moses glanced at his best friend as they both went on cleaning their guns and checking out the rest of their equipment.

Walley rolled his eyes up at the sky, so he could show how hard he was thinking, before he spoke. "I think we oughta spread-eagle him upside down between two trees, tied hard and fast first. Then I'd stick his head in a bucket of lamp oil and build a tiny fire right smack under his head. Thas so he'd have plenty of time to hear and feel his brains cookin'." In case Moses or any other soldiers weren't getting his idea clearly, Walley carefully explained. "See, it's his brains what's got to be done in first. Jist look at what he's done to us with jist his brains. Now, soon's I could hear 'em fryin' like hogside in'a iron skillet, and jist before they wuz cooked down to the size of a little hot walnut, I'd gather me a sharp stick and jab it in his arsehole; then I'd drive it as far in him as I could with a rock so big I could barely hold it; then I'd take a cavalry saber and start swinging it down between his legs slowlike, cuttin' off his balls first and then . . ."

"Seems as if you've spent a great deal of time thinking this event through," Moses said.

Walley did not catch on. "Yes, siree, besides whiskey, fresh venison steaks, and Bitch Moose, there ain't none of my time wasted thinkin' on anything else."

"If you crawl with snakes, you're gonna get blindin' sand in your eyes," Moses said. While Walley and several other troopers were trying to figure this out, Moses went on, "I just want to shoot him clean and pure. One shot exactly between and one inch above his eyes. Just one perfect shot. That's all."

That put Walley to humming and composing again to the regret of all within hearing range.

> Ole Nana done killed a thousand men
> We gonna get 'im, but we don't know when
> When we do, we're gonna throw him in a big iron pot
> and cook 'im done and let him rot
> Then we gonna feed 'im to the outhouse rats
> And we gonna . . .

Some men of I Troop were saved from having to hear more as an outpost guard raced his horse into the encampment, followed by a wildly ranting Mexican farmer spurring his exhausted horse unmercifully, trying to keep up. The overwrought farmer finally rattled out that Nana had attacked the community right under the army's eyebrows and killed his wife, several children, and four hired hands.

Lieutenant Valois had as his new assistant commander 2d Lt. George Ritter Burnett, fresh out of West Point and anxious to build a reputation with the battle-seasoned Ninth. He asked Valois if he could check out the farmer's story. Valois was experienced enough to know it was true without checking. However, he did not feel ready to commit his entire unit when Nana had probably already escaped. At any rate, he was comfortable sending Burnett out because he had assigned Sergeant Moses, his buddy Walley, and their squad to accompany him. This would give the young lieutenant some long-experienced support and guidance.

Burnett and fifteen Buffalo Soldiers mounted and, along with the Mexican farmer, moved swiftly three miles to the farm. When they arrived they found that not only had the wife and hired hands been killed, they had been mutilated. The children had simply been shot.

A crowd of Mexican farmers had gathered now at the site of the slaughter. Nana's raid had been decisive in several ways. The farmer, who had been helping a neighbor, had heard the shots and screams. He and several others had gathered up their weapons and tried to go to the rescue. This was exactly as Nana had expected, so he had had another group of warriors sweep down from over a low-lying hill and had rounded up all the unattended horses and mules and headed them out toward the Cuchillo Negros Mountains—which were actually rocky foothills of the northern section of the Black Range.

The farmers had been frantic, firing shots that only slightly wounded one Apache before they were out of range. Then they had realized, too late, that over half their horses and mules had been stolen behind their backs.

Burnett sent a scout riding hard back to the fort to inform Valois that they would be in pursuit. But now there were about thirty incensed Mexican men and teenage boys ready to join the pursuit of the killers.

Moses had mostly, by necessity, become immune to the butchery of grown men and women; but as he saw, scattered about the farmyard, the seven small children, he felt a quiet, nauseous anger growing in him. He knew, as second in command of the unit and the most experienced leader, he would have to remain calm and assured on the surface.

He read the sign on the ground; he also realized that this much careful planning and maneuvering meant that Nana's widespread raids had brought him up short of horses, as well as food. That meant they were in for a hell of a fight.

Moses's thinking was eerily correct. Lieutenant Burnett would get more than one chance this day to establish a reputation.

The trail where the killers and the stock raiders had joined was wide and clear. They were heading west to the Cuchillo Negros, ten very long miles away across rolling country.

Sooner than they could have hoped, the troopers had the Indians in sight, but still out of rifle range. Now they were closing on them and would soon be able to do battle. The newcomers' fear was replaced by the natural excitement of the chase. The chase. It had always been the same.

Nana had some of his men drop back under the yucca-topped hills and fired the first delaying shots. One Mexican's horse was shot out from under him and another received a bullet that shattered his lower leg. The downed horse was flailing about, kicking and raising his head trying to get up. Moses rode to it, drew his pistol, and stopped its suffering.

The father of the young Mexican was trying to stop the

flow of blood from the leg artery. Private Walley dismounted, cut the young man's shirtsleeve off, and formed a tourniquet above his knee, twisting it tightly with a piece of dead cedar stick. He and the father helped the youth back upon the horse.

Walley said, "Tie him on his horse. He's gonna faint on you. Loosen up the rag now and then." That's all he could do. He mounted and caught up with his troops as they gathered behind the protection of a cut bank.

Moses was relieved when the lieutenant split their forces in three parts so that they would have riders coming in on the flanks of the delaying fire.

They moved across the hills, fighting small, sporadic skirmishes, while Nana's main group moved on ever closer to the fortress rocks of the Cuchillo Negros.

The cavalry troopers were not the only ones suffering wounds. They found one dead horse and a pool of blood from its Indian rider, but as always, the body was gone. Moses knew the Apache was dead from the amount of leaked blood.

Walley had taken the shot with his Sharps scoped rifle. After so many years, and so many rounds, part of a shooter follows the bullet when he is on target. Walley knew he had hit the Apache right in the throat. He was thrilled that he had made such a long and difficult kill. Not only that but the farmers and the soldiers had been able to ride over a mile before being forced to charge from the flanks at the ambushing Indians. One more Apache was slightly wounded and one soldier and one farmer had flesh wounds but could still ride ready to fight if they could close with the enemy.

It was center-high sun now and the horses were all beginning to lather and blow from the hard riding up and down and way around to keep the group attacking. It would seem many times as if invisible spirits were firing at them.

One of the three replacements had a horse shot out from

under him and yelled at Sergeant Moses, "What do I do? What do I do without a mount?"

Moses said, "Put your horse out of his misery and walk."

"I'll miss the battle."

"No, son, there'll be plenty of fightin' left over when you get there."

Private Bolten shot his horse and followed, frightfully, on foot, trying to be a good soldier before he was a dead one.

Up ahead, the horses had been choused into the higher foothills. No matter what, Nana had won that first crucial part of the battle.

Now he set up his main body of men in a staggered position, scattered over almost half a mile, with lots of rocks for cover. They waited, watching below as the delayed action moved toward them. His grandson, Kaywayhla, looked through the glass and gave him a count and the movement of all below. Nana hunkered down, peering into the growing blur before him. Without his grandson he knew he would soon be unable to see well enough to direct a battle.

"Grandson, look for a dark man with very wide shoulders and many golden stripes on his upper arms."

Young Kaywayhla moved the glass ever so slowly as Nana had taught him. In about ninety heartbeats, he said, "I see him, Grandfather. He rides well."

"Ahh, yes, he is a fighter, that one. He survives where others fall."

"We must kill him today then, Grandfather."

"I do not know. Now you see this man for me. I have seen him many times over many years." Nana spoke as if to himself or the Great Spirit. "The bullets in his gun are meant for me."

In a shocked voice, the boy said, "I will kill him first. I will not let him kill you, Grandfather. I will crawl with the lizards and cut his throat until his head falls off."

"Not today. Soon, maybe." At this moment though, the old man felt a strange contentment and a pride in his grandson's offer. No matter what happened here, three of his men were driving the captured horses into the Black Range's hidden places. There, Lozen would take over the herd and see that his wives, children, and kin of blood and spirit would be fed and mounted on animals still strong enough to keep moving. Constant movement was their only way of survival.

However, the cavalry had also caught on that constant movement was the only way they could beat the Warm Springs Apaches. The harsh, unforgiving land made this almost impossible for the mounted soldiers. There were five hundred thousand square miles of high foothills of the Black Range, encompassing the Gila, the San Mateo, and San Pedro Mountains undulating in waves like a vast stone ocean. The solid surfaces were impregnated with billions of sharp, unavoidable, protruding stones and many species of cacti and other flesh-puncturing vegetation that crippled humans and their horses. While the soldiers and their horses suffered through these barriers, the Apaches raced on and on, often afoot, joining up again with their own band to fight another hour. Hard earth, hard men. Before the Warm Springs Apaches were finally starved out, they could race afoot farther than the best cavalry horses. Their toughness and endurance was marveled at by the Buffalo Soldiers and all their other multiple enemies. Hard earth. Hard warriors.

Nana had known for a long time now that the outsiders' coming was endless, but he was still surprised that they had finally learned the Apache trick of scattering forces and making the enemy move and wear down, too. Nana still had the advantage in single battles as long as they could reach the edge of their homeland.

And that is where they were now, right on the edge of what Victorio and Nana had proposed over and over to the U.S.

government as their true homeland. This was the northern edge of the reservation that would be big enough for them to survive in. But their offers had been refused each time, so they would go on fighting for their own part of Mother Earth until the Great Mystery in the sky made the final decision.

Nana's hearing was dulled, but he could hear the enemy getting ready to join them in battle. Thanks to the power the Dreamer had given him, the warriors' ribs might be sticking out and their hungry bellies shrunk and growling, but they had the ammunition to make a ferocious stand.

Nana's weary heart raced and he was ready. His grandson could feed the old man's energy, and he put the glass in its container and laid the barrel of his rifle over the rock. Maybe he could get a shot in before his grandfather ordered him to ride back and forth with him as he gave battle orders to his warriors. He used his grandson's perfect vision to guide him now.

Just before the battle of Cuchillo Negros was in full fury, Nana said a prayer of thanks for Kaywayhla's eyes and all the help they gave his people. It would be another good day of fighting the invaders. His hungry insides were smiling as they rode, the old man and the young man, who had been a child just a few moments ago.

Amid the growing intensity of the sound of gunfire, the two forces became locked in battle. The terrain was such that Moses and his men could no longer outflank the Apaches. They were in protective rocks. He would have to cross exposed ground to move nearer.

Lieutenant Burnett ordered the farmers to lay down covering fire, while he and his troopers assaulted the left flank.

Nana's grandson saw the soldiers leading their horses into the staggered angles of arroyos and small canyons. He passed all these movements on to his grandfather. The old man moved to cover the troopers' maneuvering, crawling when possible.

Nana's group moved into position to close a trap on the oncoming soldiers. He sent a young warrior, who was a fine shot and very brave, to lead the Indians into a surprise position. His inexperience and his eagerness to fire down on the unsuspecting troopers caused him to give the order to shoot too soon. Even though the fusillade blasted down from three angles, the ambush was too early. It was all that saved immediate disaster for the troops. As it was, the Apaches began individually crawling down through the brush and rocks.

The soldiers themselves were able to fight back with some cover, but most of their horses were left exposed and they had begun to fall, screaming their terrible death sounds above the almost incessant gunfire. Stalemate.

Suddenly there was one of those inexplicable battlefield occurrences. The approaching soldiers had inadvertently driven a jackrabbit ahead of them. Now he raced back and forth, whirling in panic, running this way one moment then leaping back. For a full minute there was silence as all watched this confused, scared animal. Not one shot was fired. Everyone was speechlessly rooting for the rabbit to pick an escape route. Finally he did, scurrying right past Moses and over the top of Private Justin to freedom. For just a tiny, flickering moment, the warriors of both sides had forgotten about killing one another. They watched the rabbit until it vanished from sight and then returned to their duties of destruction.

The Apaches, one at a time, with their disguises of grass, sticks, animal skins, and whatever else fit the landscape, had achieved the advantage of position.

Two soldiers were already wounded. One had had a finger shot off. It dangled in his way, so, Lieutenant Burnett swiftly severed it completely off, wrapped a kerchief around it, and the soldier went on firing. Another was struck in the left cheek. Bits of splintered bone hung from the bullet hole as the blood slowly washed them away. Though it looked like he would live, the shock had made him unable to fight for the time being.

At this moment, Nana gained control. His warriors had Moses and his small, but elite, unit pinned down as well as the farmers. Instead of gaining Lieutenant Burnett the reputation he had earlier hoped would advance his career, this untenable position looked like certain disaster. The heroics were forgotten. All he wanted to do was survive and save his men. He asked for a volunteer to take a message to Lieutenant Valois, who he knew would be on his way.

Pvt. John Rogers, a trumpeter, offered to go. At first he tried to crawl back, but was stopped by heavy fire. Knowing he was trapped and would die where he lay, he was on the verge of going mad. Perhaps he did, to some degree, for suddenly he leaped up, ignoring the bullets thudding into the earth and zinging off rocks inches from his body, and made a dash for his horse. He hurled himself into the saddle and rode as hard as he could to deliver the critical message. In spite of the heavy fire, Rogers got through, even though his horse received a wound to a rump muscle. He breathlessly explained Burnett's desperate needs.

Valois and the remainder of I Troop were to occupy the hill overlooking the trapped Burnett. He waved his men forward, charging headlong at the hill, hoping surprise would be on their side. Nana and Kaywayhla had seen the Valois tactic, and Nana had moved his warriors from the left to counter it. Sergeant Moses also saw this varying movement as the fire eased up some on his small unit. They struggled back around and through the contours of the earth to join Burnett.

Most of Nana's men now raced to positions on top of the commanding hill. They beat Valois to it and began laying down fire so intense they dismounted Valois and the ten men on the point of the attack, killing two horses and wounding Corporal Eaves twice. One bullet took off his right ear and the other shattered his left forearm. He still managed to fire with his revolver.

Valois had no choice but to retreat down the hill. It was a confusing moment as the Apaches sensed victory and moved to demolish the lieutenant and his command. The cover was sparse below in the flats. Some men actually sought protection behind prairie dog mounds. It looked as if the Apaches had gathered enough forces and momentum to finish off Valois and his exposed men. The positive side of this was that the attack on Valois had taken the heavy firing away from Lieutenant Burnett's trapped troops.

Burnett mounted, riding back and forth, giving encouragement and orders to his men and the Mexicans to storm the Apaches to save Valois. They charged valiantly, but the retreating Indians turned on them and lay down extremely heavy fire from the higher ground. The move saved Valois. He was able to retreat to better cover and establish a new line, but by now Burnett, Moses, and the unified group were in almost as precarious a position as Valois had just been in. The battle furiously increased with the outcome seeming to favor the better positioned Apaches.

Nana ordered his grandson to stay protected in the rocks. He hurriedly limped down to encourage his warriors to continue the attack while the odds tilted so strongly in his favor. Along with his men, he was firing at blurs below, but afoot he wasn't much use as a warrior. His ability to drag his impaired ankle and foot and his worn, grinding bones was severely limited, but his presence was more powerful and inspiring to his men than ever. They fought like demons against the soldiers because of his spiritual nearness.

Burnett swiftly and coolly read the situation and shouted

at Moses to organize a retreat. They fired carefully but steadily as they moved backward, keeping the enemy from routing them.

It looked good for just a fleeting moment. Soon they could reorganize and attack again.

Then occurred one of those backdoor, unexpected things that change the course of battle.

Four wounded soldiers had become trapped. One of the men cried out a plea that could not go unheeded. "For God's sake, Lieutenant, don't leave us here."

Burnett was near being overwhelmed, and the Apaches, hearing the cry, were closing in to finish off the four troopers. It was a seemingly impossible situation, but Apache or cavalry man, they could not deny such a personal cry for help.

Private Walley was firing his scoped Springfield at those nearest the wounded troopers. He was having some effect all alone with his sniper fire. Burnett asked for volunteers to help him try to save the men. Moses and Walley joined him in the rescue. It was a moment of madness.

However, that thing –that entity—that occasionally took control of Moses did so now. His eyesight telescoped out and found the enemy, and a cover trail radiated in a pale blue light for him. He and Walley and Burnett scurried from one slightly protected position to another, laying down such accurate fire that they stopped Nana and his warriors for a moment. Two of the wounded ran, fell, crawled, and ran again and reached the safety of a small arroyo. The other two were too severely wounded to help themselves.

One of the wounded, a Private Brindle, a "bunkie" of Walley's, raised up on one elbow and waved toward the nearest Buffalo Soldiers, Burnett, Moses, and Walley.

Walley yelled, "Here, Sarge," and tossed his repeating rifle and his ammo belt to Moses. As Walley raced back to the horse line, Moses fired at intervals. Burnett kept up his steady fire as well.

Now under the steady work of Burnett and Moses, Walley spurred into the breech and, with that force that comes in supreme situations, grabbed Private Brindle and somehow jerked him up behind him onto the horse, reining his mount in a whirl and, with lead cracking overhead and kicking up dust around him, reached the same arroyo as the other two wounded had found.

Three out of four saved was remarkable, but suddenly, the fourth man, Bolten, alone, surrounded and dazed from a creased head shot and wounds to his shoulder and buttocks, raised up on his hands and knees, then struggled to his feet, weaving and stumbling toward the Apache lines. It would be only a few moments before he would be killed.

Burnett, near the horse line, leapt on his horse and charged into the very center of the melee. Now Moses knew exactly where to move. Carrying two repeating rifles, he came into that moment of floating movement where one is all alone and yet totally with the entire world.

On foot, he moved forward, firing until one rifle was empty, racing in the wind like an air-borne antelope, and settling like a dropping eagle in little protected spots. He emptied one gun just as Burnett reached Bolten. Then he plunged through the air, barely touching the earth, to his last cover spot. Somehow, Burnett had got Bolten over his saddle, belly-down, and, riding behind the saddle, raced into the dust previously churned up by Walley.

Moses fired methodically, with such accuracy that only a few Indians were able to get aimed shots off at Burnett and Bolten. Burnett's horse was hit in the front shoulder, but under Burnett's spurring and urging, it kept going. Burnett did not know he had been shot across his back. The bullet had only torn a large muscle and deflected off his upper rib cage and exited. He moved and slid down a game trail of the arroyo to safety. The horse's hind legs bunched under him and his front ones shoved forward as they hit the bottom of the arroyo below the line of fire.

Now Moses heard his rifle click empty and knew there would be no time to reload. He was alone in the trap. Everyone else was now safe. So, leaving Walley's empty repeater behind, he instantly whirled and raced, zigzagging, rolling into cover, then ran toward the floating dust left by Walley and Burnett's horses.

The Apaches, realizing that a total victory had been denied them by one white and two black troopers, fired at Moses now in such eagerness and anger that the bullets hit both in the air and on the ground within inches of his running, dodging body, but not one found his flesh. In the thinning dust, going downhill, Moses now escalated his speed. When he hit the arroyo edge, he fell and rolled off into its bottom. He had fallen only twelve yards from the others. They were busy tending to wounds so they could move back and join Valois.

Moses came out of his pale blue-and-tan dust-haze and, although breathing heavily, was actually suddenly calm with thankfulness. Just for a moment he rolled over on his back and stared for billions of miles into the late afternoon's blue, blue sky. Then he knew what the faraway pale blue haze had been made of. He spoke with his lips only a simple thanks. Then he got to his feet, loading his gun as he walked to join his battered comrades.

Lieutenant Valois had set up a powerful new line, and with several sorties had moved the Apaches back to their first natural redoubt in the higher foothills.

Leaving behind three men as a temporary rear guard, Nana led his warriors, with the wounded tied on the backs of horses, into the Black Range. They must move from now on. Only in constant movement could they survive at all. All things carefully taken into account, Nana would call this a fine day of fighting. In Valois's first ill-fated charge, Nana's warriors had captured several of I Troop's horses, saddles and some ammunition.

As they buried their dead in known caves and crevices and covered them with expertly stacked rocks, silent prayers were said.

Now they rode as a small group toward Lozen and their remaining, waiting families. Their hearts and spirits thanked the Great Mystery for the bounty of captured four-legged food and transportation. They would fight again.

There had been many cavalry and Apache battles at the Cuchillo Negros, but this would be the last of consequence. For their extreme bravery under heavy enemy fire and much else, Lieutenant Burnett, Private Walley, and Sgt. Moses Williams were nominated for the U.S. Army's highest award—the Medal of Honor—for their actions that long day of August 16, 1881.

Twenty Three

PERHAPS FIFTEEN MINUTES BEFORE THE HEROIC CHARGE OF Walley, Burnett, and Moses, Sheela finished reading from Walt Whitman's "Passage to India" to the Valois daughters, Danielle and Stacy. They sat on the floor, their blue eyes enraptured, captured by the poem and Sheela's mellifluous voice projecting those wonderful words into their ears and their young imaginations.

> Sail forth—steer for the deep waters only,
> Reckless O soul, exploring, I with thee, and thou with me,
> For we are bound where mariner has not yet dared to go,
> And we will risk the ship, ourselves and all.
>
> O my brave soul!
> O farther, farther sail!
> O daring joy, but safe! Are they not all the seas of God?
> O farther, farther, farther sail!

It was a good moment. Mama Mayo Lou was in the kitchen, starting the evening meal. Christine Valois was in a small study, drawing designs for costumes to be made for an upcoming musicale she hoped to present for I Troop upon its return. This abode of female workers and planners for the children and the men in the field had a soft, steady comfort to it. Everyone was doing what they loved and were expert at in a calm, almost mellow, way.

Then Sheela suddenly felt a coldness ripple through her body. She shivered. Her hands shook as she turned the page. She closed the book and held it tightly so the girls would not see her trembling. She did not understand what was happening.

She placed the book on the elbow table and said, "Please excuse me, girls. There is something I must do."

She moved swiftly, but with some weakness, to the kitchen. "Mayo Lou, would you look after the girls, please. There's . . . there is something I must do, now."

"Sho', honey. You go right ahead."

Sheela moved on to Christine's study for the first time ever, knocking and then entering before Christine could answer.

"Madam Valois, there is something I must do with Reverend Pree. Please excuse me. I'll be back in a bit. Please go on with your work. Mama Mayo is taking care of the girls." She turned and hastened out before a wide-eyed, open-mouthed Christine could utter a sound.

She exited the Valois quarters, taking the steps from the porch two at a time, swiftly walked, then ran, toward the chapel. Reverend Pree was just leaving to go to the infirmary for his daily ministrations to the ill and the dying and the few wounded who had recovered.

Sheela grabbed the captain's hands and led him back into the chapel. At the front pew she knelt, saying as definite as a commanding general's order, "Kneel and pray with me, right now. Pray hard. Pray as hard as you can."

"And what shall I pray for, dear girl?"

"You must pray for our men. Our men. All of them, and especially my Moses. I felt a sudden coldness deep in my soul, and I know Moses is in grave danger. It was a message, Reverend. I know it was a warning of danger. Of great harm. Oh, please. Help me pray."

He did. Silently.

Sheela was unaware that she faced him on her knees, hands together under her chin, praying aloud. "Oh, dear God, protect those brave men from harm. Please place a shield around them that will defy Apache bullets and arrows. Let them all return to us, precious Lord. Help them through all ordeals so we can be together once again. And . . . and . . . oh, I know it's selfish, sweet Lord, but take a little extra special care with my Moses, my husband-to-be. Please don't take him now. We all need him. All of us, but especially me. If nothing else, let me see and hold him once more. Oh, please, dear Lord. I beg you with all my heart, with all my soul. I plainly, humbly plead with you to protect and return him whole and in good mind. Thank you. Thank you, great Almighty. A million thanks and appreciation. Amen."

Then Sheela opened her eyes and saw that Reverend Pree's lips were still moving silently. She remained motionless, staring at him as he softly uttered, "Amen."

He opened his eyes and looked into hers, which had changed from panic to serenity. They both smiled at one another in private understanding. They stood as one.

She kissed him on the cheek and said, "Thank you, Reverend. I know we took care of it." And she raced out the door.

In the compound she slowed to a fast walk and every now and then did a zippy little skip. Then she did two complete joyous whirls as she made her way back to her worldly duties with a happy heart.

Twenty Four

NANA MADE SEVERAL SMALL RAIDS—PURELY FOR SUPPLIES—ON farms, freight wagons, and other targets, while leading his weary band into the Sierra Madres of Mexico to join his nephew, Victorio. They could heal there, safe from the soldiers north of them. But now there were the Mexicans to worry about. They had been pushed into the Sierra Madres by several units of the Ninth and Tenth Cavalry, but inexplicably the Mexican government had sent word to the cavalry not to come farther into Mexico. They obeyed the command.

Several times each day, Lozen stood with her palms up, turning slowly like the sun in a full circle. No enemy was near, but they kept sentries out just the same. It was Lozen's power that had never let her uncle, Victorio, or her "grandfather," Nana, down. It was a brief time of peace. Horses had been ridden near to death in Nana's last raids. These were replaced with captured, fresh mounts. If they recovered their strength they could be ridden again, if not, they would be eaten. The attack on the farming community and the increasing numbers of horses taken at the battle of Cuchillo Negros had saved Nana's band from hunger and capture.

Although the newspapers, the telegraph, couriers, and scouts had reported Nana's raids in loudly protesting headlines and angered voices, the battles were mostly officially overlooked by the army's high command. These battles, supposedly reported to Santa Fe and Washington, were simply ignored as if they had never happened. However, to Moses, Walley, Valois, and all those cavalry and infantrymen who slogged and spurred across the searing deserts and harsh and unfriendly canyons of the mountains, it seemed that "war with Nana" was their entire world.

Major Morrow, with A and C Companies, had fought and trailed the Warm Springs Apaches several illegal miles into Mexico many times. His bulldog perseverance had cost dearly in shot and worn-out men and horses, but at least he had temporarily pushed most of the Apaches from the territory.

The Apache men now gathered strength, just as the women gathered seeds and mescal buttons for baking. The young men went on hunts for deer, rabbits, squirrels, lizards, anything for a change of taste. The horses and mules grazed in little nearby valleys on good grass. The area chosen for this retreat recreated a small moment of the life that had once been so long, long ago. The location was centered around secluded springs where all could water. It was the time of last happiness. A few, such as Nana, must have sensed that this would be the very last fragment of the old way of living.

Even though he was in his mid-to-late seventies, lame footed, half blind, his body demonized by rheumatism, stiffened by thousands of miles of horseback riding and many bad falls and war wounds, he went out scouting with his grandson, Kaywayhla.

"Before the man of the golden-striped arm gets me, there are some things you should know, Grandson."

"He will never get you, Grandfather. I swear to you I will draw his blood first."

Nana raised a hand to calm the enraged youth. It worked
instantly. He said, "You see, Kaywayhla, when two warriors
are face to face so they look into one another's eyes, then one
shall die on the spot. However, when two warriors see into
the story told by 'eyes at a distance' that is very rare. It must
be accepted as a gift of meaning from the Great Mystery.
One must be patient for the moment has long been seen and
chosen."

As they rode across rolling hills between jagged hard-faced
mountains, Nana pointed out ways to survive even though
Kaywayhla had been studying such things all his short life. In
barren spots the old man clambered painfully from his horse.
He pointed out a thin, dry stalk, no bigger than a matchstick,
and he dug. Soon he came up with a root, which he carefully
peeled and sliced, sharing half.

"You see, these are like the Mexican farmers' potatoes, but
better tasting and placed here by the Great Mystery just for
us." He showed Kaywayhla the mescal and mesquite beans
turned into fine food by roasting, and told him of the nutri-
tion of sunflower seeds and many more often invisible herbs
and nutritious plants as well as medicinal ones.

Kaywayhla absorbed every nuance for he sensed an ur-
gency in the old warrior. A passing on of things to keep the
Apache from vanishing away like Lozen's love, the Gray
Ghost rider, had, like the breath of the slain does, like the
spring flowers of the desert to the summer sun, which in a
brief change of season went from being uncountable to none.

"I do not know all things. I know few things, but those few
I know well. When I was young I fought for peace. The little
spot of land surrounding the heart of our land, Ojo Caliente,
we were offered it many times but only as bait. The restrictions were too many for our hearts to absorb. Now that I am
old, I fight to kill. I know no other way. The paths have long
ago been covered over with the blood of deceit.

"The meat of the deer, the elk, the horse is sweet because they eat only sweet grass and vegetation and drink good water. But we men eat ourselves into uselessness except food for the coyotes, crows, worms, and buzzards. No, we do far worse than that to each other . . . we eat one another's souls.

"I am not sure what brings this thing to us men over and over and over without an end in sight. The beginners, the first ancestors, came from the sky, far, far away, in a flaming arrow that circled and circled until it struck and penetrated Mother Earth and fertilized her and she started giving birth to all living things. Some tribes came up from the many wombs of Mother Earth to the surface. In the long-ago time we were all the same. I think maybe it is the White Skins' little, round timekeepers that have caused this shattering of sanity. The soldiers go to bed by it. They get up by the time-makers. The miners dig by it. They are slaves to the little iron disks they carry on small chains in their pockets. What terrible demons do they hide in these little circles? Where does it come from? This is one of the many things I do not know, my Grandson.

"You see, Grandson, from the first spring of life through twenty summers it seems like the forever time. That is because you see and experience new things almost every breath. Then, from twenty to forty summers, you try to understand and apply what you've observed. From forty to fifty summers seems like one spring to one winter only. Then, from fifty to the closing of your earthly life, it passes as swiftly as a deer being chased downhill toward bushes where the greatest hunter of all awaits its arrival." He paused thoughtfully and continued. "There are fewer than two hundred warriors, women, and children of the Warm Springs Apache left, Grandson."

"Will we all be killed, Grandfather, until there are none?"

"No. That is what I wanted to tell you. We will fight on and on. And somehow, in some form, we will be in our homeland. So do not worry. All will be revealed. All will be played out as is meant."

Then, a few days later, Nana and Kaywayhla sat side by side looking out over a deep canyon of jumbled and jagged rocks. It was so deep that it had purple shadows even though high sun had only just passed over. They sat on a rimrock, the old bent legs and the straight, strong ones, side by side, hanging out over the edge of the abyss. Their horses were tied behind them, swatting at imaginary flies with their tails.

A sudden silence ensued as the old man stared beyond the canyon's curve to the north, where ripples of mountains like an army of giant stone reptiles marched motionlessly on and on into the blue then hazy, dull yellow of the last horizon. There he saw with his mind vision the miners, the merchants, the farmers, the soldiers, the towns, the railroads, the ceaseless hundreds and thousands forever coming, invading their homeland, devouring the forests with flame and saws and axes, digging holes in the ground like massive worms, soiling the carpet of the earth with the defecation of the thoughtless wealth-seeking.

The young man beside him was lost in a reverie of the beauty everywhere. Imagining how he would kill the man of many stripes, and thinking of Flower Song, who would be his first wife. He could see into her young black eyes, already full of wisdom and all the secrets of love. He could feel her hand as if it was yesterday when he had touched her palm and had whispered in her delicate ear, "You are mine, Flower Song, just as I am yours. We will raise many strong warriors, who will kill all the white-eyes and Buffalo Soldiers in the world." She had squeezed his fingers so gently he had almost missed it, and looked for just a moment into his eyes, into his spirit, then turned and tantalizingly raced away to her family's brush house, never looking back until she was at the entrance.

Then she had stopped and smiled so swiftly, so sweetly, so ethereally, he wondered even now if he had really seen it.

No, it had been real. As he concentrated it came to him, the promise imprinted for all time. His chest rose higher as he breathed the thought of her into his young, hungry loins. He was pulled back to the reality of the rocks under his haunches and the downward space under their legs by Nana's voice as he brought forth a small deer-skin pouch from inside his shirt.

"This, my Grandson, is what the white-eyes love beyond all else." He emptied several gold nuggets from the pouch into the lined palm of his hand. "They would kill all of us for this. They kill one another for this. See, how beautiful it is in the sun. Look. Look. Ahh, yes, they can purchase all their worlds with it. They can even buy others' souls with it. This beauty can deceive and make them go mad. They lust for it like we do a good seed-gathering and meat-hunting season.

"They rape the mountains, take their trees like pulling the hair from the head of an old helpless woman. They muddy the water, and dig and scrape lines in the earth all over so they can bring their trains, their wagons, their iron monsters to tear this tiny beauty here in my hand from the big beauty of our mountains. They leave mighty scars everywhere, so that the deer and even the mighty bear are nervous and frightened, no longer knowing where their homes are. Just as us.

"Now, I ask, Grandson, can this yellow iron give birth to a beautiful baby? Can this soft iron hunt deer, see the Great Mystery, and offer up prayers of thanks for the blessing of the mountains? Can these pebbles of greed tell stories of the old days, dance, sing, and make love with you?"

Kaywayhla shook his head no. "Then what do we do about it, Grandfather? Tell me what we do, and I will try to do it."

"I have heard that it has always been so with the yellow

iron and the white-eyes. It is as if the only drink they ever had was fermented mescal. No sweet water at all when they search for this. I have no answer. Maybe there never will be an answer except this . . ."

Nana hurled the nuggets out into the space above the great chasm, where they scattered apart like seeds in a wind, and then, just for an instant, seemed to stop in the air where the sun's rays could cast all its glory, changing the yellowness to tiny airborne fires before the nuggets vanished into the deepening shadows and fell into the void, as invisible as if they had never existed.

The old man and the young man sat and looked down for a spell in motionless silence. Then Nana struggled to his feet. Limping heavily to one side, he led his horse over to a big rock to help himself mount. The two rode side by side back toward camp without speaking again. All had been said and heard for now.

Twenty Five

VALOIS AND BURNETT'S TROOPS WERE MET BY THE AMBULANCE wagon out of Camp Ojo Caliente, followed by a six-up mule team pulling a forage wagon, with some extra provisions for the soldiers.

The surgeon was busy all night operating on and sewing up the many wounded soldiers. At daybreak they would have to move on to the Ojo camp to repair men, horses, and equipment before heading to their home fort for more healing and replacement of both injured men and horses. It was almost beyond belief—many said a true miracle—that no soldiers had died in the actual bloody engagement. There would be some who were never to fight again and others transferred to easier duty. Three would die later from infection. Even so, they were very fortunate. It could have been a disaster to the best soldiers in the territory. Instead, they would, with a little time, be ready to take on the elusive, ghostly Nana again.

Moses's unit was busy at Ojo repairing their equipment, doctoring horses, and allowing their minds and souls to seek peace. He now allowed himself to think of Sheela again. All the men's thoughts soon turned to the fort. When there, they complained about the food, bunk checks, and equipment, the leaders, the weather, and almost everything else, but after a day fighting old Nana it was suddenly paradise, tempting.

They dreamed too of the whorehouse, bars, and gambling dens at Leasburg, a little over two miles from the fort on the banks of the Rio Grande.

"I just cain't wait to get in a poker game five minutes after payday."

Moses and four soldiers, one a farrier, and Wahoe, a Navajo scout, were checking out a line of horses for thrown or loose shoes as well as hidden wounds or injuries. All stopped and looked at Walley, knowing something beyond reasonable thought would come out.

"Lordy, Lordee. I know I gonna win me enough money to go back to Bitch Moose's place. Dear Sweet Jesus, I hope you're listenin' 'cause a place with so many heavenly treats could have only been figured out by a shore 'nuff high command."

Moses said to the other men, "I do believe that ole Walley is in love with the impossible."

"What's impossible about it?" Walley asked.

"Bitch Moose's is impossible for you, son."

"Hey! I done learned—ain't nothing impossible. Look at ole Nana. We done fired a million shots at him and he is still alive."

"Yeah, well, we ain't never had ole Nana hemmed up in Bitch Moose's barroom. Jorge would blow him dead as last year's farts."

"I'm tellin' you, Sarge, even if Bitch Moose won't have nothin' to do with me, I'm gonna make it back there jist one more time before an Apache kills my wild ass. Ever'thang 'bout that place is the best I ever seen. The worst of her girls is better'n the best of all the rest . . . in the whole damn territory. Maybe the whole cockeyed world."

Moses knew from long, patient experience that it was time to alter the course of the talk. Walley would go on for hours on any subject that intrigued him, so he said, "I knew it. I knew it."

Walley asked, "What? Knew what?" still holding up a horse's hoof.

"That some day that itty-bitty brain of yours would tell you a big truth."

Walley asked with intensity, "Which one was it?"

The rest of the men, along with Moses, had a good giggle. Walley was busy figuring and checking the horse's hoof for at least ten seconds, then he launched again. "Hey, Wahoe, why don't you have a vision and tell us what all's gonna happen."

Wahoe went on checking the horses without looking up as he spoke. "I'm tard havin' visions. My eyes got arthritis already from havin' too many visions.

A new man, Justin, who had just survived his first combat, said, "I hope we never hear from that Nana ever, never again. My bowels got loose the first shot. I figger I'm gonna have a nervous tear down next time."

All appreciated and were surprised at Justin's honesty, but Moses knew talk like this could spread into disaster so he tried to put a stop to it as pleasantly as possible.

"We're gonna see there is no *next* time, Justin, for *us*. Next time is for *them*."

The slanted, shadow eyes of his love appeared before him and for a moment he was so weak with wanting he had to lean against the tired horse, but he could smell Sheela's spring-rain-wildflower fragrance and taste her fresh strawberry lips so strongly that the only escape was back to the horses' care, and not an animal on the line would know of the willpower and desire Moses had sacrificed for their well-being.

Twenty Six

SHEELA HAD JUST FINISHED THE DAY'S TUTORING OF DANIELLE and Stacy Valois. The young girls had tested her will at first, but Sheela had said simply, strongly, "I know you miss your last tutor, girls, but now you have me and you might as well get used to it. I think that your small unkindnesses to me are because you feel a loss. Give me time, as I've given you, and I think we'll all be pleased with the learning procedures and have a lot of fun as we grow together."

Sheela was amazed that her little talk had worked. It was the "we" that had evidently awakened the girls to the fact that she included herself in the problems. Slowly they accepted her and the respect was rapidly cementing into a bond of friendship.

Reverend Pree had been successful in getting the idea of education over to Chaplain Allen Allensworth of the Twenty-fourth Regiment, U.S. Infantry. Chaplain Allensworth carried the respect of the high command, and now educational programs were in effect at all the forts, some for three nights a week. However, due to the constant fighting duties of the Ninth, Pree had received permission to school only one night a week for troopers left behind as guardians and caretakers of the fort while others did battle. In spite of the limitations, he knew his dedicated concept of the necessity of education was taking hold.

He enlisted Sheela to help teach them. Reverend Pree was especially proud of Sheela. Not only did she have the same feelings about scholastic needs as he did, but she was a natural, giving, sharing teacher.

Some men of rank might have resented the fact that a private or corporal could possibly teach them anything, which was often the truth, but being taught by a chaplain who also was a captain and by a woman who was tutor to their troop leader's own children caused them to give proper attention and respect. Attendance was good.

The white soldiers, who mostly came from the slavery of poverty, in contrast to the Buffalo Soldiers who had, with a few exception, been slaves of their owners, began to attend classes as well. Both Reverend Pree and Sheela had been fortunate enough to find that knowledge was color-blind. They shared a certain almost gleeful satisfaction in the future prospects for their school.

This afternoon Sheela had finished teaching for the day and had led the two children to their play area so that Mayo Lou could watch over them from the kitchen. Then she went to Christine's room to help her sew costumes for the musicale she wanted to present to the warriors of I Troop on their return.

She had made many "waits" now and could feel inside her bones and heart when the troopers were moving toward home. Sheela was caught up in Christine's enthusiasm for her "specialties," as she called her varied programs of plays, music, and dance.

Sheela helped wash and dress the children for the day. She often assisted Mayo Lou in the preparation of meals. She spent three hours of the afternoon teaching the girls, and anywhere from one to many more hours assisting Christine during the day and often at night. Then she visited Reverend Pree to prepare the troopers' lessons. She also spent at least one hour a week with her laundry friends, writing letters for them and encouraging them to attend the schooling sessions. This kept her from thinking and worrying every minute about Moses and his safety, as she had in the beginning. She also felt she was fulfilling a part of her destiny with the teaching and consoling of others.

Her visits with the reverend to the hospital ward of the wounded was one burden too much for her, but she had yet to admit it. Once she had volunteered to write a letter for a disabled private, then the requests multiplied. She was soon going to have to face that she was "worked out," just as she had told Moses he was going to have to admit that he was "fought out."

Today, as she sat hemming a garment, her thoughts were on Moses. She somehow managed to continue the dexterous movement of the needle and thread through the cloth even though she felt a sudden worry. Then, as suddenly, she experienced a surprising surge of exultation. Already she was acquiring the mystical ability of long-experienced cavalry wives and girlfriends to sense the welfare and presence of their men at a distance. It would be awhile before she could be as conscious of this as Christine.

Christine said, with a soft smile, "The troopers are near. Our men, yours and mine, are whole in body and mind."

It was amazing that Sheela gladly accepted this pronouncement without question. Her hands flew with the stitching as her heartbeat increased.

Suddenly, she leapt to her feet, placing her work on the table, and raced as fast as an antelope for the front door, down the porch steps, and across the compound. Christine smiled, understanding, and followed along with Mayo Lou and the children out onto the porch.

Sheela stood alone, looking at the fort's wide open gates. Gradually others gathered on different porches and places of the compound, waiting as the ambulance wagons came in first and made their way toward the infirmary. Then Lieutenants Valois and Burnett rode through the gateway, followed by Sergeant Moses and the surviving able, anxious fighting men of the Ninth.

Somehow Sheela contained herself until Moses had dismissed his unit. Then, as he dismounted, she could control it no longer and flew to him with such force she knocked him against his tired horse. He laughed as he picked her a few inches off the ground and pulled her to him, trying to keep from crushing the lovely mass of woman. The long agony of waiting was over for a while.

Twenty Seven

THE COMPLEXITIES OF WAR AND LOVE ARE ABOUT EQUAL. MOSES thought of Sheela as his wife, his lover, the family maker, and a precious gift from God. He had entertained himself during the moments he was not forced to think of killing or surviving Nana by imagining her sweet flesh. Along with his lust for Nana's blood, his thoughts of Sheela's love comforted and kept him going far beyond the average soldier's endurance. Oh, he would kiss her ears, her eyes, her neck, her lips, the bronze streak in her hair. He would trace her graceful neck with his fingertips all the way down to her breasts, nibbling them and all of her with a slow, sensual tenderness. He knew her every curve, her sounds of love, her scent.

Sheela, no less than Moses, even with all her daily, hourly chores, did her own dreaming, some of it twinned to those of her soldier husband and lover.

However, when they were finally alone on the blankets behind the supply room, all dream visions were forgotten. For the first time they paired with urgent lust.

After they made love, Sheela asked Moses an unanswerable question. "You must have some idea when these wars will end." Her concern and love for him was so encompassing that she could not help breaking the first rule of a soldier's woman.

Moses traced the streaks in her hair a moment before answering. "Soon, I think, but first Victorio and Nana must be killed."

"Why not capture them?"

He laughed. "Oh, darlin', that would be a wonderful event, but you might as well dream of filling a water bucket with no bottom. They are both like wise old coyotes, who know all your tricks and daily invent new ones of their own."

"Well, you've been fighting for years and now you've won the Medal of Honor. Doesn't that count? Won't they give you a break from battle now? It seems to me you've earned a long furlough. And maybe a placement at a training station for a change . . . and . . ."

He chuckled at her reasoning, which made sense to her and even a little to him, but had nothing to do with the treatment of a Buffalo Soldier on the frontier.

He interrupted by kissing her lightly. Then, looking as far down as he could into her huge, questioning eyes, he said, "True, I've been put up for a Medal of Honor, but out here these things often take longer than securing a marriage permit. So-called heroics occur every battle and those have been many. Anyway, it's mostly from men getting hemmed in, having no place to run or temporarily losing their minds. All of us who have battled a long time know this. Few admit it, though."

"You're being too modest, Sgt. Moses Williams. From what I hear you should have been awarded that medal long ago."

"Ahhh, that's just camp gossip you've been hearing. In a few days you'll be hearing just the opposite."

"Never," she said. "I also think you should demand only training duty now. Anyway, you didn't answer my last question."

"I shouldn't say this, because I know you mean it, but I really do believe the wars will end soon—one way or the other."

That was what she had wanted to hear no matter how doubtful it all might be. Now they turned to each other. As close as they would know to a personal heaven on this earth enshrouded them with boundless benedictions, and they were thankful for their brief time of shared pleasure.

It was the time of healing again. It was also ordered by Colonel Hatch through both a telegraphed paper and a more thorough one delivered by a Tenth Cavalry courier to Lieutenant Valois. Five days of celebration were ordered before the last, long scoutings began again. This time none of the units would return from the field until the Warm Springs Apaches were conquered.

Lieutenant Valois was happy to prepare for the celebration, but he doubted his commander's follow-up order that they would destroy Nana before returning to the fort. They had been certain of this on every one of the countless times they had ridden out of the fort, but Nana still rode, marauding across the land. Hatch believed this almost impossible task could be done. He had battle units and scouts scattered into positions, forts, and encampments all around the Black Range. He felt that a final killing trap could be sprung with such force that not even the ghostly Nana could escape it. His troops were in place all the way into Arizona.

It was the time to give the men all the special provisions possible, and the time to order the leaders of entertainment to give their talents to making the Buffalo Soldiers and their white comrades forget, for just five days, the wearing, crippling marches and the deadly fields of gun, lance, and arrow fire the Apache warriors hurled at them. Let them eat, drink, dance, and rest, if that's what they wished. Let them have one last time to refresh, replenish themselves with fun and forgetfulness before they would march across the land and possibly die.

Colonel Hatch and Major Morrow were fine field commanders and they deeply loved and respected their men of war, even the less skillful, as long as they gave it all their hearts, their minds—yes, even their souls. For they, especially Morrow, had certainly done so, over and over.

Hatch was practical enough to know that the pressure from the farmers, ranchers, the businessmen, the miners, and above all the rich, powerful eastern owners of the mines were demanding victory. There was too much gold and other riches to be dug, too much timber to be cut into material for the towns so they could move more and more people to the West and bring them more and more profits. He thought about his men first and then all these things. They had no choice. He would be positioned as well as he would ever be within two to three weeks. If he did not move and achieve a victory now, they would be ordered to by an absent, higher command, and their losses could be, and more than likely would be, unacceptable.

So he ordered the regimental band away from the Santa Fe headquarters to tour the posts and make music for the fighting men. Even though Christine had her own small orchestra, the regimental band was not only exceptionally talented but a matter of great pride to the Ninth. These musicians were special, and they were treated with care and better supplies than the rest of the troops. There was no jealousy here, only a grateful and happy appreciation of being touched by the beautiful, always stirring sounds of the drums and horns that caused their battle blood to surge.

Twenty Eight

ALL THE SOLDIERS COLLECTED BACK PAY—AND PRIVATE WALLEY won a few extra dollars at poker because of it. But instead of going to Mesilla to see Bitch Moose, he decided he did not have enough funds to take his new buddy, Private Justin, along, so they went to the most convenient "hog ranch" at Leasburg on the nearby Rio Grande. It was called Hog Heaven by the soldiers, but more properly named Bar None by the owner.

The name was certainly apropos as the lowliest robbers, thieves, well-paid miners, and poorly paid soldiers were all welcome to drink, whore, and gamble their money away here—which they did with abandon. The whiskey, bought from professional bootleggers, was raw, cheap, and powerful. Private Walley was once heard to say that a glassful of Bar None Whiskey would make a man eat bark from a pine tree, fight a mountain lion with his bare hands, and make love to a porcupine.

The women at Bar None resembled almost everything but a porcupine. They were of every color and nationality to be found on the frontier. They were also of every shape. Although they were only a short distance from a river full of water, they seldom bathed in it. It was not altogether their fault.

Jerry "Big Belly" Bressler owned the place and employed several men of vague backgrounds. They were skilled at switching dice, dealing from anywhere they chose in a deck of cards, and selling women and whiskey as fast as they could rake the money in. So speed and turnover were way ahead of clean and comely at Bar None. The music was furnished by a fiddle, a banjo, and a drum. The players were ordered to beat out fast tunes that made the feet itch to dance and the blood surge with sin. It was the pleasure of the so-called sinning here that made the money change hands. Since no one had an abundance of cash, volume was the key to success.

In a day and a night, Walley and Justin had downed enough bad whiskey to fill a bucket, danced several miles in a forty-foot square, and fornicated at least three times with harried, hurried whores. They had five days of rest, courtesy of Colonel Hatch. Walley missed his old buddy Moses. He accepted his absence at the Bar None with understanding and respectful best wishes.

"Hell," he told Justin, "if Bitch Moose would jist have me, I'd marry her so fast your head'ud spin off your shoulders tryin' to watch."

"Who's Bitch Moose?"

"The most beautiful woman in the West, maybe the world, maybe in the . . . heavens." Walley motioned up to the universe through the *vega* ceiling of the Bar None toward the outside universe with such energy he propelled his chair backward in a crash, spilling his drink all over the dance floor.

This was not an unusual occurrence at the Bar None, but Walley had performed the act so many times over the years that two bouncers were right on him. They each took an arm and proceeded to propel him from the premises.

Justin was watching this action and to his battle-addled mind, the bouncers became Apaches attacking his soldier buddy. He ripped a leg from the fallen chair and whapped one of the bouncers across the jaw line. As he fell, Justin had space enough to splat the weapon across the kidneys of the other. It turned the surrogate Apache instantly sick and with no air to breathe. He dropped to his knees in the praying position, but could utter no words of either praying or cursing.

Other men of the establishment now moved on Walley and Justin. In certain barrooms across the West, Walley had been variously nicknamed Whirlwind, Buzz-saw and Tiger Man. His fists were driving so fast and so powerfully into his attackers that they were momentarily turned back with various pump knots and bleeding patches on their faces. Justin had broken the chair leg and now only held a six-inch stub. A group of miners joined the Bar None men. Walley and Justin were forced backward to the doorway. Being experienced against warriors like Victorio and Nana, they knew when to retreat to fight again.

He yelled at Justin, the one-Indian-battle, one-Bar-None-war-veteran, "Justin, retreat to the fort."

They exited with alacrity and to the relief of all inside. Walley encouraged his friend, as they ran up through the rolling desert terrain. "We done had e'nuff of that dull place. The fort's where the real party's happenin'."

Justin knew it would be impolite not to reply, but he had just swallowed two teeth and could not answer for fear of choking.

The battle continued for a spell at the Bar None as both Buffalo Soldier and white infantrymen had rushed to the aid of Walley and Justin.

However, Big Belly Bressler, both cunning and greedy, yelled, "Free drinks. Free drinks for all," and thereby saved more bloodshed and actually even the very walls of his low-down establishment. Even the whores got a brief rest. Some good had come out of Walley's glass-breaking fall after all.

Twenty Nine

IT WAS A TIME OF EXCITEMENT. THE FORT BUZZED WITH TALK filled with gossip, rumors, and plain fun. A guard unit would be sent to proudly escort the regimental band from the railhead at Mesilla. Before the musicians' arrival, Christine planned to hold her musicale to whet the musical appetite of the compound's residents.

Requisition units had been sent out with six-up mule and horse-pulled wagons to barter for potatoes, beans, grain, and both fresh and dried fruits from the farmers and ranchers of the area. They had returned laden. The final vegetables of the season were taken from the regimental garden. A shipment of fresh beef and mutton had been salted down and stored and was now made available to all units.

Some would miss the festivities as the work had to go on. The herders still had to range with the horses across the grasslands. To the relief of everyone, it had been a long spell since the present remuda had been raided. Lieutenant Valois had designated a small unit to follow the herd and herders with a ten-pounder cannon and Gatling guns. They always took up well-mounted positions with the heavy weapons so they could see in all directions. The Apaches were wise to the power of the ten pounders in the flatter grazing lands of Texas. The guns had proven deadly there, long ago, but were almost useless in the high country.

The cooks were joyfully doing extra duty, delighted to be able to feed the hungry troops decent food for a change and escape the gripes. They knew that the greatest Parisian chefs would have been unable to make most of their low-quality foodstuff tasty. All long-time veterans knew that this rare bounty would be short-lived and every able man would soon be sent to battle again. The camp duties would become lighter for the few remaining behind. It would then be the turn of the herders, the remount trainers, the laundresses, the seamstresses, the chaplain, and the supply room attendants to ease up a spell. Slowly the work would pick up again and the cycle would be completed when the wounded, war-pummeled, war-exhausted troopers began to return.

No one understood what was taking place better than Moses. These generous five days of rest and celebration, this largesse of food and entertainment would not be free. This was the fourth or fifth time he had experienced this in his long career. After the fun, they would be sent into a battle of finality, no matter how long it took or the cost in troops lost to lead, steel, and the unforgiving earth. The burning sun did not care, the freezing snow did not care, and the millions of acres of jagged rocks did not care. Moses doubted if the distant high command cared for anything but a hell-ringing victory, assuring their personal glory and promotion.

When Walley and Justin had told Moses they were sneaking off to the Bar None, Moses could tell by their tone of voice that they wished he could join them. The sudden realization that he was not sharing their drinking and whoring fun touched him strangely. It was a loss he knew he would never regain, but it was a feeling of sadness mixed with one of warm, comforting thoughts of Sheela. Wars and soldiers changed lands and positions all over the world, but a fine family was forever together, even if sometimes physically parted. It was comforting.

He had needed that consoling thought when he sent them on their way. "You men go and have one hell of a lot of fun. You hear? Those are orders," he had said as he watched them mount their horses.

Moses remembered Walley's grin as he said, "You knows I always obeys orders, Sarge, no matter how much it galls me. Fun it is, Sarge."

"Justin, you see that Walley gets back here in at least three or four pieces. All right?"

"Shore 'nuff, Sergeant. I'll get him back if I have to gether him up with a shovel."

Moses pushed them from his thoughts as he turned away to think only of escorting Sheela to the stables.

Everyone knew that the slick sorrel, Reno, and the heavy-quartered bay, Badger, "belonged" to Moses and Sheela. He presented Badger to her as an official prewedding present. However, there was a silent understanding that his sorrel could be used as a remount training horse or even a herding horse while he was detached to the hills. At the same time Sheela's bay was to be ridden just enough to keep it in shape.

They gathered their horses, saddled, mounted, and rode to the pistol range. There Moses patiently showed Sheela how to fire a revolver—how to point the weapon with both eyes open instead of sighting with one closed, how to squeeze the trigger. After a dozen or so shots, she had it down so well, he had to control his amazement at her accuracy.

"Are you real sure you've never fired a revolver before."

Sheela smiled shyly, cocking her head to the side in the way of curious puppies, and said, "I never said I hadn't fired a revolver before. Actually, Nelda and the General gave me several lessons while we were living in Socorro."

Sheela was stunned that she could now say Nelda's name without a giant lump of pain filling her throat. The solidity of Moses being near had helped her heal from what she had once felt would be an unrecoverable loss. Then too, she now had a new mother as well. Mama Mayo Lou, in her own way almost equal to that of Moses, knew how and, more importantly, when to give her love and comfort. Even now those warm thoughts still dazed her in a way she was unable to fully understand.

They mounted up again and the sun kept them warm in the cool breeze as they reined toward the river. Neither spoke. The horses moved smoothly under them, their muscles rippling, catching the sun in little bursts of golden light not unlike the streaks that coursed through Sheela's bountiful head of hair. A magpie screamed in resentment as it flashed its white streaks from one bush to another, moving ahead of them like an erratic and resentful guide.

The air was diamond-dust-bright, creating a vast blue shroud just for them. The cottonwoods along the Rio Grande's banks were at their deepest green, having one last fling of color before turning to gold. The soft semidesert floor muffled the sound of the horses' hooves, but even so, a lizard heard them just before they reached it, and it scooted with amazing speed, its little short legs an invisible propellant, as it disappeared in a clump of vegetation then reappeared on a rock, watching the giant transgressors move away.

Moses knew all the significant landmarks, every tree, fallen or standing, every rock of any size, for miles north and south on this part of the river. He had fought on its banks and seen blood pour into it to become part of the great watery artery moving far, far down to the Gulf of Mexico. None of this was on his mind at this cherished moment except the strength the clear air gave his lungs and the salubrious healing of his eyes from the range of colors in everything around them. There was a fallen cottonwood with two large umbrella-foliaged trees to each side.

They tied their horses. Moses took a blanket from behind his saddle, shook it out, and folded it double up against the cottonwood. It made a comfortable seat and leaning place for them to sit together and listen to the river talk in many musical voices and sing in unknown tongues of ancient things and new things. All they had to do was listen. The little waves caught up the sunshine, and deep green and blue shadows moved, undulated, flowed in eternally changing lights swallowed by shadows only to be sparkled anew in billions of instances, ceaselessly.

As they leaned, shoulders together, holding hands, they knew peace. The peace that comes from love and the beauty of the natural earth combined just for them.

The hypnotic spell of the river and their nearness to each other caused earth time to pass invisibly, silently. There was a nirvana upon them. A beguilement. And neither was conscious of how they had become naked, nor how her heart had seemed to move inside his chest to join his.

Later, as they rode again, too content to talk, they both reined their horses around for one last look across the westerly hills, where the sun was mixing it up with elongated cirrus clouds to flare golden rays through dark purple cloud shadows.

As Moses took in the awesome western sky, he said softly, "I love you, Sheela Jones-gonna-be-Williams."

She said, "And I love you, Moses, more than that."

Then they rode together back to the fort. Tomorrow the band would play for everyone and many people would dance and sing. Today though, the Great Mystery in the sky had painted an entire world of colorful magic just for the two of them. That they knew.

Thirty

THE TIME OF PEACE LASTED A LITTLE WHILE LONGER. NANA spoke and imparted confidence to his wives. He held council with his children and grandchildren, telling them stories of the time of hunting for the deer and elk instead of the white-eyes and Buffalo Soldiers. These stories were ancient history to most of his children. All they had known was running wars, hunger, thirst, and the almost daily disappearance of a loved one lost in the wars.

These brief times of relief, of rest, of playing, and of healing their young minds and bodies were precious. The constant running, in fear of starvation or gunpowder destruction, had made up most of their entire lives. Many had been born on the steep trails, their mothers birthing them, wrapping them in a blanket, and moving on with the rest or they would not be here at all. It was incredible that any babies had survived to become children, much less grow to adulthood. So now they played, or flirted, according to their age and listened in wonder to Nana's tales of the days when hunting, fishing, and gathering of seeds and roots were not only a necessity but an adventurous pleasure. Their visions could not help but portray both day and night dreams of those wonderful days returning. Nana knew this was what kept them all moving, fighting, grubbing food anywhere, anyway they could. The possibility of the old dreams, of the old days returning, must feed their spirits even when there was little sustenance for their stomachs. It was the only way to survive.

Nana rode from tipi to tipi, from brush house to brush house, on his favorite mottled gray horse. Horseback, he was powerful and in control, just as he was in council. The less the tribe saw him stiff and limping afoot the better. It made him happy to see the blur of the young running about playing games, laughing with the joy of momentary abandonment. He thrilled at his favorite grandson's rapture with the gracefully seductive Flower Song. He wished they could experience a joining before it was too late. They might never know of this most necessary and needed of all things by the young of a certain time, a certain magic age and moment.

He smiled, struggling to recall just one more time when and where that special happening had been for him. It was so many summers, so many wives, so many children, so many battles, so many burials, so distant, that it took him awhile to dredge it back. Then there it was. There by the hot springs at the secret place high in the Black Range. Ah, how sweet, how tender, how giving she had been. For just a second his old loins felt one last tingle. He could see her lithe, smooth body, hear her cries of painful joy, and feel a bit the explosion in his middle, but no matter how he strained, he could not remember her name just yet.

The horses were herded from one grassy spot to another and, with the plentiful water, were gaining weight and strength. The seed and root gathering was successful and the women talked and gossiped as if they had lived here in the Sierra Madres their whole lives. The men cleaned and checked guns, ammunition, saddles, bridles, blankets, and horse-gut water containers. Victorio, Lozen, Nana, his *se-*

gundo, Kaytennae, and a few others held quiet councils of possible war so as not to disturb the healing of the others. They had only to kill a horse or mule to feast. Their flesh was returning and helped strengthen the powerful spirits that were always with them.

As Nana hobbled to his horse and struggled up on a fallen log before mounting, he was having pleasurable thoughts of all the life around him. Even if he saw it with dim vision and dulled hearing, his mind vision had sharpened to compensate. Just for the hell of it he threw his head back and let out a surprisingly loud yell of the purest joy and shouted through sudden laughter,

"Fear not, my people. We shall live on forever."

Those who heard these sudden sounds from the old man had a feeling of rejoicing and would truly remember it all the way to the forever time.

Each day Lozen skillfully disappeared to hold the silent reconnaissance of her palms for the nearness of any approaching enemy. Thankfully, today they remained their natural color. They were safe for now; nevertheless, constant vigilance was life. In spite of her reports of safety to her brother, Victorio, and "Grandfather" Nana, there was some doubt of what might be coming from the north.

Even though it was against U.S. government rules to cross troops over the line of Mexico, it was often done when in close pursuit of Apaches and conveniently overlooked. In fact, they had been pursued for twenty or so miles across the border this last ride. So Victorio ordered Nana, Lozen, and Kaytennae to choose a mixture of the more experienced and the younger warriors for a scouting trip to the north. Nana took his "eyes," his grandson, Kaywayhla, as well.

They had several days' rations with them, lots of ammunition, and a battle spirit ready to fight any invaders. However,

Victorio, like all humans, had made mistakes in spite of his multiple great victories. Sending this scouting party out would prove to be the costliest of his life and lead to the loss of many things.

The third day out, Nana sent his "eyes" along with Kaytennae to scout ahead, for Lozen's palms had shown a slight reddening. When the main body camped that night, the scouts remained absent. Nana led his warrior band on north through the foothills of the Sierra Madres. It was late that day before they recognized the two scouts returning.

"Grandfather," his *segundo* said, "we found the white-eye soldiers camped by a spring. They even had cannon."

"Three," said Kaywayhla.

"Then we must be sure we attack swiftly and with surprise before they can put the big *bangers* on us."

"We will not have to do this, Grandfather. They are returning to the north."

"You are sure of this, Kaytennae?"

"Yes, Grandfather. Kaytennae tells it so. I watched them until they became small in the glass," he said with conviction.

Nana said, "Those white-eyes are very lucky men." All grumbled how lucky the soldiers were to have escaped the wrath of Nana in spite of outnumbering him two to one and having three big cannons. He continued, "How could fools like that be so fortunate."

"It is hard to believe."

"We could have fed the coyotes and the buzzards for a month."

"Not to mention the mountain lions and the worms."

"Do not forget the magpies and the crows."

"Ah, what a terrible day for us."

"They must have had a scout who saw us coming and caused them to tuck their tails and run for their lives like cowardly dogs."

"That must be it."

"Yes, that is it. There is no other explanation."

Lozen held her standing seance with her guiding spirit and verified. She told Nana, "Grandfather, they have retreated to our stolen homeland."

He, for one, was silently pleased that they would not do battle this day. He had been enjoying the rare time of peace and musing about his youth. He wished for just a few more days of this. That is all he would ever ask for.

As he motioned his warriors to turn back toward their own camp, he could not know that his last wish would be denied him.

Thirty One

THE MEXICAN COLONEL, JOAQUIN TERRAZAS, HAD BEEN AS-
sured that two separate units of U.S. mixed cavalry and infantry were moving to entrap Victorio from the northeast and
northwest. He had been about as successful as any of the
northern troops against Victorio, fighting many battles, but
never truly winning the one that counted to him—Victorio's
death.

With great care, and copying his enemy's tactics, Terrazas
shuffled two and three men forward at a time in a slow and
hidden encircling movement. It took two days, but at last he
had a numerically superior force ready to strike. They were
within a mile of the camp, almost surrounding it. He knew he
would never have a better chance than this to destroy Victorio and his band.

The troops moved forward slowly and were within a quarter of a mile of the camp before being seen. Then they
charged with full cries at Victorio's camp. It was not exactly
a surprise attack, but it had the same results.

Many of Victorio's remaining warriors and many of their
wives joined him in defending the meadow camp. Others had
been given absolute orders to help the remaining women and

children escape with most of the horses and mules, as well as ammunition, guns, and other goods.

Victorio knew that his "call" had come. He would stand and fight so that some others could escape to join Nana. Some later said he fell on his own knife rather than be taken alive.

Against their nature, the Apaches fought to the death, racing, crawling from one indentation in the earth, one rock to another. It was successful at what Victorio knew he must do. He died, as well as his warrior brothers and sisters, hoping that Nana would have enough fighters left and maybe enough women and children to maintain some bloodline of the Warm Springs Apaches.

Many of Terrazas's men fell before they finally found Victorio's knife-slashed and bullet-shattered body where he'd fought to the last breath. Terrazas was joyous in finally destroying the great warrior, and because of both exhaustion and prudence decided not to pursue the escaping small bands.

Nana felt Lozen's spirit. He held up his hand to stop the band. They were still several miles from their meadow camp on the west side of the Sierra Madres. Without a word, without dismounting, Lozen held out her hands and they immediately appeared as if blood would burst from her palms. She turned her stricken face toward Nana. "Grandfather, my brother, the great Victorio, has been killed." The words were like large arrows of ice shot into the hearts of the entire band.

As they trotted their horses forward, Nana was mentally instructing Kaytennae and a small group to go to the camp to bury the dead. Lozen's vision had proven exact.

It took Kaytennae and six men two days to finish the interment of Victorio and his fallen. It was a terrible task. Nana knew he should have been there to oversee it and give his nephew great prayers of honor. But now he was the last leader left. He must gather all the survivors together along with the horses and supplies they had saved. They must now raid his own caches of dried food and ammunition scattered about the land.

It took all winter and was very difficult to round up all his people. They had scattered far and hidden well. It was a frenzied time. Above all, the old man, now past seventy-five years, must show, not compassion, but certitude.

All the warriors, the women, the children had been on the raid and on the run so long that these critical chores were accomplished with dispatch.

Now he had all of them, his warriors, his family, his wards, assemble back together. They had sufficient pack, saddle, and meat animals to sustain them awhile, and because of his power over the years there was gathered from all sources enough ammunition to last as long as they themselves could. It took longer than expected to marshal and make everything as ready and right as it would ever be again.

Nana sent Kaytennae and two warriors to ride circle around the temporary camp. Lozen said there was no enemy in striking distance, so Nana recalled the scouts. What were the risks now?

There in the vast, severe, lonely Sierra Madres he summoned all his people, the Tcihene (or Warm Springs Apaches) in a half circle around where he was mounted on his favorite warhorse. The Warm Springs Apaches never danced before a simple supply raid, but now Nana must declare not just a vengeance raid, but a vengeance war, and this called for a "ceremony of beginning."

"There must be fierce dancing," Nana said. He raised his Winchester above his head and continued. "Now, I say to you people of the Ojo Caliente lands that my nephew and your great leader, Victorio, must be, will be, avenged. The blood of the white-eyes and the Buffalo Soldiers will flow like red rivers. If they still live after our bullets have found them, we will slice them like deer meat with our knives. Their flesh must suffer the same pain as our hearts. *Ahiu, ahiu.*" He yelled at the sky, and all, even the moving wounded, echoed his shout.

Wood was gathered swiftly to build a great fire. The dance always started from the east. Four men danced toward the fire and around it, as they had from the long-ago time of their earth arrival. There were singers and hide-beaters to the west. No one was ordered to dance—yet. They did not paint their faces. They moved to the rhythm of the singers, the hide-beaters, and their own coursing blood. They pantomimed how they would act in the battles to come with their guns, knives, and the few bows and metal-tipped lances left. Some men left the dance to pray, then returned. Those who had not joined had their names called, for they could not refuse to unite with the name-caller in battle or the vengeance dance. This was their unbroken code.

"Ahh, Guidan, come and join us so you can brag some more. I heard you tell your son you had killed six soldiers with one shot."

"Ahhiii, Kaywashe, what are you waiting for? You, the great talker of dog shit. You, the great belly-gutter of white-eyes. Come dance for vengeance."

None was left out. None refused. Not even Nana. And even though the old man appeared to be falling as his crippled foot caused him to lean far to the right, he danced on to the end, overcoming his age and stiffening wounds and weary heart, to finish. After the last warrior had joined, they danced even wilder, four times around the fire to the finish.

Nana organized his tribe—really a band now, there were so few left. Since there was such a small number, he included the young boys of fourteen or fifteen in his main group. Then several old men, who could not ride well enough to stay atop a horse on a lightning raid, were instructed, along with some younger boys and strong women, where to ride to avoid the inevitable retaliation of the soldiers. These secret places were known from the original time, places where warriors would return to regroup and move on to another secluded spot while the surviving warriors attacked again.

Nana made a last statement after they had organized for vengeance. "Now the Mexicans have taken near a hundred women, children, and wounded for slaves. Many of our women died fighting the Mexicans, but those to the north drove us there. We are few, it is true, but we have the hearts of many. So now to the duty of killing the destroyers of our people. We will win because none will surrender except his life to the great spirit. We are the Warm Springs Apache. We are the imperishable!"

He led his pitifully few remaining people north to the attack. Eagerly. Enraged.

The newspapers of Silver City and Central City had heralded the news of Victorio's death. There was a great rejoicing not only there but all over the territory. It was premature. Soon confused reports were printed that Victorio had been seen here, then there, and then another place, rampaging again.

When a unit of troopers near the southern U.S. border found a wagon with an arm dangling from it, they soon discovered the conveyance was full of mutilated Mexican farmers and storekeepers, all dead and some cut to pieces. Fear returned. It was thought by most of the citizenry, and their representative news sources, that the report of Victorio's demise had to be erroneous. Who else could it be? Geronimo was still a danger, but that was mostly in Arizona Territory. These few became hundreds then thousands of savages in the fertile minds of the civilians. They were chasing the wrong demon.

Nana had become a living ghost. His vengeance had given him a strength and cunning beyond any of his mighty abilities of the past. Emotional terror was created all over by the widely scattered raids of a very few warriors.

The pressure grew on Colonel Hatch again; greater, more strident, and desperate demands made by the newspapers.

Thirty Two

THE BAND DID PLAY ON AND ON. THE MUSIC DID SOMETHING special to all the occupants of Fort Selden. It was their pride.

The music varied, some selections for the Spanish influence and culture, others for the northern Yankees, and others for those of the Deep South. But the finale was a medley of national melodies of several different nations. The Russian "Meadowland," the "Marseillaise," "Yankee Doodle," "What Is the German Fatherland," "Hail Columbia," and "America." The bass drum and the smaller snare drums created in the powerful finale such a skilled, blood-pounding beat that the explosion of applause would have made the Royal Orchestra of London appreciative.

They had put in one of their finest days of playing and would remember it as being almost as splendid as the recent performance for Pres. Rutherford B. Hayes during his visit to New Mexico's capital city. Since it was the first visit to the territory by a president, the band's rendering of "Hail to the Chief," as he and his entourage stepped from the train to a platform, would naturally hold a high point in their memory. But here today their contribution to fighters of the Indian Wars, the Ninth Regiment, and, in particular, I Troop, would soon resonate in their blood, and even in their music, as long as they would play.

Christine Valois was truly in her element, and she had remembered all. She had arranged a reception for the band at officers' quarters, with Mama Mayo Lou in charge of refreshments. The new shipments of supplies and the seasonal harvesting of the garden provided delicious fare. As the band retired for well-deserved and appreciated treats, her own small, private, post orchestra mounted the temporary platform to play dance numbers

The dirt had been swept down to hard clay and all the women of the camp—outnumbered three to one—were in demand. Even the children, black, white, and brown, danced in their awkward, enthusiastic play.

Christine had seen that lanterns were hung for the early evening dancing. The mess hall was set with small tables of meat, sauces, vegetables, and sweet rolls. The company cooks kept the large coffeepots hot and replaced them as they were emptied. There were various bottles and flasks appearing and disappearing as quick snorts of alcohol were sneaked here and there, with some surreptitious mixing of it in their coffee.

At about ten o'clock in the evening, when straight above was a black star-flecked sky, and the lanterns cast a soft, orange glow around the compound, Sgt. Moses Williams danced closely with his love, Miss Sheela Jones. He was always amazed at how her huge black opal eyes absorbed light. They glowed and flickered like little replicas of the oil lanterns. They did the same in sunlight or moonlight. Sheela, Moses had decided, was a gatherer of light.

How softly the music caressed the cool air they breathed! They stepped and whirled in a rhythm. It was their moment of bliss, as if the violin had been invented to play only for them. They were perhaps, for a moment, selfish in their closeness, their aloneness in this frontier crowd of survivors. Nevertheless, they whirled so slowly it was almost like the hands of a clock. The feeling of love between the fortuitous pair was palpable to all. They were left a special space to the west side of the other dancers. A place all their own.

Also attending was the sergeant from the Twenty-fourth Infantry, whose unit was temporarily stationed there. He, out of some perverseness, jealousy, or insecurity, made the first mistake of the evening. He had swallowed only three secret slugs of whiskey, so drunkenness was ruled out as an excuse.

Just the same, he said a little too loudly to some companions, as he pointed and stared at Sheela, "Man, I'd like to get that one in the bushes. She moves like a . . ."

His second mistake had been made when he said this in the presence of Private Walley. The next most definite sound heard was a growl coming from Walley's throat, and the long, lean muscles that drove the fist into the infantry sergeant's face made a "whap" that could be heard across the room. He had struck with such force that the broken nose had splattered blood over four people before the momentum carried both the attacker and the attacked to the ground.

Since Walley had landed on top, he continued his fist work on the hapless sergeant until Justin and others succeeded in dragging him from the sergeant's unconscious body. Getting Walley off was one thing, but stopping him was another. Walley flattened the first two of the sergeant's men who had pulled him off and knocked his new buddy, Justin, about six feet backward on his butt. Justin shook his head and found that his legs and arms crumpled under him as he attempted to rise. Then one word from Sergeant Moses was all it took. "Walley."

The private froze at the command in the voice from the person who had saved his life so many times. Then the Military Police of the Ninth took control, and Walley gave in without further struggle as they rushed him off to the guard-house.

His voice came back with only one regret, "Hey, Justin, you got a free punch comin'. I didn't see you."

Justin rubbed his numb jaw to feel if any bones were broken, saying, "Whooee, I sure hope he don't get a good look at me next time."

The Twenty-fourth Infantry sergeant was helped away to the infirmary to be washed up and have his wounds disinfected. There was not much that could be done about his broken nose. He would have to breathe through the very mouth that had spoken the foolish words about Sheela. Although the ignorant soldier would live to fight other enemies, for the moment he thought he was dying, and later, when he suddenly had to sneeze at the pungent smells of the medicine, he wished he had.

The orchestra started a fast-paced Scottish two-step, and the dancing went on without incident and with pleasure for all till midnight. Then Lieutenant Valois ordered taps called. It had to be done twice to get all the happy revelers to bed.

Walley had been in the stockade so many times that he felt right at home and slept like an exhausted hunting hound. The beat-up sergeant had to drink a whole glass of whiskey before he could find a sleep of nightmares, where boulders kept falling from the sky right at him, turning into big, bony fists just before they struck. If he felt sorry for himself later, it would all be wasted. There were many men across the West who often remembered making the mistake of angering Sergeant Moses's best friend and still his closest companion in the great Apache chases.

Thirty Three

NANA HAD BEEN JOINED BY TWENTY-FIVE WARM SPRINGS Apaches who had taken leave of the safety of the Mescalero Reservation. They had all fought together at one time or another and, to his way of thinking, the new warriors gave Nana a mighty army. Even so, he would not be alive if he had been a fool. He knew, unlike the civilians, that there really were several thousand of the enemy scattered across southern New Mexico, with nothing on their minds but killing him and every single member of this army of his.

Nana was a great field leader, and using as a counselor, Lozen, the finest tactician of his Ojo Caliente tribe, he laid out a plan that would continue to terrorize the area to avenge Victorio's death.

Since Nana could name any draw, canyon, arroyo, game trail, or sacred spot in the entire area, he could send his warriors out two and three at a time to make quick, killing strikes. They would go out forming prongs. Then, after the strikes, they would turn and, hiding the best they could, return to a designated spot in the foothills of the Black Range. In fact, they would meander back and forth from the southern Floridas along the west side of the Black Range all the way north to the San Mateo. It was an immense area to cover. Nana wanted the enemy to think it would take many, many warriors for them to be in such widely scattered places in such a few days. It worked better than he had hoped. There is no rumor dispenser that compares to that of war, for one's life is at stake every second. His widely scattered raids kept the populace in a panic for, indeed, his warriors were seen everywhere.

It took Herculean efforts to move, protect, and feed the last of the tribe behind their constantly assaulting warriors. Moving camp to camp, attacking and returning again and again, took an enormous physical toll on all. Although Nana had ordered death to the enemy white-eyes as the first order of battle, when there was a reasonably safe opportunity, his warriors were to acquire horses and mules above all else because the constant, wide-spread raids diminished mounts just as it did humans. There could be no proper revenge without fresh animals. He often, with Kaytennae and his grandson and one or two more, led raids himself. A leader leads.

Sometimes Nana would send the group out with Lozen, while he stayed behind and moved the women and children to the designated gathering spot. Once, when his "eyes" went with Lozen, Nana told him to watch for the "golden striped arm with the broad shoulders," and he added that Kaywayhla was not to risk anything when he spotted the man, because this one was meant for Nana alone.

Lieutenant Colonel Dudley, who had been relieved of field command, was now put back in action. Even this detested commander would be hailed if he downed Nana. Dudley, mistaken again, did not believe all the rumored sightings— and sometimes genuine ones—could be taking place without Victorio and his warriors being alive. Being overly exuberant, he was foolishly trying to answer every sighting by dispatching pursuit units. This was exactly what Nana wanted—the scattering of troops so that his two or three men could strike and run without having to face a coordinated force.

After many units had ridden mounts until their horseshoes wore out, and the men moved dazedly, their eyes burned half-blind looking for Victorio's nonexistent Apaches, Dudley finally got real evidence of their presence.

A white man and two Mexicans were riding a wagon loaded with barrels of pickled fish about twelve miles east of Fort Cummings when they were attacked. The bodies were burned and the heads of the men slashed to ribbons. A couple of prospectors wandered upon the grisly scene. They studied the site and reported that it must have been a "huge" band of Indians who had done this horrible thing.

A couple of hours later, near the same place, a mail stage-coach was attacked and the stage driver killed. The attackers had cut the man open and then the mailbags, scattering the contents over a large area for the wind to dispense farther. They took or destroyed all the express freight. And were delighted to pound to bits the drums and beat the horns of the Twelfth Infantry band into odd rock-sculptured shapes, laughing heartily at the sound of the metal twisting and smashing flat. The Indians captured four mules from the attacks.

When Colonel Dudley arrived with a large contingent of men and found these atrocities, he went into a quiet rage. He dispensed Companies C and F, led by Lieutenant Humphries, supported by supplies on ten pack mules, with orders to "pursue until taken."

But it was the army that was taken in. There had been only three of Nana's men at each assault, although the raiders had purposely ridden round and round, back and forth, making so many tracks that there was no way the troopers could factually read the earth. The plot had worked as Nana planned.

During that very same week, a considerable distance to the north, and east of the San Mateo Mountains, six soldiers of Company D were attacked while escorting a small wagon supply train from Fort Craig to camp Ojo Caliente. One soldier was killed and one received a bullet in the tibia, shattering it for good. The civilians and the remaining soldiers pursued the Indians—only two—but even as they were being chased, the Apaches killed a buckboard driver and stole two horses near Hillsboro.

Nana never let up on himself or his people. The movement and the onslaughts went on every single day somewhere in the far scattered hills, villages, farms, and ranches. Travelers of all kinds were victims. Nana lost warriors and horses just as the soldiers did. The army could keep replacing their losses, but that was nearly impossible for Nana. A few more Mescaleros came to join him, but these were to be the last. There were a few Apaches scattered through the mountains in small family groups that made up the last of his replacements. No matter. None of this bothered him; it goaded him to fight harder, ride longer, and revenge Victorio's blood by severing every artery, by whatever means possible, of the eradicators of his people.

Nana's warriors shared his vision. They rode so far, so fast, and struck with such surprise and ferocity that all the other peoples of the land—Spaniards and Mexicans of the ranches, villages, and farms—joined in bands with the whites. They organized small armies of their own. They were just as tortured, just as frustrated as the army in suffering sudden violent losses and just as swiftly they chased tracks that seemed to be made by invisible whirlwinds—tracks that broke apart and vanished into the hills. When they did find blood—even without the body it came from—they lusted for more, some to near madness.

Nana had created an amazing psychological warfare with bloody and butchered bodies. Near chaos took possession of both his civilian and army opponents.

At a council with Lozen and three other elders, he said, "They run around with their guns, shooting at shadows like fools."

Lozen knew—they all knew—that finally their numbers would dry up like a five-minute rain shower in a desert sand dune. However, knowing this did not matter now.

Nana told his followers, "We are not only avenging Victorio's death, this is for all of their kind from the time when the Spaniards worked our people to death in the mines, and the white-eyes dug huge holes and put axes to the trees of our hunting grounds, and the army fired cannons, rifles, pistols, and chopped our hearts apart with sabers. This is the time of our last vengeance for all. This is for our dead, for their spirits in this and other worlds."

There was nothing else left to say.

Thirty Four

THE TIME OF REST WAS OVER. THE DRILLING OF HORSES, SOL-
diers, and guns began again with a fervor never before felt at
Fort Selden. The pressure on the high command had filtered
down to the fighting men.

Moses had not questioned Valois about the length of Walley's stay in the guardhouse, but he would, at the right time.
He missed their friend C.C. just as he had yearned for all his
other friends killed over the years. But Walley became more
important to him now as their time against Nana had to reach
a closure soon. Like Sheela, he had become so much of a
playing, warring companion that there was a bond deeper
than ever before.

Despite his dedicated professional past, Moses was for the
first time having mixed emotions. At the same instant he
craved to go head-on with Nana, he worried about surviving
to hold Sheela again. He was also torn between hoping Walley would be stranded in the guardhouse to certainly survive
the upcoming battles, and his strong need for Walley's
courage and deadly weapons accuracy. He felt selfish at these
thoughts, wondering for a moment if he needed Walley just
to help secure his own safe return to Sheela. He felt guilty

not following her request that he ask for camp duty. Even though he knew she was right—and growing adamant about it—he could not quit the pursuit of Nana now. Not now. All the years would have been wasted. His soldier's blood weakened at the thought of quitting when he was so sure the battle was nearing its end. He made a silent prayer that she would understand.

He decided to request Walley's release when they were ready to move out. As to Sheela, he could only carry her warmly in his heart as a realized dream. He knew that these conflicting thoughts had to be conquered and made secondary to his real duty, otherwise he would not be capable of taking care of his men properly—or himself.

Then there was his own personal matter of vengeance. He had seen a thousand times how Nana had outwitted them and destroyed Cpl. C. C. Smith (his other best friend) and other damn good soldiers and men with the bombardment of stones from the sky. The fact that he had been helpless to save them, or even make the attempt, is what held his thirst for Nana's blood ongoing. His mind's vision had never softened about this heinous act upon his friends, his wards, and himself. These thoughts brought him back to the reality of his duties, his soldierly obligations, and he drove his men and himself even harder seeking a performance of perfection that would finally destroy the old warrior.

Sheela also busied herself as never before. She gained confidence daily that she would make Moses a good army wife. This belief had come with much difficulty. Far beyond her childhood remembering, the things she had loved the most had been taken away from her. Moses had turned that around at Bitch Moose's. Occasionally, she could not help musing on this. Where would she be if he had not been there at the right moment? What really would have happened to her? The thought was always too much of a burden to handle, but she took solace in the fact that the mind-muddied remembrance and her nightmares of the Sweetwater massacre and her escape were becoming increasingly fewer.

She busied herself by learning, by tutoring, by helping Reverend Pree teach, by all the other visits and assistance to the laundresses, seamstresses and the infirmary. She had found companionship, love, and comfort with Mama Mayo Lou. Although she did not feel real love for Christine Valois, she did like and respect her. She felt a strong warmth toward the children, Danielle and Stacy, and she could tell they returned that feeling by their growing respect for learning and for their teacher.

There was so much more in her life now, so much more than she had ever even dared to dream. Then why was she suddenly becoming frightened, with terrible moments of insecurity tearing at her like countless little sharp-clawed demons? She was able to force away these fears by studying the professional composure of Christine.

Finally one day, as she felt the time of Moses's departure nearing, she ventured to ask Christine.

"Miss Christine, how long did it take for you to adjust . . . well, get used to Lieutenant Valois's departure to the battlefields?"

"Oh. Oh, my dear, a long time. But there is no choice is there? So you learn to accept."

"Well, ma'am, for me it was easier earlier, but now . . ."

"Of course, dear, it is a natural feeling. We cannot totally rule our destinies; but if one cannot make the adjustments, then I guess one should marry a chef instead of a soldier. That is our choice."

"I know that, but . . . well, I just can't stand the thought of losing Moses."

Christine suddenly realizing how serious Sheela was, put

down her sewing, asked her daughters to go to their room to finish their studies, and said, "You are not going to lose him, dear. When I first married Gustavo, we were at war with those Comanches in Texas. Every time he rode out of camp, my heart turned cold. But he kept returning and returning until I realized, I accepted, that he was a professional at what he did and damned good at it. So you see, after a certain number of battles you adjust. You must become a professional at what you do. You must be just as busy and dedicated to your duties as they are to theirs."

"Yes, ma'am, I know you are right and I'm trying my best to contribute."

"And indeed you are doing a fine job. That is the real secret though, keeping busy at your work, your own contributions, and feeling pride and contentment in that. It shortens the wait and eases the mind. Remember, dear, that Sergeant Moses and the lieutenant have been together ever since the late war. They have proven themselves to be the best."

Christine had just done her duty the best way she knew how, and it certainly had not been the first time. Her words helped give, or rather enforce, what Sheela had already surmised.

However, the next day the thought of losing Moses suddenly struck her in the middle of her reading to the girls. She felt the tears burn behind her eyes and threaten to gush forth. She felt frightened and ashamed. She willed herself to act normal as she excused herself. She barely made it to the kitchen before her tears burst forth on Mama Mayo's big soft shoulder.

Mayo Lou took her in the same mighty arms that had consoled so many. She caressed her and rubbed her back with love and comfort. She knew what was wrong from having suffered the same experience so many times herself.

Finally, Sheela's body stopped shaking and she moved to

the table where Mama Mayo had been peeling potatoes. She picked up the knife and continued the chore for her with shaking hands.

"Oh, Mama, I'm such a coward. After all you've lost, you must be ashamed of me."

"No, no, honey. All them losses ain't really losses. I still got 'em here in my happy heart. They're with me all the times. Anyways, you ain't gonna lose that Moses. Cain't no Indian nor nothin' else hurt him or it would'uh already happened."

"Oh, Mama, I know he's a great soldier, and he's already told me the Indian Wars will soon be over, but I can't help it. I can't stand for him to ride off again. I love him so much I can't think of living without him. I just *can't* stand the thought. I'm not going to."

"I knows, dear child, I do knows how much it hurts, but you gotta be strong for him, don't you see? If he's worried 'bout you, he can't concentrate on killin' them Indians and keepin' hisself alive for you. Don't you see, honey, what I means?"

Sheela put the peeling knife down, pushed the damp strand of hair back from her face, and somehow shined a big smile at her dear friend. Sheela took Mayo Lou in her arms, patting her, reversing their roles temporarily.

"I'm being a foolish and spineless little baby."

"No, you ain't, honey. Youse bein' natural. Sometimes tears fallin' outside make the insides feel better. I s'pose I oughta know, huh?" They stood apart and had a little laugh.

"I s'pose you do, Mama. I feel better. Thank you."

"Come here, honey, I got something I been meanin' to show you."

Sheela was feeling much better as she followed Mama Mayo into their bedroom. Mama Mayo got down on her knees and reached under the bed, pulling out a canvas bag. She struggled a little getting back to her feet. She lifted the bag onto the bed. She opened it and carefully took out something heavy. It was wrapped in canvas cloth and tied together with twine. Slowly, tenderly, she opened the parcel.

Sheela stared at a full cartridge belt on top of a carefully folded cavalry uniform. She lifted the belt that had a holster with a revolver on one side and a scabbard with a cavalry knife on the other. She laid them aside and picked up the wool cavalry jacket and put her face into it, breathing deeply. Then she clasped it over her massive breasts with both arms, saying, "Even hard as blood is to warsh out, I can still smell him. Cpl. Herman Eubanks, a whitey, was my last man, Sheela, and he's 'long side me, inside me too, all the time. You don't never lose real love, honey. I loved ole Herman jus' like you loves Moses. I ain't got no use for that there," and she pointed at the gun belt, "but I know it makes him feel good to have it 'round. So's I jist keeps it even though I'd ruther throw it plumb away."

For a moment Sheela had such a warm love for her friend and her dignity that she almost cried again out of gratitude. She felt blessed to be surrounded with so much love.

She went back to her tutoring, and it took more courage than she had thought. She could reveal no fear to the wide-eyed youngsters and must go right on reading to them. Then she wondered for a moment at the end of a verse who their hearts would go out to some day—a day when their own men would close a door behind them to go to their duties. She prayed silently that they would not be going away from them to a war.

Reverend Pree had learned long ago to give his blessings and encouragement briefly to the wounded and the dying. This time control was necessary so he could be available each day with enough mind and soul left to give comfort to all. The hospitals were simply earthly hell. Treatment and medicines were crude. The doctors and assistants seldom lasted very long without taking to alcohol. It was just too much for them. When the wounded finally were hauled, or carried, from the far-off battle sites by horse- or mule-drawn wagons, their shattered bones and busted insides had usually become so infected that gangrene had set in by the time they arrived at the infirmary. The crude amputations and splinting of bones— often with little sedative—killed many from pure shock. The stench of rotting flesh was indescribable and unforgettable. It permeated clothing and skin. Every breath taken drew the death scent into the nose, mouth, and even the brain in nauseous repugnance.

At first, Sheela had simply followed behind Reverend Pree and added a smile and her natural soothing presence. Just a light touch or a pat of her hand gave solace. In spite of the fact that all the doctors, their helpers, and even the reverend wore masks of varying kinds in a futile attempt to escape the enveloping smell, Sheela refused to do so. Unknowingly, she had set herself apart by trying to impart the appearance that all was normal here in this place of suffering. She thought if she acted as if the stench was not there, it wouldn't be. She paid a very high price for it.

She took on too many duties. Her first mistake was writing a dying soldier's last letter home. Soon the other survivors timidly asked for this precious service as well. Often she would vomit after her duties there. And even though she always took a bath to rid herself of the clinging, invisible emanations of death, they would not go away. Amazingly, the yucca soap her Navajo friend gave her seemed to have been created for this purpose. She also borrowed a bit of Christine's imported perfume to dab under her nostrils. It only made it worse. She tried stuffing her nose with rose water–soaked cotton, but it was too conspicuous. Then finally she gleaned an idea that had promise. Her friends in the sewing room gave her bits of tightly rolled, dark blue wool to insert in her nostrils. If she put them in just right they almost looked like a shadow and were less visible to the wounded. She had to practice breathing through her mouth and controlling the nasal sounds of her voice. By speaking a little slower and softer, not one patient ever seemed to notice. It had been worth the trouble. She managed to comfort and encourage now without heaving afterward.

For a while the sounds of the hospital were as wrenching as the smells. There were low, pulsating moans from some; others would be still and silent and then let out a piercing sound of unbearable pain. Then, too, there would be the sound of repeated cries for the medic or for their mothers. But the noise that pulverized nerves came from the operating room. The shrieks from the sawing of flesh and bone were a horror, but their sudden ending was the worst of all, for one could not know which of two things it meant—death or blessed unconsciousness. Sheela slowly conquered this by thinking of the hospital building as containing a symphony of painful sounds and notes, which she truly believed was directed by one of the devil's demons. Then after a while, like all who gave succor there, the sounds became a background only. There was no other way for the aides to mentally survive. Many did not.

Another thing she learned to control was not flinching at the sight of often bloody, filthy wrappings over the stub of an arm or leg. If she turned away abruptly, the injured, who was fully conscious, would notice immediately, for they were often above their physical pain, suffering mental horrors from the loss of the limb—or limbs. Sheela was determined to overcome this somehow. She tried to look at the man that was left and, if possible, engage him in a pleasant visit about his home and homeland, wherever it might be. Of course, when this approach worked, it often led to the shy requests for a possible dictated letter home.

"Tell Mama I am fine, but I'll be a . . ."

She would often verbalize for them, ". . . a lot happier, however, when you're back eating one of her wild plum pies that you've missed more than anything else."

"Yes, that's it . . . more'n anything else, I miss that wild plum pie."

Other things the wounded and maimed men were anxious to know about were their new or little sisters or brothers, how the catfish were biting, and who had been raccoon and rabbit hunting, and who had been by to visit lately. She would put all these things into their letters.

Reverend Pree had warned her, "Sheela, my dear, you have a kind heart and you must not let yourself become involved with any specific individual or the gifts you are capable of presenting these poor souls will be used up and you will be unable to help others just as needful."

Oh, how true his warning was. Every day, when she saw life in weary, pained eyes illuminated at the thoughts of a message, a contact, back home, she could not help feeling a strange warmth envelop her heart. Then, on the next visit, if that bed was empty or another shattered body had replaced it, she felt a moment of intense loss. She had, on the whole, mostly arrived at the reverend's truth and did her best to act accordingly. It was never far from her mind that someday she might walk in and find Moses lying there, bloodied and maimed. She tried to erase these visions but could never completely conquer them.

Then it happened. Three visits in a row. Private First Class Jakes, who had all his limbs but was wrapped around his middle in an odd way, was helping Sheela with all his available strength to write his family and his hoped-for wife. Suddenly, he choked hard to hold back the tears, but the sudden heaving and shaking of his body from that effort created a spasm of emotion beyond his control.

Sheela placed a hand on his sweating forehead and soothingly and softly said, "It's all right, Jakes. It will be all right sooner than you think."

In a moment he had gasped back most of the flow of sorrow from his eyes and throat. He took one of her hands in his and turned his stricken eyes to her so that the whites showed on each side of the dark pupils, emphasizing the young man's inner torture. He cleared his throat with much difficulty and spoke words that broke her heart.

"Miss Sheela, I ain't a man any more. I ain't even a boy. I ain't never . . . you know . . . I ain't never had a woman. Not never. Now I never will. Ain't no amount 'uv sewing or doctoring on me is gonna help. I'm finished."

For the first time, Sheela could not speak words to ease the dreadful knowledge in this twenty-year-old boy-man's eyes, which stared at her, pleading for impossible help. She could only squeeze his hands in both of hers, kiss him on the forehead, and walk away with her eyes blurred with moisture. She was unable to give to anyone else that day—not the patients, not her Mama Mayo, not Christine and the girls, not to Reverend Pree, not even to Moses. She hid. She tried to hide from herself.

During a fitful night of dreams, she saw the face of an old Apache raising his rifle to fire on her husband. There were other visions of the legless, armless, headless soldiers lying about on a battlefield muddy with blood. She came fully awake determined to save Jakes.

Usually she only went every other day to the infirmary, because the hour or so it took put an extra burden on Mayo Lou having to care for the girls. But today she could not wait. She was no longer repelled by the almost unspeakable condition of Jakes. She spoke aloud to Mayo Lou, who listened with big eyes and confused silence.

"I must go and try to impress upon Jakes, even though he'd probably be incapable of understanding without his wounds, that there are many kinds of loves left to him. Beautiful loves. There are visions of grandeur all over the earth and all kinds of different foods to give his palate sensual pleasure. There are so many delights in watching all the wild animals, the flight of birds, to create wonder. I will . . . I will convince him of those wonders that are all waiting for him." She knew the odds made her message almost hopeless, but could not stop herself.

She walked across the compound with a certainty in her stride, an undeniable purpose in her entire demeanor. She strode straight to his bed. It was empty and made up with clean covers. Dr. Miller was bandaging a patient at the next bed.

Sheela asked, "Where is PFC Jakes?" She could not imagine him dead because Dr. Miller had posted an optimistic report that his infection was diminishing.

The doctor said, "He died last night without a word or a sound that anyone heard. Surprising, really. He was rid of infection and was healing well."

There was no use for words. She knew he had simply willed himself to die. A great sadness possessed her. She said a short prayer, then composed herself and went down the row of beds, doing her best inspirational day's work in the ward she had ever done. It had drained her energy, however, and she went to bed early without eating and slept for a while. Then without realizing she was breaking all her patterns and rules, she returned to the ward as if guided by a force nearly as powerful as any god.

When she got to bed number seven—the bed where Jakes had died—she faced an even greater jolt. A young man was asleep there, and he was missing both legs and one forearm. There was nothing new about missing limbs, eyes, noses, chins, or private parts. However, this young casualty looked almost exactly how she felt Moses might have looked fifteen years earlier.

She sat on the edge of his bed and looked at his sleeping countenance. He had the same firm jaw line, the same high, Indianlike cheekbones as Moses, and after a while, when he awoke, she felt as if she was staring into the eyes of her lover, her love, her very own Moses. She never knew how she contained her composure, but so did the young corporal from A Company. His name was Marly Madden.

Even though he was still under the influence of a sedative, he gave her a big, white-toothed smile that came as fast and as bright as sunlight and vanished in the same manner. In that instant before he turned inward again, she had absorbed the smile into her soul just as she had done with Moses.

"My little Moses," she said, with a strange meaningfulness.

He slept. She stared and stared and then made up her mind on a matter of great significance. She left the ward just as she had arrived—with purpose.

Moses drilled with his men so hard, and Sheela was so exhausted, that they just waved at one another as she watched him enter the mess hall. Her plans for the next day had all been worked out in her head. She would be finished tutoring Danielle and Stacy at almost the exact time Lieutenant Valois's aide-de-camp, Sgt. Luther Wilson, rode up leading the commander's brushed and saddled horse. Valois could easily have walked to the drill area, but he was a cavalryman. Valois rode proudly to join Lieutenant Burnett and Sergeant Moses in inspecting the horses and firing drills of the men of I Troop, Ninth Cavalry.

Sheela timed it so as to walk out behind Valois and go to the stables to brush and rub down Badger. Moses was riding

Reno today, but he would leave him behind for Sheela in case he did not return from the last great chase of war with the Tcihene.

After she finished brushing Badger down, she inspected his mane and tail, checked his iron shoes, and fed him an extra ration of oats.

Lieutenant Valois rode up. He always brushed his mount down before walking back to headquarters. This activity made him feel that he was one of his men, and he surely hoped the troops felt the same.

It was a time of great risk for Sheela. She knew her upcoming actions could get her sent back to the laundry or, worse, barred from the fort forever.

The lieutenant dismounted. "Well, Miss Sheela, did my darling little genius daughters give you any trouble today?"

"No, sir, they are a joy to work with. I think maybe I'm becoming the pupil now."

He laughed. "That's how Sergeant Moses often makes me feel."

They could banter for twenty minutes, but all those, and even the seconds, had run out.

"Sir, please forgive me, but I must speak what's on my mind."

He stopped caring for his mount, looked full at her, sensing the seriousness in her voice. "I've not known you to do otherwise."

"Well, it's about Moses. I . . . I don't feel my husband should go on this raid. He long ago earned the right to be drill sergeant here . . . a permanent post drill sergeant. It is not fair to ask him to go beyond . . . beyond any imaginable call of duty."

He looked at her silently for what seemed like several summers to Sheela and finally said, "It cannot be."

"Why? I pray you explain to me. What else does he have to

give that he hasn't offered up so many times they're uncountable . . . his life?"

"I spent years trying to explain the 'why' to Christine to no
avail, and then one day she simply understood. I only have
this moment to try with you. Just this one moment. Not
years. Moses chose to be a soldier. That is what he is. One of
the best that ever lived. If all his wounds, all the losses of
close comrades, all the years he has spent leading up to this
chance of possible fulfillment by destroying Nana and ending
this war is taken away from him, then his love for you will
never be the same."

"Forgive me, sir, but I do not believe that. That is pure soldier's talk. I grew up in the same house with a retired general,
and I recognize that talk when I hear it."

"That may be your truth, Miss Sheela, but what you have
just heard has *always* been true. The men of I Troop depend
on Moses more than they do on me. Whether you believe it
or not, the loss of hundreds of our men over the years must
not be multiplied by risking his absence. We all, you included, must accept that."

She was silent, laying her head up against Badger's. She
had made the only gesture left for now. She had faced it. "I
appreciate your being candid with me, sir. I do not agree, but
there is nothing left for me to say on the matter either." She
paused a second. "Am I fired?"

He smiled at her now. "I'm not that much of a fool. My
wife would leave me, my children would never speak to me
again, and either Mama Mayo Lou or Moses would ambush
me before you were out of sight."

"Thank you, sir. I'll handle it the best I can then."

"Know you will."

"Sir, I don't feel our talk should be mentioned to Moses."

"Of course not. My word on it."

They walked back to headquarters together, laughing at

the special sayings and activities of the two daughters whom
they both loved very much.

At last, the day before the day she dreaded so much, had
come. This Sunday Reverend Pree's chapel was almost full.
The soldiers and everyone else felt a closeness at this parting
they had never shared before.

Lieutenant Valois sat erect and proud beside his shining
clean, little ladylike daughters and his elegant wife.

Lieutenant Burnett and his wife, Sue, sat behind them.
The young bride of only two years was trying to put up an appearance as strong as Christine's, but her man had only been
in a few battles. Along with Moses and Walley, he had proven
himself and earned a Medal of Honor, winning the respect of
the men in spite of his being a West Pointer. Just the same
she was as fearful of the coming day of departure as Sheela.

After the service Moses was going to approach Valois about
Walley. He did not know how he was going to mount up and
lead these men into death's stomping grounds without the
wonderfully crazy Walley by his side. If somehow Nana got
him first, he was sure Walley would fulfill his killing duties.

The people present at the little chapel in the adobe fort
had half-thoughts and doubts and only halfway absorbed the
words of God. Reverend Pree was desperately trying to con-
vey the spirit of those words so that each one present could
receive succor for their own special needs.

The reverend asked Christine and Sheela to come forward
to perform. They had all been practicing secretly for several
days.

Christine moved to the battered old piano eagerly. This
was her element. She was proud to bring this surprise to all
there. It was difficult for Moses to turn loose of Sheela's
warm hand. He was a little stunned already, not having the
slightest idea what was coming. Was Sheela going to preach

or pray to music? He knew the range of her capabilities was wide, but what new thing would he find out today?

The reverend was smiling in anticipation. He had personally tutored Sheela for this special moment. Sheela stood just in front of the piano, where she opened a song book. She faced the crowd seriously, then turned her head and nodded to Christine. The music began at the exact right beat. Sheela illuminated the room with a smile and began to sing, "Cast Thy Burden on the Lord." Her voice rose and lilted in soprano tones, filling the church with joy.

Moses felt his body dissolve into the wooden bench. His pounding heart was raised in the saintly air of the church by Sheela's divine voice pouring out in musical prayer.

Cast thy burden on the Lord, Lean thou only on His word;
Ever in the raging storm, Thou shalt see His cheering form;
Cast thy burden at His feet; Linger near His mercy seat;
He will gird thee by His power, In the weary fainting hour;
Ever will He be thy stay, Tho' the heavens melt away;
Hear His pledge of coming aid; "It is I; be not afraid";
He will lead thee by the hand gently to the better land;
Lean thou strong upon His word; Cast thy burden on the Lord;
A-men.

Sheela's silken, hallowed voice had caressed and penetrated all of the listeners, the indentations and cracks of all the wooden *vegas,* benches, floors, and walls built by the strong, dedicated hands of the Buffalo Soldiers. At the end there was a silence of thankful awe. Then, unlike any time in the history of this place, a few hesitant hands clapped. With the nodding of his head and sudden vigorous smacking of his hands, the reverend freed the worshippers to applaud and yell in delight and appreciation.

Sheela was pleased, surprised, and embarrassed all at the same time.

After supper, Moses was called to a meeting with Lieutenants Valois and Burnett, a sergeant of infantry, and his commander, Lieutenant Parker of C Company, Thirty-eighth Infantry.

Valois explained that what was said here must be kept to the members of the meeting only. The high command could no longer suffer the ignominious raiding by Nana and his followers. All units in the field now would continue the pursuit until he was defeated. There would no longer be any period of rest. Valois pointed with his saber to a map of the territory and explained how troops would gradually be moved into a corridor all the way from Camp Ojo Caliente to the Mexican border. Somewhere in that rugged rock, small canyon-filled foothills, some unit, some individual, must bring Nana down and stop the fear and panic. He relayed the orders couriered by Colonel Hatch through Major Morrow that they must take Nana before he reached the Mexican border. The army could not cross over.

There were very few questions to ask. Valois had made it clear; destroy or die in the attempt. There were no other choices.

Moses stayed on after all but Valois had left. "Sir, I must ask a favor of you."

The lieutenant felt his heart seem to stop. Had Moses found out about Sheela's request? He looked at Moses, appearing calm, waiting, knowing the sergeant never asked anything unless it was important. "Yes?"

"I need Walley, sir."

Moses missed the deep gulp of air the relieved lieutenant took. "We all need fighting men like Private Walley. A hundred of him and the wars would have ended years ago. However, we must discipline a soldier who has never been able to confine his fighting to the field."

"I understand that, sir, and believe it or not, so does Walley. You see, sir, I've known for some time now that I will put my gunsights on Nana. Please don't think I'm crazy, sir."

"Anyone who would sell you short as a soldier, Sergeant, would be the crazy person."

"Thank you, sir, but it is something I've known for a long time now. I need Walley by my side to get me to Nana."

"I believe you mean this . . . this premonition?"

"Whatever you'd like to call it, sir."

Valois turned and studied the map a moment then faced Moses, smiling. "Just between us, Sergeant, I don't blame Walley for what he did. Defending a comrade's wife's honor should be a priority. Especially such a wife as yours will be. I will let him join us, but to save face with the new men he will have to spend a week in the brig when we finish our duties."

"Thank you, sir. He'll probably need the rest anyway."

Thirty Five

MOSES AND SHEELA HELD EACH OTHER ON THE BED IN THEIR sanctuary behind the main supply room. I Troop would leave the fort at sunup the next morning. The ambulance wagons were readied. The forage and supply wagons were loaded. All their wheels were greased and tightened. The horses and mules to pull them had been well-rested and fed. Knives and sabers had been sharpened and boots repaired. All guns and equipment had been oiled and checked over and over for flaws. The men had been healed, trained hard, and were well rested. Everything was as ready as it could be made as far as utilization of war necessities was concerned.

There was nothing left but the farewells to those left behind.

Sheela had her own war to fight. She was trying with much effort to act like a good soldier's wife. It was not always working, but somehow she had managed to keep the turmoil to herself.

Moses followed the lines of her streaked hair with a soft touch as he said, "There are so many things I don't know about you. So much I want to know about you. You sang beautifully. I didn't even know you could sing."

"Thank you, but the singing didn't seem like much to me."

"Well, it sure as hell did to the rest of us."

"It was Christine and Reverend Pree who helped me or I could never have done it . . . get up in front of everyone like that."

"Well, you're too modest. I'm gonna brag on you whether you like it or not."

She changed the subject and her tone became serious. "I know I'm not supposed to ask this, Moses, but when do you think you'll be back?"

"Now you know there's no way to tell for sure. We'll head back when I get Nana."

"You? Why you? There're thousands of soldiers after him. Why you?"

He wished he had not said it, but it was too late now. "I don't know how to explain this even to you, but we're—me and Nana—joined in some way. One or the other has to win. Either I get him or he gets me. It's ordained."

She took his head in her hands and stared into his eyes. Then she said with a sad finality, "Yes, I believe what you say is true."

"Please don't worry, Sheela, I will win. Walley is being freed to go along with me. I Troop has a tough, bright leader, and we have the finest men and horses anywhere. I won't be alone. There will be plenty of protection."

"Of course," she said, not believing it.

"It's only a matter of putting the sights between his eyes and pulling the trigger, and then, my beautiful baby, we'll be heading home. All I gotta do is just softly pull the trigger."

"Just pull the trigger. That's all there is to it? Well then, if it's gonna be all that easy, why can't I just come along and watch?" She knew she was saying the wrong things, but she could not force herself to be false no matter how she tried. The thought that Nana might be the one to center his sights on her Moses and simply "pull the trigger" was more than she could silently bear.

"I will take you with me in my heart." He placed one hand on his chest and continued, "You'll be there with me; every minute, every second, every breath, you'll be right here inside me." He almost said, "as long as I'm alive," but managed not to.

With a swift movement she turned and kissed him with desperate hunger, as her hands sought to pull his hard body all the way into hers and keep him safely there forever.

This was the time of forgetting, the time of feeling and loving, and they were fortunate enough to be here together trying to forget the worries of war. Together.

Thirty Six

I TROOP MOVED INTO THE LOW FOOTHILLS, HEADING NORTH. IT had been decided they would be based at the Ojo Caliente camp, sending their scouts in all directions. Then, if there was no contact or fresh Indian sign, they would start moving south to intercept Nana.

Moses had told Lieutenants Valois and Burnett that he did not believe, in spite of all the reports to the contrary, that Nana would take to the high mountains again. When asked what he based this assumption on, he explained that the far-flung attacks would take so much energy that it would be impossible for them to climb so high and back down so often to make that many raids. The two officers looked at one another and, to Moses's surprise, nodded in agreement.

"In that case, you're suggesting we save our energy and scout the foothills only?"

"Yes, sir."

"I think you're right, Sergeant," Valois said.

"And I, also," said Burnett. "It will speed up our sweep south by at least ten days."

"Or more," said Valois. "But first, we must be sure he is not at Ojo. That is the heart of his homeland."

Now as I Troop moved ever nearer their first destination north, the troops loosened up and made small talk to make themselves relax, at least enough to relieve the natural, growing tension as they moved nearer to battle. Somewhere, someday, out here in an unknown spot, the great old Indian must die. All, more or less, hated him, but there was not one who had fought, or even tried to fight him, who did not give him respect.

The rhythmic sound of horses' hooves, the creaking saddle leather, the almost unheard, unseen, hum of insects, with the Black Range dominating the far horizons like a mighty humpbacked whale, gave a strange peace to this movement of men and horses.

Walley had started his low, mumbling hum, which meant he was composing music and, worse, lyrics to go with it. Among all these battle-toughened men there was only one who had the courage to stop this ineluctable flow of creativity, and even Moses would not interrupt unless it was about to get out of hand.

Suddenly Walley felt his newest composition was ready to be recited. He removed his hat for this rendition, certain this would be his masterpiece.

"Ole Nana's killin' everybody try'n to take back his land.
Ole Moses is gonna go up and shake him by the hand.
Then he's gonna whirl him in the air an' kick him in the face.
Informin' the old coyote bastard this ain't no longer his place.
Then Sergeant Moses gonna throw him plumb over the
    mountain.
When Nana hits the ground the blood gonna splash jist like a
    fountain.

We all gonna ride up and piss in the hole where he hit.
Then we gonna laugh and holler and celebrate till we have a fit.
No more Nana means no more fightin'."

Moses knew one thing for certain: he could alter Walley's train of bad verse by asking, "You been thinkin' about Bitch Moose much lately? Maybe you got lucky and somebody shot ole Jorge. Or hell, maybe it could be they've split up by now, leaving that big ole door kicked wide open for you."

"I tell you, Sarge, there ain't hardly a minute goes by I don't think about climbin' up on Bitch Moose mountain."

"Yeah, that's a lot to think about all right."

"You got 'er there, Sarge. Someday she's gonna be ole Walley's. The *whole* mountain."

"All it takes is unflinching belief."

"Hey, I got it."

Those soldiers who rode in a line of twos across the seemingly endless rolling prairies within hearing range were relieved at the change in the conversation. They could actually listen now without trying to feign deafness. Of course, they were all a little jealous that they had never been able to afford Bitch Moose's whorehouse offerings. It sounded like heaven was supposed to be—with its streets of gold. They daydreamed of going there someday, but they knew it was too far away and too unpredictable for definite plans.

Walley was suddenly very serious, "Hey, Sarge, I want you to promise me something."

"Yeah?"

"If ole Nana gets me 'fore he does you . . . well, I want you to tell my sweetie that my last thoughts an' my last word wuz her name—Bitch Moose."

"Done."

* * *

The next day, as they neared the camp of Ojo Caliente, Walley became even more serious. "Sarge, to tell you the truth, I been scared part of ever' Indian fight we been in . . . and that's a bunch."

"What makes you think you're the only one?"

"Well, I reckon I ain't, but sometimes I mighty near shit my britches."

"*Everybody* does that. It's just part of the dirty job."

"Yeah, I know that, but for some reason I'm gettin' scareder this time that I ever done before."

Moses had been long-trained to ease the fears of I Troop, but this honesty caused him to pause a spell. Then he said, "Well, Walley, when you've been fightin' one of the smartest, toughest warriors who ever lived and you're suddenly close to the very last shot to be fired by one side or the other . . . why it's just natural to get a little edgy."

"I s'pose that's right."

"Sure it is. I'm just as scared as I am anxious to put my sights on him."

Just then a Navajo scout came back and reported to the officers that the trail was clear of any fresh Indian sign all the way to Camp Ojo, and that the infantry troops there reported that the last attack in the area had been on a sheep ranch headquarters over a week ago.

Even so, being just a week away from Nana caused the troops to become silent. They were having difficulty refraining from thinking about how they would be fighting him this time—hopefully the last time.

As they rode over a hill they could look down on the blue, silvered Alamosa River and see the camp squatted there as if trying to hide. Its adobe colors blended with the earth like those of a chameleon.

Walley broke the silence. "You know, Sarge, we been here

at Ojo Caliente so many times over the years that I'm beginnin' to feel plumb at home."

Moses knew he should not be voicing what was in his mind, so he said it as softly as possible. "Yeah, Walley, I've thought about that quite often. I'm the same way. Now don't you think it's strange we feel like that? This is Nana's home, but now we've made it ours. Then somebody else will come along someday and make it theirs. It doesn't hardly seem fair, does it? Nana's people were here first."

"Well, Sarge, it's kinda purty country, but if I had my druthers, I'd just leave it for ole Nana."

Moses spoke even more softly than before, "Just between me and you, Walley, it'll always belong to that terrible ole bastard. He just ain't ever gonna get a deed to it."

Thirty Seven

SHEELA WAS SIMPLY NUMB AFTER THE TROOPS RODE OUT. SHE could not see things clearly because her thoughts, her body, her being craved to be with Moses. She had moments with Danielle and Stacy, when she was reading to them and their blue eyes were wide with the wonder of the new worlds they were experiencing, that she felt relaxed and even happy. These moments were few compared to all the times her world was fuzzy and full of fear.

Nightmares and dream visions came to her as she slept. Twice she awoke in the arms of Mayo Lou, who was consoling her like a baby, knowing the pain of imagined loss that wracked her body and her heart.

In her dreams she constantly saw Nana—even though she did not know what he looked like. Nevertheless, his face was there and he was drawing a bead on Moses. Then she would scream herself awake or experience the nightmare horror of seeing Moses's body on the ground, face down, dead.

Somehow, when the morning sun lit a new day, she was able to make her rounds of consoling those soldiers still in the infirmary, do her teaching with Reverend Pree, and visit her friends of hard labor. Some of them had husbands in the field with I Troop, and they tried to console Sheela and each other.

When she could find the time, it did help to ride Badger around the training grounds. Occasionally she would ride out and look across the faraway blue ranges of mountains, thin against the horizon and deceivingly peaceful. She would stare and try to project herself into the foothills to Moses's side to warn him of her constant nightly dream visions.

She prayed and she talked into the southwesterly winds to him. But the winds would blow her voice away—not toward him.

She was working on a plan. It was in her favor that she had chosen to help so many at the fort. Everyone was used to her moving about the entire compound and even the outer grounds. She always carried a wicker basket with books and sweets for the wounded or her friends, including the supply sergeant. This made it easier for her to secure one object of soldier's clothing at a time. She hid the pieces of the uniform under a haystack, along with a blanket, some hardtack, and jerky.

The cartridge belt with the revolver and knife that had belonged to Mayo Lou's last husband, Eubanks, was another thing. Even though Mayo Lou had said she did not care for it, Sheela felt guilty about taking it. Without the gun she might never make it to Moses in time to save him. It would have to be done at any risk.

She took the gun belt from under Mayo Lou's bed and hid it under her own bed, knowing Mayo Lou would never look at it again. Then when Mayo Lou was busy cooking, she put it in her wicker basket and secured it along with everything else in the blanket. The next day when she took her ride, she would not return.

They all dined that night together. Christine insisted when

her husband was away that Mama Mayo and Sheela join her
and the girls.

As she poured Mama and Sheela a glass of wine, Christine
said, "I don't know what's causing me to feel like a small celebration tonight, but let us toast to the end of the war so our
men can join us in peace forever."

Mayo Lou was pleased and showed it with a smile and a
warm chuckle that shook her more than ample breasts. "To
the end of this ole war . . . an' all wars."

Sheela clicked her glass to theirs, saying, "And . . . and . . .
may our hearts go out and be with our men until they return
safely."

She felt some surprise at Christine's breaking out a bottle
of precious wine. It was almost as if she knew what Sheela
was planning to do and was showing her approval. Since they
customarily consumed little alcohol, the three became quite
giddy before the bottle was empty and only picked at their
suppers. Even the girls were swept up in the emotions and
joined in the conversation as equals.

"Mama," Danielle asked, "when Daddy kills Nana, will that
stop the wars?"

Sheela was surprised at Danielle's knowing the importance
of Nana to everyone here and the entire territory. Not once
during the tutoring and play talk had either one ever uttered
anything about the war, much less Nana's name.

Both Christine and Mayo Lou knew that children were always a surprise at how much they knew, but Sheela had yet
to learn this eternal fact.

Christine talked to her daughter as if she were an adult. "It
is his duty. We all know your father does his duty as all good
soldiers must."

Stacy joined in. "Maybe Nana will just run away and Father won't have to kill him."

Christine said, "That would be nice, dear, but you can be assured that your father intends to end this war once and for all."

Christine chattered on with the two women, planning entertainment and refreshments to help I Troop celebrate and heal when they returned.

Although Sheela easily joined in and contributed to Christine's plans, she was making her own at the same time. Tomorrow morning she intended to fetch the blanket loaded with her provisions for the trail and ride to the far hills to warn her man and save his life. The visions had been horribly clear. There was no other way.

Thirty Eight

NANA'S AGED BODY HAD THINNED AND GROWN FRAGILE FROM
countless battles, lack of food, horse falls, and plain exhaustion. He wanted to make one more raid close to his home of
Ojo Caliente.

"Just one more time," he said to Lozen and later he told his
old wife, Nah-dos-te, the sister of Geronimo, "I tell you, my
woman, it is almost over, but a raid near the heart of our
homeland will have fully revenged Victorio."

Nah-dos-te wanted to tell him one more time might be the
one that finished them, but she only said, "Let us do it then
and find a new home in Mexico."

Even though he knew that Lozen, Kaytennae, and his wife
really did not want him to go on this last raid, he could not
help himself. He, Nana, kin of Victorio, must finish the vow
himself.

Since it was to be the final attack, he took the last of his
warriors and asked Lozen to lead the women and smaller
children and move slowly southward. Upon the war party's
return they would all ride at the greatest speed they could
muster to a treasured spot high in the Sierra Madres.

Nana took his grandson along. He would need his "eyes" through this raid and on their escape run. In the hills above the mining camp of Chloride, only a few miles from Ojo, he readied his small force of surviving warriors, some as young as fourteen. Two of the older ones had brought their wives into battle with them. That was the only way, except for Lozen, that women were allowed to fight. Of course, in defense of the band and tribe, they all fought just as ferociously as the men.

The miners, having been attacked here before, had guards posted on three sides, perhaps a mile apart. Nana sent Kaytennae with a bow and arrows to take out the first of these men. The grandson watched through the long glass, which was carefully screened by twigs with leaves tied on it so no reflection could give them away.

"Grandfather, Kaytennae is moving up a draw toward the guard. He is not seen. Now he crawls from one bush to another. The guard's horse has heard, but the stupid guard is leaning back against a tree smoking a pipe. He has not noticed the horse raising his head or the ears working. What a fool, Grandfather. Does he not know smoke always moves and gives him away?"

Nana's old heart beat faster. He wished he could be the one to send the arrow. It must enter the throat where it joins the body so as to cut off any possibility of a loud cry of warning. The next best thing to being there was his grandson's eyes relaying the action into his mind's vision.

The success of the final raid to fulfill Victorio's vengeance hung on the accuracy of Kaytennae's arrow.

Kaytennae had thought about this as he first crept forward and feared failure, but now as he eased closer with his belly flat to the ground as a lizard, he only thought of the spot on the man—that indentation in the front neck from whence speech, songs, and warning cries come. If the arrow was true, there would be no cry. There would only be a death rattle.

He peered through the leaves of the bush, only forty feet from the guard. Oh, how easy it would be to hit the spot firing a rifle, but of course, that would alert the miners. That is why he had been sent with the weapon of their past.

He, like Nana's grandson, found it hard to believe—but was glad—that the man ignored the warning signs of his horse tied only ten feet away. He moved as slowly as a desert terrapin in notching the arrow then set it with one hand against the bow. As he pulled the string back, the old hunting instinct and experience of his youth returned. He centered his eye once more through the leaves on the death spot.

Now! In one swift motion, he raised his eyes. Centering on the neck, the spot, the target, he felt as much as he saw. The arrow seemed in frozen motion to Kaytennae, but it moved to the spot, right into it, and split the voice box, separated the sixth and seventh vertebrae and drove into the tree, hanging the man there. The blood gushed out around the arrow shaft from the force of his lungs' air struggling to cry out. Too late!

Kaytennae crouched, raced forward as he extracted his knife. With invisible speed, he slid the cutting edge along the arrow shaft where it reached the red-spraying neck and sliced all the way back to the tree. The head fell sideways and rolled downhill a few yards. The body slid down the tree, then pitched forward, belly first. The horse had snorted and pulled at his tie-down, but Kaytennae was on the reins instantly. Muffling the horse's nostrils, he led it swiftly down into the draw, where he mounted and rode back with a fine trophy horse.

Everyone knew what to do now. They quickly tied the fat horse with hobbles so he could be picked up on their return from the attack. He was so fat they would probably eat him. Their other mounts were lean and drawn. Their meat would be stringy and tough.

They spread out along the draw and waited for Nana's grandson to give the signal. They waited, ready, as he peered over the hill, carefully, then he turned and motioned forward at the same time. He sheathed the glass and raced to his own horse. He had been ordered back by Nana to unhobble and have the trophy horse ready for flight.

Before the other two guards could see them—since they looked outward from the camp—they struck their usual glancing blow. Two miners dumping rocks on the waste pile were hit and died instantly. Another stepped out on the porch of a little outbuilding, raising a rifle as Nana rode at full run sideways and shot what was, to him, a human blur. The blur was struck in the edge of his heart, and the bullet tore a shattered hole in the shoulder blade before it exited.

A woman and a nine-year-old child crawled out from under the side of a tent. They tried to escape into the timber behind, but one of the Apaches spotted them. Followed by his fifteen-year-old nephew, they rode down on the scrambling pair, firing through their backs before running their horses over them.

Nana could see that the corrals were full. That would be treasure far more precious to them than all the metal the miners could ever melt down. He yelled for Kaytennae and half of his warriors to go for the horses. The others knew to cover. The guards were charging from the low hills. They were too late. The horse raiders were already driving the captured ones on their back trail.

Nana followed that group now. Five warriors covered them, retreating and firing as the miners dashed out of the mines looking for their weapons. Both guards' horses were shot out from under them. One rolled over its thrown rider's head, his skull broken apart like a clay pot, squashing his brains out his ears as a half ton of horse hit him full force.

The miners were helpless to pursue the raiders. They had two horses left, but were still running back and forth around the camp in panic and confusion from the noise of the firing and the screams of the dying.

By the time the miners caught a horse and sent a messenger to Camp Ojo Caliente, over three hours had passed. Nana and his band—with a few fresh horses and mules—were already many miles to the south. They would also leave many tracks.

Nana's old heart beat to the rhythm of his horse's hooves. Victorio's vengeance was now complete. He must head south through the rocky hills and run a gauntlet of soldiers and civilians all wishing to kill him and obliterate every single one of his fragile band. He knew it. He would fight accordingly.

Thirty Nine

I Troop split into the three spearheads agreed upon earlier. Moses commanded the center unit on the trail left by Nana after the attack on Chloride. According to the scouts, the trail was about a day and a half old.

They rode hard. There was no evidence of trickery from the ground sign. The small unit was moving swiftly, actually gaining a little on Nana. It had to be Nana. He felt it.

Moses felt a new surge of energy, fired up by hope. It was the great hunt. And even though he tried to dismiss it from his mind, out ahead of his unit moved the greatest trophy of all, Nana. When the unit struck the sign of Nana's warriors joining the camp of his entire band, all the Buffalo Soldiers—even the new, scared replacements—and the remount horses seemed to sense a possible victory.

They took note that Nana was not splitting his small force. The Apaches were all moving together. Doing so they were slowed. By the second nightfall, Moses and his men had ridden almost forty up-and-down wearying miles, but they had gained on Nana. Moses felt they could close with his fighters before the sun rose the next day.

Moses knew that Nana would set out guards for the night

in strategic spots. He also knew he had to stay close on the trail of the elusive, canny, old warrior. There were many other units scattered about the land wanting to be the ones responsible for Nana's demise.

It was more than that to Moses. This was a personal connection that could only be resolved by a face-off with this unprecedented nemesis. Nana was the puzzle of his soul.

The camp by a small spring was extra quiet for a while. After eating the sparse food, feeding extra rations to the horses, and setting out guards, Moses crawled under his blanket too anticipatory of the next day to sleep, too tired not to.

Instead of Nana dominating his mind, as was natural, it was Sheela's face that floated before his closed eyes. She smiled and then turned serious, trying to say something to him over and over, but he could not catch her words. He could smell and taste her sweetness almost to the point of pain, but he could not read her lips as her vision floated in and out of the blue mist.

Just after daylight, they moved out. According to the prior plan, Moses's unit would be in the middle of the great fan-spread formation of the troops. Now was the time to make the greatest ride of their lives, and Moses had told them so just as they mounted.

"All right, men, we are fed, watered; we have plenty of guns and ammunition. Let us ride until we catch him and then let us fight him to his death. Death to Nana!"

There was a stirring rumble emitted from all the Buffalo Soldiers' chests and throats. The horses felt it and moved nervously for a moment.

Moses sent the Navajo scout and Justin out on a double point about fifty yards apart. The terrain was so varied in its convolutions that sometimes the scouts were only a few yards apart and other times they were spread as much as a hundred.

They rode on, just south and above the mining town of Hillsboro and into a little more rugged country. It was obvious now that Nana was not going anywhere near the great heights and massive canyons of the Black Range.

When Moses saw this, he said, "Walley, Shit-su-ye is headin' to the Sierra Madres sure as hell." The troops had picked up a few Apache words and occasionally referred to Nana as Grandfather.

"Lordy, Lordee, Sarge, we gonna get 'im 'fore he gets there . . . ain't we?"

Just as Walley's last word was spoken, a single shot was heard ahead, then several more. Moses spread his unit and charged, seeking cover in a little draw that wove around a small mountain like a young woman's breast. There he, Walley, and five more men ran head on into a loose remount horse. They caught it quickly and formed a horse line.

Moses then sent two men up around the mountain in the rocks to the left and three others to the right into a small brushy draw. He, Walley, and bugler Dutton advanced down the draw, carefully protecting themselves with embankments, boulders, and covering their movements by moving next to brush whenever possible.

Then they found their Navajo scout. His body hung over a dead piñon limb that had fallen to the ground. He'd been shot in the gut and one ear was hanging loose in the blood. It flopped as he raised up, pushing his wet, red-soaked hands against his stomach.

Justin's horse had been hit smack between the eyes, dropped dead where he hit the gravel and small rocks of the bottom of the draw. Justin was unhurt except for a bruised shoulder where he had fallen. He had not felt it yet, and was using his horse for protection, firing upward at a cedar- and brush-covered hilltop. A bullet struck the dead horse and ric- ocheted off its rib cage, causing Justin to duck behind the whole body.

Moses halted just a yard behind the opening and ordered, "Justin, stay down till I tell you different." Since he was in a direct and open line of fire from the hilltop, Justin obeyed that order with pleasure.

Moses said to the bugler, "Hold position here, Dutton. You can fire at any targets of opportunity, but stay put." Moses signaled Walley to move out and get ready to use his scoped rifle. "Walley, soon as you get into position behind that clump of rocks over there," and he pointed to them, "I'm gonna draw their fire."

Walley scooted forward behind the brush. At a small open- ing, just before he reached the rocks, a shot kicked gravel over his scrambling legs. He plunged his lean body forward and reached cover. Slowly, very slowly, he eased the rifle into a ten-inch indentation in the rock then settled his body in solidly and got into a perfect position to look through the scope. His trigger finger was ready. Now he saw where the enemy fire was coming from, but he could not make out a target.

Then part of the unit spread to the east, firing three shots at the enemy hill. Walley and Moses waited for return fire. It did not come. They waited. They waited more. Silence. Then even closer on the ridge two shots were fired at their men to the east. That froze them for a moment.

Moses watched Walley, rifle steady, muscles bunched like a bobcat ready to leap on a rabbit. Then Moses saw the tini- est movement of the bushes. It could have been made by the wind, but long years of experience had taught him that it was out of rhythm with the wind. He motioned to Walley.

Moses leapt forward, zigzagging from one bit of cover to another, deliberately leaving himself open in between. The shot came. It had furrowed the outside of his leg just enough to act as a propellant.

Walley saw the gun barrel pull back. He centered and fired, knowing he had struck meat. Moses fell right by Walley's side behind the rocks.

"Get 'im?"

"Yeah. Got 'im."

"Good boy."

The troops moved forward. Walley and Moses laid down covering fire. It was a tiny, vicious little war now. There was no way they could know how many enemy were ahead, and only Walley was sure of a kill.

Justin yelled, "Can I fire now, Sarge?"

"Blow their asses off, Justin."

Then as Moses shot at what he hoped would be flesh even if the eyes could not see it, he said to Walley, who still searched the hill with the scope, "That Justin sure does obey orders."

Walley fired again. "I think I got a busted hand with that 'un, Sarge."

Moses signaled Private Dutton, the bugler, to blow a cease-fire. He did. The sound that Moses seldom ordered seemed to bounce alive from one slope to another and then lose itself in space somewhere toward Nana's tribe. Everyone held up with great difficulty, waiting for the bugler to sound attack or withdraw. Nerves pulsated. Death had been served up here in these beautiful hills of grass and bushes with wild things hiding, hushed, listening in holes, crevices, and stands of trees to the human madness around them. Some, such as deer and elk, had already fled over hill after hill to the safety of a higher canyon.

Silence again. Interminable.

Then Moses knew that the delaying attackers had moved on. He signaled the bugler again, and they all moved forward toward the Indian's hill. From three points they closed, but there was no return fire. They had lost one man and one horse. They looked for Walley's kill. They found two small spots of blood, some disturbed earth, then discovered a body buried in a pile of rocks. They did not disturb the site, but were strangely moved by Walley's visible success.

Even with every particle of Moses's physical and spiritual self full of awareness, even eagerness, to kill Nana, a sudden unaccountable thought invaded his mind. He recalled the countless pools, smears, and drips of blood from the bodies of many distinct breeds of Indians, and the blood from white people of many divergent countries, and the blood of the Spanish and Mexicans, and the blood of black men. Fresh or dried, there was no difference. None. And now he knew that all their spirits were the *same* color of very pale blue as well. The blue spirit trail at Cuchillo Negros had saved several men's lives, including his own. He had seen it many times before but only recently realized what it was. The blue spirit was where his *warrior's warning* came from. He hoped it held up now with Nana when he needed it the most. He puzzled. So what was this insanity of forever killing? There had to be an answer, but, as always, it escaped him as his attention returned to the duty of the moment.

Moses stood looking at the rocks in the crevice where he knew the dead enemy lay. The mystery of Nana's band never leaving any wounded behind still held, but for once they all knew where at least one dead warrior lay.

Again, Moses felt a surge of confidence, knowing Nana's people had weakened and slowed enough so they could not hide the burial spot—only the body. But then he felt a tinge of dismay that they had been able to even accomplish this burial at all when the delaying party had obviously been outnumbered and outflanked. The little firefight had been costly to both sides.

The Buffalo Soldiers had suffered one dead scout and one dead horse. Moses had a furrowed, but usable, leg. Private Means had a bullet lodged in his calf muscle. The lone medic cut in and extracted it from the back side of the leg while Means only let out one scream. His wound was medicated and bandaged. He could still ride but could not run afoot and fight. Moses let him make the choice of returning to seek out an ambulance wagon below or move on with them. He chose to go along. So with one mount dead and one soldier dead, they broke even on horses and men. All were still mounted.

Moses allowed the medic to cut off the top half of his boot and smear his leg with some disinfectant and bandage the furrow as well. It would be sore later but had to be ignored for now.

They mounted up, sent out two new scouts, and moved more cautiously until they cut sign on Nana's main trail again. The loss that Moses felt the most was the fact they had been slowed by the ambush. They would never be able to close in battle with Nana's main band today, but for sure tomorrow.

The unit rode forward, winding up and down, along game trails, and into graveled gully bottoms, around hills and over them. They gained back a portion of the yardage lost before night stopped both the Indians and the Buffalo Soldiers.

The men had less to eat this evening, and so did the horses because Moses had ordered an overfeeding the night before, being sure he would catch Nana this day if his horses held up under the hard, driving pace. They had. He had not. Everyone on this pursuit would be a little weaker when the sun came around again.

Forty

SHEELA WAS GRATEFUL SHE HAD LEARNED TO SPEAK PASSABLE
Spanish while helping out in the Socorro mercantile with
Nelda and the General. The two sheepherders were hesitant
to give her any information, but when she began speaking
their language and accepted a cup of coffee and squatted by
their campfire to drink it, they began opening up a bit.

They would not say for sure if they had seen a band of
Apaches hereabouts but finally told her that just that morning the soldiers from Camp Ojo Caliente had passed over the
low hills to the west, heading south.

Both their heavily weathered faces crinkled into wide grins
when she told them she had information to save her fiancée's
life. A lone woman dressed as a Buffalo Soldier riding to save
her lover struck a chord of appreciation in the two men, who
were separated from their own families for two-thirds of each
year in this dangerous land. Her madness and her courage
somehow felt in rhythm with their own.

One of them, Luz Martínez, volunteered to accompany her
and get her moving on the trail. His saddle horse had a lot
slower gait than Sheela's dark bay. However, she felt that it
was critical to know she was on the right trail.

Finally they were en route. She had some difficulty keeping her mount slowed to match Luz's. Luz rode around among the many tracks and trailed them awhile to help her feel comfortable that she could follow it.

Then they reached a used campsite. There had been cooking fires and unused cut wood and brush and lots of dung where the horses had been fed on line. Luz followed only a hundred yards or so and explained and pointed out to her where the trail split into three prongs of tracks. She was puzzled and Luz explained that this was done to minimize ambush from the Apaches.

She explained that her man was a sergeant and a great veteran soldier.

"Then I think you must choose which trail to follow, señorita. You know this man. I do not."

She was torn, but suddenly said, "The middle one. Moses would be in the middle of it."

She looked for affirmation from her guide. He said, "I think you have made the best choice."

They parted, reining their horses toward their separate duties.

"Muchas gracias, Luz."

"Por nada, señorita. Vaya con Dios."

And they moved away without looking back.

She had thought, because of their forage wagon and ambulance, that she could easily overtake them. She rode up on a hill and saw that all of the I Troop's wagons had pulled out to the lower hills, where the landscape was smoother, thereby falling so far behind they would be useless to the fighting men until the chase was over.

She rode on, not bothering to look for Apaches. If she was taken, so be it. Otherwise every particle of her being, every ounce of the bay's ground-swallowing, running walk must be dedicated to getting to Moses before Nana did him in.

She had to watch the trail carefully; twice she had let her worrying change to the comfort of holding Moses close to her once again. She craved him so much it caused a numb pain. She had lost the trail. A sweat, cold as a north wind over frozen snowbanks, beaded her forehead and the nape of her neck. Her heart thumped so hard with fear of failing Moses, her breath seemed to be knocked painfully out of her chest. Then she found the trail, vowing never to take her eyes or her horse from it again.

On and on she moved, curving around sudden upraised hills, down graveled gullies and rocky canyons. Of course she knew that Luz had not wanted to speak of it, but she was following two trails in this one. Underneath the cavalry's were the markers of Nana and his band. Knowing this did nothing to alleviate the tightness growing in her throat that she might be too late. If so, she would go on and pursue Nana and shoot him down herself. Moses was her life. If Nana took him away, then she would be happy to die taking the old warrior's life. She touched the steel of the revolver to reassure the purpose in her heart.

She had another hollow, lost feeling when the middle trail split into three again. She tugged lightly on the reins sitting back in the saddle to stop the horse and think. They must have gotten close to Nana to cause maneuvers like this. Her eyes followed the center trail again. Then, ahead perhaps three-quarters of a mile, she saw three buzzards circling lower and lower. Her breath seemed to stop. There was death there. Maybe it was an Apache, she encouraged herself, riding forward with jaws clenched, revolver in her hand.

The horse tracks split in many directions now. She was frightened at the confusion, but when she rode upon the dead horse, its belly already beginning to swell, she was oddly relieved. The shell casings showed that a battle had taken place here.

She rode on down the curving rocky gully until she saw several horse tracks crossing and crisscrossing, but they moved on ahead nevertheless. The tracks soon left the draw and headed up and around a grassy hill with small, scattered cedar trees, yuccas, and bushes.

She rode slowly now, for there were many tracks on the far side of the hill, but she could only make them out clearly in open, dirt-covered spots. There had been Apaches here for she saw the difference in the moccasins and hard-soled boots of the troopers.

Then she saw a dried pool and a smear of blood that had already turned brownish black. Someone, a soldier or an Indian warrior, had died here.

She dismounted, surprised at how stiff and weary her legs felt once on the ground. She tied the horse securely to a cedar tree and walked in circles, trying to find the cavalrymen's trail. Finally she found it. She marked the direction with three round rocks, taking no chances of having to hunt it again. As she struggled back to her horse near the rock-outcropped hill, she realized the sun was setting. She would have to stop and wait for morning.

She fed Badger the last of the grain, but she could not take a chance of looking for water in the swiftly coming night. She had one canteen of water left. She poured half of it in her cap and held it under the horse's muzzle. He only got two swallows and then sucked air. It would have to do. Surely they would come across water somewhere tomorrow.

She sought out a grassy spot just below a shelf of cracked and weathered rock, and wrapped herself the best she could on top of the saddle pad with her own blanket. Her exhaustion came at the same time as the semidesert turned cold.

She ignored them both and thought about Moses. He was reaching to caress her hair with love exuding from his eyes. Just as she was getting comfortable with her lover's image, another floated in and took it away. Nana rode into her vision with a raised rifle. He shot at Moses. The image of love and the image of death permeated her visions, interchanging all night, endlessly. At last the hard-riding days on the trail and the contrasting dreams wore her into such an exhaustion that she fell asleep.

She was awakened by a strange noise and something heavy striking the heel of her blanketed boot. She scrambled to a sitting position, her hand on the revolver. To her astonishment a rock raised up from the outcropping and came tumbling down the hill toward her, its flat side stopping it about two feet from her body. From her sitting position she could see just over the edge of the outcropping. Another rock raised and fell back two or three times. Then it was tipped over on its side. She was paralyzed with fear. Was she still asleep? Was this a nightmare?

Then she saw something that was not rock raise to the top of the ledge and disappear. Sheela thought her eyes had worn out and she had gone crazy staring at the twisting trail so many hard miles. That was it. It had to be.

Then she heard a gurgling sound of a human choking and was sure she was going to faint, but the hardness of the earth was real beneath her.

Inch by inch the thing rose up now. She was staring into an Apache's bloody face with much of its lower jaw missing where mixed blood and liquid rolled down in strings from the hole that had once been a mouth.

He was crawling out now with a knife in one hand. She could not seem to think or move from the figure. She was like a hypnotized prairie rat staring at the approach of a rattlesnake. Then the gurgling and rasping of throat and lungs intensified into a horrible sound.

The resurrected Apache was desperately gasping for air. He had crawled out of his grave and could only make it to one knee. The black eyes had only one purpose in them: kill. There was not enough strength for more, but it was just enough to launch himself toward her in a rattling, bubbling howl.

She fired straight into his heart, then again, as the first one straightened up his upper body. The second jerked his frame again. He looked at her. She saw the hatred turn to nothingness as he fell forward, driving the knife with such force into the edge of the rock shelf that the blade broke. It pinged off the rock like a ricocheted lance head.

She emptied the other three bullets into the top of his head. They were wasted as far as the Indian was concerned. He had been fatally shot with her first bullet. She pulled the trigger, clicking it on empties over and over. At last she realized the warrior was truly dead. She had just killed her second man in self-defense.

She forced herself to calm down. Before she rose to her feet, she reloaded the gun methodically, putting it back into the holster. She stood up and strapped it back on.

Then she said aloud, "Thank you, Mama Mayo. Thank you for the loan of it." She saddled up, securing her blanket and the few supplies left, mounted, and urgently rode past the three lined-up rocks. She did not glance back at the body. She had seen it long enough to do for several lifetimes. She would think about all this later, but for now she had to ride very hard until she caught up with and saved her man. There was no other thought now.

Forty One

NANA RODE HIS DAPPLED GRAY ALONGSIDE HIS GRANDSON, KAY-wayhla. Lozen was riding ahead to scout the highest hill left in their vicinity. Kaytennae was flanked out to protect in any way necessary.

Nana had carefully surveyed the last remnants of the Warm Springs Apaches. They were down to so few, only a band remained. The wounded who could not ride and had no hope of reaching Mexico's Sierra Madres were sacrificed and interred wherever they faltered enough to jeopardize those still able to move.

Some would have looked at the tiny little band of men, women, and children and felt pity. They were haggard, thinned by the long rides and constant battles. Even if they had had ample food, there was little time to eat it. Most limped from bullet wounds, horse injuries, and from torn muscles and broken bones. They were desperately trying to move into the safety of the Mexican mountains. If they could make it there with no more losses, there was a slim possibility that they would have enough of the band left to survive.

Where others might have looked on this dazed, shuffling band with pity, Nana observed them with great pride. They were unparalleled survivors. Never in history had so few fought so many with so little and over so great a distance. Nor had anyone covered as much rough terrain and outfought and outwitted so many tough veteran soldiers and civilians. He had crossed and crisscrossed the mighty Black Range, the Mogollons, the San Mateos, and Floridas, often moving his band seventy miles in a single day—a seemingly impossible distance to those in pursuit.

Nana was never to know the exact size of the forces against him, but these consisted of eight companies of white infantry, the same number of Buffalo Cavalry, along with two companies of Navajo scouts. There were around four or five hundred civilian miners, farmers, ranchers, and even businesspeople armed and chasing and seeking vengeance on Nana just as they had on Victorio. Over two thousand men were after him.

In his youth Nana was said to be able to drive an arrow completely through an elk, and he had once run down a deer on foot and cut its throat. But now he was bent and could barely walk. He was still mobile in the saddle, however. He had led his band from deep into Mexico and back many times. They had ridden across rugged mountains and deserts all the way north to the villages of Garcia and Seyboyetta, west of Albuquerque, coming within a hard day's ride of Santa Fe.

Although he had lost men and women in battle over this massive map of land, he had never lost a single decisive battle. Not one.

Nana had covered and fought over three thousand miles in just two months. Even though his old body was racked with pain and disabilities, he was outwardly optimistic and cheerful with his grandson.

As they rode following his best two remaining warriors, he

said, "Hello, rock. Good morning, bluebird. How are you, brother coyote? Good luck to you, yucca plant. It's good to see you, mescal, and you too, tree cactus. Blessings on your growth, little cloud. Thank you, wind, for all the seeds and pollen. There you come over the horizon, father sun, without which none of us would exist. Ahhh, Great Mystery, thank you for the sun."

Now they could see Kaytennae scanning the world as far as he could see to protect Lozen as she took her locating stance. As they rode up, her hands came together, pointing back in several directions.

"They come from many directions now, Grandfather. And there are many."

"So I expected, Lozen."

"They have been like that for a long time now, haven't they, Grandfather?"

"Yes, but we have made them count their horses many more times than they have us."

Nana set both his grandson and Lozen looking through the glass that folded into itself. They looked south first at the rolling ground toward Sonora, Mexico.

"How long is our trail, Lozen?"

"The way we move now, a day and a half. Maybe two."

Now Kaywayhla, in a prone position, was moving the powerful instrument slowly from the northwest to the northeast. At last he stood up and said, "Grandfather, Lozen is right. There are many. They come like slow arrows, all pointing at us. Some are two days or more behind us, but one small band, the one we have been fighting all the time, is less than a day away."

"Grandson, is the closest band of soldiers led by the broad-shouldered, striped armed one?"

"Yes. He and nine others are nearing us."

They all gave Nana a quick look when he said, "That is good, for destiny must be fulfilled. Only the Great Mystery can make it or change it. It is not for us to decide."

Nana knew what was left for him to do. He reined down the hill toward the fragile little band—all that was left of the once mighty tribe of Warm Springs Apache. Even if the white-eyes would offer them a reservation now, it would do no good. They were too few. And it was too late.

Forty Two

MOSES HAD BEEN ABLE TO KEEP THE HUMAN AND HORSE CASU-
alties about even for perhaps fifty miles. His attacking force
would somehow change horses and stay on the move. He
was familiar, to a degree, with the land they crossed, but had
nothing of Nana's knowledge of it. He wished Lieutenant
Valois or Burnett would catch up so they could mount a final,
sustained assault. The pause here would have to be brief for
he knew Mexico was only an ordinary day's ride away. Of
course nothing was ordinary with his unit. They had been
moving ahead now under constant fire for almost a hundred
miles.

Nana deployed his small number of rear-action warriors
with amazing skill. The warriors themselves—whether young
or old—were the greatest of his survivors. They would fire,
move, fire, move again, then vanish into the carefully chosen
draws and small canyons to take up another hidden position
farther on.

Moses had lost count now of his dead and wounded. There
was one thing for sure though; the horses suffered more than
the men. They were much bigger targets for one thing, and
they could only go by the guidance of their masters. When

the soldiers guessed wrong or were outmaneuvered, the horses fell first. Nana had turned a lot of cavalrymen into infantrymen.

Somehow the units of pack mules had caught up again. They must eat and get ready for the final charge. It might be their last chance at Nana.

Moses had scattered his men with scouts on both flanks. They had chewed jerky and taken water from a muddy spring. Moses was checking with his field glasses to see if, just by some chance, support was on its way. The remaining mounts still in battle condition were only eight in number. They were tied on a horse line in a protected swale. A pack mule carrying food supplies had been moved to a forward position behind some brush to facilitate this last feeding of the exhausted men. The troops were bruised and skinned from top to bottom from hitting the ground, crawling forward, over and over from one little protection of rocks or earth depressions to another, countless times, avoiding death. Most of them had had horses shot out from under them and the resulting falls had bruised even their insides. Half the distance of the hundred miles of fighting had been spent on their bellies, moving forward like desert reptiles.

Private Wilkins had been bitten in the neck by a rattlesnake and had been choked to death by his own swollen flesh.

They were all drawn down in the belly from lack of food and water. Their eyes were dropping back in the sockets as if trying to hide from the blinding sun. And the very thought of moving cramped muscles forward again seemed impossible.

Moses crouched low, moving faster than even he believed possible, winding his way through the best protection to the top of the highest hill.

First he lay behind a small, rocky outcrop and carefully scanned the entire area with his naked eyes. He located his two forward scouts. He spotted his two flanking scouts being relieved so they could go eat. He strained to see any possible enemy, but could not.

He moved slowly, very slowly, getting the field glasses ready. It was natural now after all the battles. He had seen too many men fall from making a quick movement. With eyes slightly blurred from lack of sleep, he eased the glasses to the hundreds of thousands of acres behind them. He could make out a fair-size force finally coming their way. His guess was that Burnett and Valois were joined now. For a foolish instant he was uplifted by the sight of them but realized they were still several hours behind.

He blinked his eyes over and over to try to clear his vision. He could see three other dust trails of infantry and cavalry back in the distance. They were far out of the final closing but had no way of knowing this.

As he made the complete sweep he found the tiny band of Warm Springs Apaches moving slowly toward the Sierra Madres. My God, he would have to move out now if they hoped to close. He could not wait for Burnett and Valois to catch up. Every minute counted.

He recognized a butte that was right on the Mexican border. It was only a few miles away. Nana would know that. They were riding parallel only a few miles east of the Arizona border as well. Even though a fraction of pursuit time was being lost, he could not help but look once more at the infinitesimal size of Nana's remaining tribe, what he could see of them.

He did not have time to linger on them long enough to discern their rate of progress, but knew it was very slow. They were about finished. His men could still stop them. For just a moment, as his mind conjured up the large numbers of scattered units pursuing this one little speck, he had a feeling of profound admiration for Nana and his vanquished people. However, that was shattered by the sound of a gunshot on his left.

He saw his scout, Sam Hightower, rise up only a hundred and fifty yards away. He was attempting to return fire, but instead hurled his rifle in the air and fell back and down the slope, stopping spread-eagled on his back, motionless, facing the interminable sky with unseeing eyes.

Moses moved his rifle barrel swiftly on a movement to the left, perhaps fifty yards away, and fired, but he knew he had not found flesh just as he knew his sentry was dead. It was all he could do to keep from charging downhill and up the other side, hoping to get a shot at the attacker.

Instead, he focused the glasses and caught a flash of a rider disappearing into a draw. The Apache had escaped after having fired one round, killing one good soldier.

As Moses charged back down toward the mule—whose area constituted a temporary command post—he said aloud to Nana, "You old bastard, you've got me down to nine men now."

He counted once again the eight usable horses and one mule. He was premature. A shot tore through the brush, striking the mule in the left side of its ear. Another hit it in the shoulder and entered the chest cavity. The mule fell, kicking desperately, trying to regain its feet. It squealed in pain and despair. One of the packers shot it between the eyes with his revolver.

Moses's sentry on the right fired two shots at the vanished sounds. While their attention had been drawn to the left, Nana's warriors had somehow moved by the right front sentry and destroyed the mule—their last method of delivering supplies. It did not matter now. The last run for Nana had finally arrived.

Swiftly, Moses chose seven men, besides himself. With Walley right behind, he led them forward in a forced trot. It was a slow one for sure, but Nana's band was also moving slowly. The agony of wounds, broken bones, and cut flesh from years, very long years, of endless fighting and pursuit was catching up with both sides.

Moses forgot caution. That was over. He was certain the last of Nana's rear-action warriors had consolidated to help the pitifully few Apaches escape into the sanctuary in the Sierra Madres.

Moses turned in the saddle, yelling, "Men, they are only three or four hours ahead. We can finish them now."

The voice they had heard, obeyed, and respected so long gave a charge to their spirit. This was transferred somehow to the horses. Their spent muscles felt an upsurge of power and they increased their pace.

Moses, on point now, knew they were moving faster than Nana's crippled band. At last they would have their final confrontation, just as it had been meant to happen since they had looked into each other's eyes and souls.

Forty Three

THE EARLY EVENING BEFORE, SHEELA HAD SPOTTED LIEUTENANT Valois and the remaining contingent of I Troop making camp and sending out sentries. Her first impulse was to join them. Her second told her that the commander would not let her move ahead alone, if at all. So she rode quietly around them, fearful of losing the trail in the half-moonlight.

The bay was tired to the point of collapsing, but she urged him on, talking softly, "Dear, Badger, you must be as strong as your namesake. You must move on to save your master, Moses. He has cared for you like his own child, and I love you just as much. It will soon be over. Then we can all rest in peace. Do you hear me, Badger? Peace. Blessed peace for all." The horse moved its ears, listening to the singular silken voice and did, in fact, *feel* the message and valiantly moved toward the place of finality.

She met two soldiers head-on. They held a wounded companion up between them. He had taken a bullet in the side and one in the upper chest and was babbling about his mother and the state of Georgia. The blood frothed and bubbled from his mouth as he spoke, reliving youthful days for the last time. He seemed unaware of any presence. The two helping soldiers did not even try to guard against Sheela, who could have been an Apache. One had had two fingers shot off. The other was limping badly from a foot mashed by his dead horse falling. They were moving, weaving slowly to the rear, hoping for medical help.

"Is Sergeant Moses ahead?" she asked tentatively.

They stopped. The corporal with the crushed foot slowly raised his eyes as if he had just now realized her presence. The half-moonlight caught the white and dark pupils that stared at her blankly.

"Moses? Sergeant Moses? Is he alive?" she insisted.

"Yeah. I s'pose he is. Was the last time I seen 'im. Chasin' ol' Nana . . ."

Her great relief was shattered as the young Buffalo Soldier, held up by his comrades, let out a gurgling, pleading last cry. "Mama, oh, Mama, I . . . I . . ." And he slumped down between them. They let him stretch out on the ground; then the soldiers folded one arm across his chest and sat down on each side of him.

A knot of pain wadded between her stomach and chest.

Sheela kicked the horse on ahead, knowing she was on the main trail. The chance meeting of the soldiers by moonlight was jolted from her memory by flashes of riding the wagon west on the long Santa Fe Trail with Nelda and the family. Even Bitch Moose came through the undulating mists, smiling, cajoling. Then there was Moses. He was trying to tell her something. There was Mama Mayo Lou, smiling her great smile, with her powerful, comforting arms open for her embrace. Then over and over, telescoping back and forth, rode Nana. He raised his rifle and its sights were on her Moses. It all faded and came again. She saw his old arthritic finger on the trigger as it squeezed . . .

She was on the ground and had been asleep. She held the horse's reins in such a tight grip that she had to prize her cramped hand free a finger at a time. It was daylight.

She and Badger had not eaten for twenty-four hours and it had been ten hours since they watered. But she knew, somehow, this was the day. There would be no other. There could be no other.

Without any sense of the stiffness and the pain in her body or the rumblings of her stomach, she mounted the near-finished horse and prayed and urged him into movement.

"Oh, God, don't let me be too late," she murmured. "Give strength to dear Badger. Help him carry me forward to Moses. Oh, Precious Lord, I love him so . . . so much."

She rode up to a dead mule and saw some soldiers digging a grave for a comrade. It wasn't Moses. She rode right on past them, her eyes on the main trail now.

One of them looked up and recognized her. He said, "Oh, Miss Sheela . . . whatcha doin' here . . . in that uniform? Where . . . ?"

The words gave her impetus, and she willed it into the stumbling bay horse and kicked the poor heaving beast forward. The cavalry cap was knocked from her head by a low limb. Her streaked hair fell down as the sun showed over a hill and gave it a glow. She moved on up the ragged, winding incline.

She could tell by the fresh tracks around the rocks that she was nearing him. She said to Badger, "See those tracks? We're almost there."

She took her comb from the saddlebag and to prove her confidence in her man's survival, she combed her hair first with one hand and then the other in a desperate attempt to allay the unimaginable . . .

* * *

The sun was clear of the hills now and, with only an occasional interruption, shone full on her from an infinite cloudless sky. The aura around her head was angelic in its reflected glow. She was a breathing masterpiece painted by the great father sun. There was nothing left in all the world to do but ride till she found Moses.

Forty Four

NANA HAD NO KNOWLEDGE OF THE U.S. GOVERNMENT'S ORDER for the army to stop at the border. What he and Lozen were struggling toward was simply the rock bluffs and the deeper canyons to form a delaying action so the few remaining members of his band could escape into the Mother Mountains. There, he hoped, a few of the old ones would also have survived.

He was sure that if they could hang on another couple of hours they might be able to join his brother-in-law, Geronimo, in one of those high-fortress spots they both knew so well.

Now he and Lozen commanded from the rear. It was more like *herding* the debilitated band. Nah-dos-te, in spite of her age, rode like her husband—with authority. She had one lame eight-year-old boy in front of her in the captured army saddle and a year-old baby strapped to her back to relieve the burden on both their exhausted mothers.

An old man had died in the saddle a mile back and had fallen from his horse. Lozen and Kaytennae had lifted his frail body back on the horse and tied him in the saddle so he would not have the dishonor of being buried by the enemy or eaten by buzzards. They meant to inter him in a crevice somewhere ahead. Everyone was wounded or injured in some way. They moved slowly without a single moan or cry of pain. Only the horses' hooves and the creaking of saddles and the noise of weapons adjusted for readiness over and over could be heard.

There was no need for words from Nana and Lozen. Their presence was enough to inspire the last particle of strength left to be exerted.

Finally they topped out over the edge of the rocky incline, and it was only a little over a half-mile slope downhill to the edge of the wind-creviced buttes.

Two-thirds of a mile back downhill, Moses caught a glimpse of movement disappearing over the rocky rise. He simply said, "He's there, men. Dead ahead." And all tried to urge their horses to more speed. If successful, it did not show. Not only were their muscles used up, but not even the powerful will of Moses could speed them on. Nevertheless, they were gaining. Moses strained to project his being from the saddle to the ridge, but he would have to struggle there in person. He knew that both he and Nana were, with all the creaking and creeping movement, running out of yards, out of inches, out of time.

Nana motioned Lozen and Kaytennae and his grandson to him.

"Kaytennae and Kaywayhla, you will go with me to make a last stand so Lozen will be sure to reach the rocks with the last of our people. If we are lucky and brave, we will slow the soldiers and rejoin them."

Lozen held out her hands and her palms instantly turned red and her hands swung together and pointed toward the as yet hidden troopers.

She did not want them to go, but said, "You are right, Grandfather. The white-eyes must be delayed for us to reach the safety of the rocks."

"Well then, I have no choice anyway, Lozen. I do not wish to take my grandson, but I need his eyes to get Stripe-arm."

Kaywayhla looked into the eyes of Flower Song, his love. She turned her eyes back to his, signaling their deep feelings for each other.

They all understood. The three rode away to meet the enemy, just one more time. They were mounted on the best of the horses taken at Chloride. These horses had strength enough left to be kicked into a lope.

Kaywayhla knew what to do. He coaxed his horse into a run. He dismounted and tied him to a yucca tree below the crest of the hill. Nana and Kaytennae rode up and stopped right next to him. Crawling on his belly with his rifle, Kaywayhla chose a spot between the rocks with thick clumps of bunch grass. He pulled the telescope from the holder on his leg and extended it almost in one motion. The time of waiting was over.

Nana's face showed no discernible emotion. He knew he did not have to speak; his grandson knew when to inform him. They had worked, these young eyes made ten times sharper by the glass, uncountable times.

"He is there ahead of all. There is but one just to his rear. The rest are scattered back behind. All come to us."

"Ah, that is good. Now listen, Grandson. As soon as you see Stripe-arm fall, mount your horse and race back to our people. Flower Song awaits your return."

The two men, one very old, the other, Kaytennae, nearing middle age, rode unseen down a side gully toward the enemy.

Kaywayhla eased his rifle to his side and then put the glass back on Stripe-arm. He could easily, he was certain, drop Stripe-arm's horse with one shot and then kill the buffalo man with another. His young body suddenly burned for the kill, but it was not his. This kill belonged to his grandfather alone. Nana had waited a long time and many long rides for the time of killing the one coming toward him. Kaywayhla controlled himself with difficulty and kept the glass on Stripe-arm.

Kaywayhla was dismayed as the sergeant's horse tripped and fell. He had stepped into an unseen crack and twisted over, breaking a foreleg. The man behind him dropped from his horse, pulling a knife from his belt, and cut the horse's throat. Kaywayhla had to admire the quick thinking. They were not going to give their position away by a gunshot. Stripe-arm was already on his feet. Both men were moving forward afoot now.

Nana and his longtime *segundo* rode up out of the gully into a grassy swale. There was scrub cedar and yucca scattered about. Kaytennae rode up behind a yucca clump that crested the rise and saw the horses led by two soldiers afoot angling up the rocky, curving incline almost toward them.

Kaytennae turned and waved his arm, signaling Nana to take his position. He moved on down and made ready to complete the ambush. Nana eagerly rode to the chosen spot. He could see the blurs of movement and make out that two human forms were leading.

It was the time to kill.

Nana rode to the opening between the yucca clumps and a greasewood bush just high enough so that he could fire and expose the least amount of himself and his horse as possible. He raised the fully loaded repeating rifle and pointed at the blurs with both eyes open.

Moses strained, stretching every part of his being forward. He could feel Walley's presence behind him as he had for so many years. Suddenly, a shocking thought came to him and he could not help but voice it to his best friend.

"My God, Walley, old Nana has no way of knowing we're not allowed to cross the border after him."

Walley never had a chance to answer.

That instant an icy feeling grabbed the back of Moses's neck and the strange hum hit his ears to form the ancient warrior's warning that only those of long combat time recognize.

Moses yelled, "Down!" and fell, seeing a movement up and to the left. Nana. The eyes of Nana. Big as the world. He crashed into the rocks so hard the breath was jarred from him. The firing continued and he slid his rifle over the low stone and tried to find Nana. A bullet struck the rock and zinged upward into space. A piece of the rock was chipped thin as a razor blade and driven into his right cheek. He did not feel it as the blood oozed and slowly ran down his face. The firing had moved back below them now. He heard a horse scream and twisted his head to check Walley as he heard random shots coming from the rear troops.

Nana exulted without showing emotion as he saw the two leading blurs fall at his first shot. He pulled off two more at the spot and then charged down toward Kaytennae, stopping to empty his rifle as Kaytennae had done. The ambush had worked well. Very well. Horses and soldiers were down and some were futilely firing back at the empty space the two veteran warriors had occupied. They both were kicking their horses back downhill as fast as they could toward the tiny band beginning to move into Mexico. They reloaded their rifles as they rode. Nana never gave a thought to his grandson, for he always followed orders.

* * *

Kaywayhla felt the exulted spurting of his own killblood as Stripe-arm and his comrade fell, but he forced himself to hold the glass in position.

Moses was gasping for air as his dazed eyes saw the unthinkable. Walley had been struck in the left forehead and lay, staring up at him, totally motionless, with unseeing eyes. Moses wanted to charge up the hill and rip Nana and everyone of his band into bloody strips with his bare hands.

Kaywayhla was both dismayed and enraged as he saw Stripe-arm raise his rifle above the rocks. Without any thought except vengeance for his grandfather, he grabbed his rifle, shoved the barrel into the grass bent by the telescope, aimed, and fired.

Moses, even in the shock of losing his best friend, saw the movement just before the bullet cracked above his head. He fired at the motion and saw the rifle jerk up and back, and knew he had struck meat. He reached and took the scoped rifle from under Walley. A rage came from knowing Nana's bullet, which had been meant for him, had killed his closest friend. He had selfishly insisted on Walley being released from the guardhouse only to die by Nana's bullet. He charged, weaving from habit only, as hard and as fast as he had ever moved before. He carried the Sharps sniper rifle in one hand and the repeater in the other. If he'd had room left in his brain for it, he would have been amazed, for no bullets came his way.

He was nearing the crest and whatever finality was destined between him and Nana. It was all down to a few moments, and it would be over now, one way or another.

Sheela felt Badger faltering beneath her. No amount of projecting her will or physical urging could bring anymore strength to the courageous bay. He had given her his all. Badger had passed, and stayed ahead of, all but Moses, and had gained ground so that they neared his tiny unit now. She had caught glimpses of them ahead and knew they were nearly catching up.

Suddenly the bay stopped. His sides were bellowing in and out and there was a rattling, whistling noise as his used-up lungs strained for just enough air to keep his heart beating.

Sheela knew. She dismounted, saying, "Thank you, Badger, and I'm so sorry," and she, too, stumbled past him and fell to her knees. She jerked about, getting to her feet. For a moment her deeply fatigued legs failed to coordinate. In fact, her whole body was out of sync with its various parts.

Nonetheless, she somehow forced herself forward like a marionette propelled by wires held by an awkward beginner.

Then the firing started up ahead, and she heard the screams of horses and the shouting rage of men trying to kill each other.

"Oh, God," she cried out, "Moses! Moses! Moses!" She managed to increase her clumsy forward motion. Each time she fell, she arose more determined. She never quit shouting his name. After all this time, all the rocky, dry hills, gullies, and small canyons she had followed and crossed, she must not wind up a few minutes—or maybe a few seconds—late. If so, she swore she would curse both God and the devil until she fell dead from exhaustion, anger, and sadness.

Moses reached the crest. He crawled on his belly, dragging, peeling his elbows to keep both rifles protected from the rocks and dirt. He peered through the bunch grass at the very crest. He saw the rifle on the ground first and then the body a yard farther on. It was a frail child. He had one arm twisted partially under his body. The dark, dimming eyes stared straight up into the sky as if he had looked for some fantastic entity from the mystery of space to come for him.

Moses recovered swiftly, lifted and pointed the scope downhill toward Mexico, where he saw the remaining few Apaches trying desperately to reach the rocks and safety.

Nana and Lozen were herding them ever closer. Nana rode in a constant half-arc behind, wishing his body would expand to completely cover them until they could be made safe. He had heard the two shots. Now he looked for his grandson among the band. Of course he was not there. Nana kept looking back for him, torn between riding to his favorite person in all the world and keeping his loyal, old wife, Nah-dos-te, and the few others moving toward possible escape.

Moses got Nana in his scope sight with difficulty because of the old man's constant horseback movement. Twice as he was turning to arc again, he centered for an instant and almost squeezed the trigger, but he could not afford to miss. He would never have time to reload and resight again before they vanished.

At that moment the body of the child stirred. One hand searching for his rifle. When he could not find it, the young, bony arm moved into the air, reaching out with inestimable effort.

The lips moved over one last word, "Shit-su-ye." The hand fell into hard desert dirt. The slender fingers clawed at it twice, then were still.

Moses was not consciously aware of it, but the entire war changed for him in that instant.

Kaywayhla's horse suddenly broke loose from the bush and raced downhill toward Nana. As he ran near enough for

Nana's old eyes to recognize him, Nana froze. In that very fleet moment Moses had Nana perfectly in his sights. His finger instinctively tightened on the trigger. Inexplicably the rifle barrel tilted above Nana, above the bluffs, and only when Moses saw blank blue sky did the gun fire.

Nana heard the sound of the gun and the last word ever to be spoken by his grandson in his mind-ear and saw clearly Kaywayhla's empty saddle at the same moment. The great old warrior whirled his horse around, facing the prone Moses, who had brought the scope sight back down on Nana, making no attempt to reload.

Then Nana raised his rifle above his head and let out a cry so loud that it could have come from the throats of a hundred young warriors. It was a sound of great anger and despair— a cry so ancient and knowing, so haunting in its helpless seeking, it was a cry to all the world. Nana's little band heard it and understood. Moses heard it and understood. Its message broke apart and dissipated, wasted away in the immensity of space around a solitary eagle circling in the sky.

Then Nana could not help himself. Growling like a steel-trapped cougar, he turned toward Moses. Then, another cry, sharp and pointed as a lance, pierced his half-deaf ears, "Nana! Nana! Don't. We must save our young for seed." Lozen's words were always true and to be heeded. His people still needed him.

Moses held his eye to the scope, watching, knowing the great old warrior had turned around with his soul wrenched in half. Nana rode on, shielding the last of the Warm Springs Apaches with his exposed back, almost daring Moses to kill him, until he, too, vanished with them into the all-embracing stones from whence they had come.

* * *

Moses rose now and picked up the limp child and, for a reason unknown, the telescope. He muttered softly, "My God, he's just a baby."

Moses's war was no more. It was finished.

He moved along until he found an oblong indention in a face of rock. He tenderly placed the boy's body in it, folding his thin, young arms around the twig of a body. He laid the glass eyes between them; then, methodically, he moved about on his hands and knees, gathering rocks and carefully working to fit them permanently in place.

At last Kaywayhla, Nana's favorite grandson, was properly interred. Moses knelt by the wall of rock. He wanted desperately to say the proper prayer but could not find the words.

He cleared his throat. "I'm truly sorry, Nana. And it's too late." He arose, gathered his weapons, and moved erratically, limping, back down the hill to bury Walley.

Sheela passed a dead horse and then another, a soldier's foot extended from under it. She moved on and then sank down, doubled up next to the dead horse's breast. She was still awake but trying to gather some remaining particle of will to rise again.

Moses reached the first two men and asked numbly, "Where's Walley's body? I'm gonna bury him myself."

One of the soldiers, a medic, pointed to a body in a sitting position, leaned up against a near perpendicular rock.

Moses moved to it. The body spoke.

"Did ya' get 'im, Sarge?"

The shock of a living Walley was small, pleasant, and temporary. Too much had happened for a resurrection to impress him now.

He answered softly, before kneeling to check out the miracle of Walley being alive, "Missed him."

"Oh, shit." They were both quiet a long moment; then Walley explained, as he made a motion from the entry point around his head to a bloody exit just above his ear, "Too hardheaded even for ol' Nana's bullet. It went under my hide, 'round my head, and come out here."

Moses said, "If you keep on behavin' like this, you may make corporal yet."

"*Again.* Corporal *again.* That's what you mean, ain't it?"

Moses rose to go check on the rest of his men. One was lying behind some bushes where he had crawled, leaving a smeared trail of blood, and was dead from a shot in the guts. Now he knew what his duty was, but he could not count how many of his men he would find. He tried once more and failed. The altered chemicals of his body had anesthetized his thinking tissues.

He moved forward zombielike. He saw the figure of a soldier trying to stand up, then dropping to his knees, then raising his head and moving forward in a crawl. His long, streaked hair fell all about his head. Long, streaked hair!

Moses's mind numbness disappeared as fast as it had come upon him. Could it be Sheela? In a uniform? How? He must be dead. He must be a spirit. All the recent moments had to have been a delusion, mad visions. Nana had killed him after all.

Stunned, he picked her up as the familiar voice said, over and over, "Moses, is it really you? You're alive . . . you're bleeding. Did you kill Nana?"

"I missed."

He felt her fingers tenderly remove the slice of rock from his face. And he felt the lips kissing his wounded cheek and the salt taste of the blood as they moved to his mouth.

"Oh, God, Sheela. It *is* you. It really is you."

"Yes. Yes, it is me, my darling. Oh, dear God, thank you. Thank you, Badger. Thank you world. My Moses is alive."

He pushed the tear-wet face away from him to look at her. Her eyes swam in dark warm ponds before him and her lips smiled, moving in emotion. He felt and caressed her hair and then stared into her eyes and beyond again. His tired heart seemed to have suddenly warmed to the melting point.

Moses took Sheela by the hand and led her to the last of the unwounded soldiers and said to him, "Please, soldier, go patch up Walley and bury the dead."

"Yes, sir, Sergeant, fast as we can."

Then Moses put his arm around Sheela and pulled her to him. She reached around his waist with a tight hug as if she never intended to let go. They moved limping and weaving toward a drooping Badger. Moses took the reins, pulling the horse around, and he followed them, moving his legs like they were made of sawed-off fence posts.

They all three walked awkwardly, out of balance with the turning world. They moved on over a little rise, slowly disappearing from the view of the survivors of Sergeant Moses's remaining contingent, I Troop, Ninth Cavalry, in the bottom of New Mexico just above the Mexican border.

The eagle kept circling because there was much of curiosity happening below him. Lieutenant Valois's troops, with food and water and medicine, were coming close to a head-on meeting with the man, the woman, and the horse. In the far dusty distances, many groups of men on horseback, and on foot, moved toward a final merging. They were too late. Only Sergeant Moses of I Troop had seen the last of the embattled old Nana and the few Warm Springs Apaches. He alone, from the soldier's side of the great vengeance war, had been the final witness.

As the three took more difficult steps toward the multitudes of troops and supply wagons still advancing in wasted anticipation, Moses stopped.

He slid his arm from around Sheela's waist and stepped in front of her. He placed a hand on each of her shoulders and observed her at arm's length for a long moment.

Slowly shaking his head, he said very softly, "Sheela Jones"—and a little grin crept across his face—"you *really* are a mess." He gave her a quick hug and they started on down the slope. Then he said over his shoulder, "Loosen up, Badger, we're all goin' home."

The horse tilted one ear as if in understanding.

Afterword

OFTEN IT IS DIFFICULT TO REMEMBER THE ALL-IMPORTANT GEN-
esis of an idea by the time it has become a book. It was no
different with *Faraway Blue*.

In the open-weather seasons of 1957–58, my father, W. B.
Evans, and his brother and partner for fifty years, Lloyd
Evans, and a Denver geologist, Den Galbraith, were working
a silver claim in the Hillsboro-Kingston mining area of south-
western New Mexico.

I have always been in love with the wonderfully historical
western town of Hillsboro. So I drove down from Taos, not
only to visit my kin, but to enjoy one of my favorite areas in
the foothills of the vast Black Range.

They had two mules that pulled the loaded ore car from the
mine. One was a saddle mule. The first day I borrowed it and
rode up into the high foothills of the Black Range, immensely
enjoying the views and the semiwilderness. I remember find-
ing many old mines and prospect holes, resembling the pock-
marked face of a giant with a forehead ten miles across. And
even though I had a great sympathy for the skeleton-bending,
dangerous work of the miners, it suddenly came to me how
the Warm Springs Apaches must have felt. Some of their

most precious water holes were now occupied by armed strangers; the surrounding hunting lands had been scarred with explosive powder and steel picks. The timber that was needed at that time had been cut to shore up mine tunnels, build the mine camps and towns, and used for heating and cooking and a hundred other necessities. It must have appeared to the Apaches as if the mountains had been skinned like a huge buffalo and all the countless tunnel and shaft wounds revealed as other indignities.

It was no wonder to me that they had fought so long and relentlessly in a futile attempt to save and reclaim what they deeply felt the Great Mystery had reserved for them.

Although sporadic mining has continued in the Hillsboro locale until today, it is the tourist, hunting, and cattle ranches that keep the area extant. The timber has mostly grown back and in some sections, including parts of the Gila wilderness, it is so thick, nothing much in the way of feed, for either wild or domestic animals, grows. But the unimaginable history and beauty still hang thick in the air like thousands of invisible spirits.

I had spent most of my creative life writing about the northeast quadrant of New Mexico, a slice of southeast Colorado cutting through a portion of the Oklahoma panhandle and down the northwest part of Texas. I called this the "Hi Lo Country" in many of my books and short stories—most in fact. I had acquired a slight knowledge of how Nana felt in his struggle by fighting for thirty-seven years to get a film made from the *Hi Lo Country*. It is now done.

About 1980, I began steadily visiting and becoming even more enamored of the Hillsboro-Kingston country and the unique people who live there. During those early years of beginning obsession, I started writing about this location, visiting off and on over the years with rancher Jimmy Bason and his historical F + Ranch in the heart of the Warm Springs

Apache land. Then I went on to situate the second book of my mystical *Bluefeather Fellini* duo in the area.

I did a great deal of reading about this vicinity, and every now and then I would see a brief mention of a Medal of Honor–winning Buffalo Soldier, Sgt. Moses Williams. In some way that I'm unable to explain, there was a spiritual connection with this veteran of countless frontier battles. He wouldn't let go.

A little later I read brief mentions of an old Warm Springs Apache, Nana, who had miraculously fought against the incursion until he was near eighty. He had an absolutely amazing, genius-touched, tactical ability and unbelievable courage. Not only was he old, but for that time, he was ancient. He had a badly crippled ankle and foot, serious arthritis and rheumatism, as well as being half-blind and deaf.

Slowly, these two spirits grabbed me and with their tenacious wills took possession of my being. So sometimes, in short breaks from other works, I began to wonder if they had fought against one another in other instances than the battle of Cuchillo Negros—where Moses won the highest military honor, but Nana won the battle.

To my pleasant surprise they had engaged in so many little wars against one another that I realized I'd have to telescope many of these and simply ignore others. There were just too many fights, even though the army high command failed to fully record many of them. It is no wonder: Nana was a great embarrassment to the army.

Anyway, I had more rich material than I could possibly use.

Finally, I was ready to write a sixty- to one-hundred-page novella, or short novel as these successful works should be called. This *essence* of writing was what I valued most, whether doing it myself or reading the few writers still trying this most difficult of all written media.

I must say, with total conviction, that the powerful spirits of these two warriors took control of me and the resultant historical novel. There were many times I would have to read back through it because I wouldn't fully realize what had gone down on the pages. At last I simply gave in to these forces and went along comfortably, gratefully, with them. This novel was a journey of literal revelations. Moses and Nana coauthored it. Of course, in a novel, no matter how close you stay to the historical record, the characters will take over and lead the writer to the situations and endings that *they* wish.

Fort Selden is a famous fort in history. I'm sure both Moses and Walley would have enjoyed knowing that other great war heroes followed them there to that adobe-walled compound. Maybe they did know. ¿Quién Sabe?

Capt. Arthur MacArthur commanded at Fort Selden from 1884 to 1886, after the Ninth was moved to Fort Riley, Kansas, for what was satirically described as a "well deserved rest." The statement was made in all seriousness at the time. The captain was accompanied by his wife, Mary, their son Arthur Junior, and a two-year-old son Douglas. Arthur MacArthur won the Medal of Honor in the Civil War. His youngest son, Douglas, would win America's highest honor in World War I, and would go on to become one of the most famous and controversial generals in American history. Many military historians think he was the nation's greatest. One can only wonder how he would have fared matched up against Nana under the conditions that Colonel Hatch had to face.

The well-tended remains of Fort Selden, at Radium Springs, just off Interstate 25, a few miles north of Las Cruces, New Mexico, still has a haunted feeling of many brave presences, invisibly and eternally riding the parade grounds.

In reality, recorded history has it that Pvt. Augustus Walley was born into slavery on March 10, 1856, in Reistertown, Maryland, and spent his childhood in slavery until the end of the Civil War. The white Lt. George Ritter Burnett cited Walley for the Medal of Honor. He didn't receive it until nine years after Cuchillo Negros, on October 1, 1890, along with a Certificate of Merit for Bravery. It was fourteen years before Sgt. Moses Williams received his medal, and Lieutenant Burnett waited sixteen years for his award. Walley did finally make first sergeant and fought with the Ninth in the Spanish-American War in Cuba. Here he was recommended for another Medal of Honor for "Great Gallantry" when he dragged Major Bell of the First Cavalry to safety under intense fire at San Juan Hill. The officials didn't know what to do since the rules of the time allowed only one Medal of Honor, so they gave him another Certificate of Merit for Bravery.

He spent two years in the Philippine insurrection with the Tenth Cavalry and retired from the Buffalo Soldiers in 1901, having spent twenty-nine years of admirable service to his country.

Between enlistments, Moses Williams worked as a janitor in the Capitol Building in Washington. He volunteered to fight with the Ninth in Cuba, but was turned down because of his age. He did reenlist in 1891. It is both interesting and thrilling to peruse copies of a few letters by and about Moses Williams obtained for me by Brig. Gen. (Ret.) Michael Cody of Albuquerque. They reveal that Sergeant Moses had a good handwriting. He requested reenlistment as a married man and the adjutant general gave his permission. His final request for retirement was handwritten and was granted on April 30, 1898. Sergeant Williams's last request of the army was that they furnish him transportation to his home in Vancouver, Washington.

Nana, along with his brother-in-law, Geronimo, was imprisoned in Florida and at Fort Sill, Oklahoma. Nana lived past ninety years, never giving in completely, aggravating his guards, and coming down hard on younger Apaches to stand up for their rights, until he died. If there had been, in all of recorded history, a warrior leader who surpassed Nana in miles, or moved horseback in such rough, crippling terrain and weather, I have never read or heard about him. Considering the few warriors under his command, the conditions faced every day for years, his age and physical condition, as well as the thousands of well-trained soldiers and heavily armed civilians who never stopped pursuing him, I cannot help but believe he was the greatest warrior of any kind who ever lived.

Moses Williams fought over eight years across Kansas, Oklahoma, and West Texas against the fierce Comanches, the Kiowas, the Kickapoos, and Apaches, as well as Mexican bandits and U.S. robbers, rapers, and murderers. He put in over six more years in southern New Mexico doing the hardest of labor and fighting over and over with what was thought to be the greatest warrior of all, Victorio, and finally what must have seemed like an endless running war with the indomitable Nana.

As historians finally start researching the life of Moses Williams, I feel he will be found to have been a fine counterweight to the incomparable Nana.

The valiant Moses did not get to enjoy his so richly deserved retirement very long. He died of a heart attack while being treated at Vancouver Barracks on August 23, 1899. His age was not given on the birth certificate.

Among over one hundred personal items listed were: a pen and holder, nine books, a pack of playing cards, a fur cap, a walking stick, and fourteen two-cent stamps with writing paper. Ord. Sgt. Moses Williams, Buffalo Soldier, was buried at Vancouver Barrack, Washington, Grave No. 393. The value of his entire possessions was listed at $23.00.

The locations of the battles, the Apache warriors, Moses, Walley, and all the U.S. officers were real; Sheela Jones, Mama Mayo, Bitch Moose, the officers' wives, and other characters I have simply dreamed up or are composites of people I have known or, maybe, met briefly throughout my own battles and life experiences, but they became as real to me as Nana and the hard land he rode across.